JERRY F. WESTINGER

A Bad Time to Meet the Family

I

Part One

Chapter 1

The wall clock chimed softly for seven. Ceci glared into the dressing table mirror, dissecting her reflection for the slightest flaw it might betray her with. Any errant strand of hair, any blemish uncovered, any smudge of color where it didn't belong was an intolerable threat.

Tonight had to be perfect. Every night had to be perfect.

Her nose twitched, and she grabbed one of her carefully bleached curls. Maybe it was her mind playing tricks on her, but she picked up a hint of vinegar. She took the bottle of Sallician rosewater and scattered a few more drops on her head, as well as her wrists for good measure. Such an expensive perfume should not go to waste. Even if she wasn't the one who paid for it.

The clock chimed again. It was now a quarter past. Alendro, who had agreed to be there at seven, might have actually arrived by now. Ceci spent another five minutes picking out a pair of sandals, then found an air-thin shawl to go with her sleeveless dress. She put on her slender gilded headband, leaving a single lock hanging before her forehead, and as half past seven rolled around, she left the room.

The Three Oxen was one of the finest inns in the city of

Tarnecia, free from noise and drunken revelry, even in the later hours. As Ceci glided down the carpeted stairs to the entry hall, there was only the murmur of consummately polite conversation from well-dressed men in plush chairs. The lone person on foot awaited Ceci by the end of the staircase.

He stood six feet tall, with features that may well have been dreamed up by a sculptor. His broad shoulders were wrapped in an equestrian drape of wine red brocade, befitting an aristocrat of his station. Both his hands rested behind his back, putting the musculature of his bronzed arms on display. The black of his boots matched that of his lush hair, but couldn't outshine his dark eyes, as he welcomed Ceci with a lethally charming smile.

Alendro Benuarte was Perfection in human form, and no one knew this better than he himself.

"Did I keep you waiting, my love?" Ceci breathed as she reached the bottom step.

In place of an answer, Alendro wrapped his hands around her waist and kissed her on the lips. As he pulled away, he beamed with satisfaction, much in the way a collector may revel in his latest acquisition. He stroked her forehead to tuck away the lone curl Ceci had left out for him. "You look—"

"Beguiling? Breathtaking?" Ceci raised her eyebrows to an impish arc and sank her voice lower. *"Ravishing?"*

"—like a whore."

Ceci threw her head back and laughed. "Do you want me to go upstairs and get changed? Or would your father terribly mind the further wait?"

"Oh, I'm sure he would." Alendro sighed, entertaining the thought. "But I do think we should get going." He kept one hand on the small of Ceci's back as he led the way to the exit.

It was well into the last month of spring, but in Tarnecia, the season had barely started. The city lay in the shade of the Quierney mountains in West Ardonne, almost half a mile above sea level. Every so often, a stiff breeze swept the narrow streets, and Ceci made sure to shudder dramatically with each one, giving Alendro ample excuse to rub her bare shoulder.

Their goal was only a short walk away at another inn, where Alendro's father, the legendary former captain Harmon Benuarte, awaited them for dinner. Even Ceci had heard of his name, as the man who fought the final battle at sea during the last Werrish conflict. Someone like him would hate being held up, particularly by someone like her.

The street turned into a staircase under their feet, as it followed the slope of the mountain. With each step, Ceci swung the end of her shawl in wide movements beside her.

"What do you think he'll call me this time?" she asked, touching the tip of her forefinger against her cheek in mock pensiveness. "A leech? A flea? A tick? I don't believe he's called me a tick yet."

"I think he's warming up to you. The last time he and I spoke, he called you a magpie."

"Well, from him, that's practically a compliment!"

"Indeed. Perhaps you should start wearing thinner clothes, just in case."

Within a few minutes, they arrived. The inn was the largest in the city, with two entire floors dedicated to feasting and drinking. Music and cheers blared through the wide open entrance, as well as the numerous windows in every direction. Ceci moved to enter, but Alendro held her back.

"I have something for you." He reached into his pocket and produced a velvet bag tied with a white silk ribbon.

Ceci gasped and opened her gift. It was a necklace this time, made of solid gold like all the others. What made it more special was the row of small crystals fitted into the front part. At first glance, they appeared to reflect the sunlight many times over—but a closer look revealed that the light in fact came from inside them.

A necklace with thaumaturgic quartzes. The eighth ridiculously expensive and gaudy trinket in as many weeks.

"It's absolutely wonderful. Shall I put it on right now?" Ceci asked needlessly. The only purpose of these gifts was to be seen by the man whose money had *actually* paid for them.

Alendro took the chain and helped it on her. As he fastened the clasp, he leaned into her hair and drew a slow, lazy breath. Another pleased smile crept to his lips as he smelled the rosewater—the gift from the week before.

While Alendro dallied behind Ceci's neck, she grabbed his forearm, pretending only now to notice the bruise on his wrist. "Is that what I think it is?"

"How am I to know what you think?" Alendro asked with barely feigned innocence.

"You've been slumming again." Ceci pouted. "You told me you wouldn't."

"No, *you* told me I shouldn't."

Slumming was a popular pastime among young people with too much money and free time. The routine was simple enough: hire some men as bodyguards for a night, get them drunk in a rough part of town, pick fights with the locals, then make bets among themselves on the ensuing brawl. Most well-bred brats preferred to stay out of the scuffle and grew out of the habit in their early twenties.

At the age of twenty-six, Alendro showed no sign of losing

interest, and he delighted in showing off his legionary training by throwing himself into the fray. Ceci could imagine what chance some drunk commoners stood against someone trained by the cream of the Ardonnese forces. Nonetheless, she also knew that noble or common, the price of life was never more than one dumb mistake. And she needed Alendro alive. She needed him badly.

"I'm going to worry myself sick about you," she pressed. "What if you get into trouble?"

"A rich man is only in trouble when he wants to be, and only for as long as he feels like it," Alendro quoted the saying without a hint of the bitter irony that common people would recite it with. "But if it bothers you so much, you'll be happy to know I won't be doing it for a while. I need to be in good shape."

Ceci's curiosity piqued. "What for?"

"In two weeks, Father and I will be traveling to Lake Forterne to join my uncle and his offspring at the Benuarte villa for the First of Summer. There will be feasts, games, and parades. None but the most intimate family circles are welcome."

Ceci buried her chin coyly in her shoulder. "Sounds nothing like a place where I would belong."

"No, you most certainly wouldn't."

Ceci had no doubt that Alendro was already picturing his father's reaction when he found out she would be coming along for the celebrations.

Alendro gestured toward the door. "Shall we?"

In response, Ceci threw an arm around his shoulder. She kissed him on the cheek, leaned against his broad chest, and followed him inside like the picture of ardent infatuation.

Yes, Alendro Benuarte was indeed perfect. He was well bred and well mannered. His title, wealth, and beauty made Ceci the envy of every woman wherever they went. He was a gentleman in public and the right kind of savage in private. And most importantly, he didn't love her—which, in turn, meant he wouldn't go running after her if she suddenly vanished.

Ceci counted the days until the gathering at the Benuarte villa, hoping that with each new morning, she would get one step closer to the man she was going to kill.

Chapter 2

"I'm telling you. The second one is never as good as the first."

Corlis was crouched behind the bar, arranging cups on the bottom shelf and half-listening to the conversation that went on a few feet away. It was late evening, and the Lame Mare was empty save for him and the other two. Officially, the inn had closed a half hour earlier, but some guests had earned the right to stay behind while Corlis finished the day's cleaning—as long as they drank and paid for it.

One such guest was Porla, whose thick fingers drummed on the counter with a sound like a six-horse carriage. "Why wouldn't it be?"

There was a brief delay before the response as the man next to her emptied the last of his beer with little concern for how much of it ended up on his red tunic. He then slammed the empty tankard upside-down on the bar and carefully wiped the froth off his face. Like most Werrish men, Ladec took great pride in his facial hair, but he hadn't opted for the usual handlebar mustache. Instead, his thick blond whiskers ran along his upper lip and down the sides of his mouth, in a horseshoe shape that he affectionately called his "loin brush."

"The spark just isn't there, you know?" he said, while Corlis stood up to clear away his tankard. "The first time, you never quite know what to expect, and everything is exciting and new. But by the second time?" He snapped his fingers. "Gone, like that."

Porla tutted. "I don't agree. Yes, the first time everything is new, but that's exactly why it's not quite right. You're both figuring out what you're doing and what you want from each other. The second time around, you can keep doing what's right and fix what's broke."

She ceased the drumming and finished her own drink. Her flat face with the telltale reddish-brown hair and freckles of the Mountain people stood in stark contrast with Ladec's straw-colored locks and elongated jawline. Just about the only thing they had in common was their love of women, which they often discussed at length by Corlis's bar.

"Ah, but that's just it." Ladec raised a sage finger. "How do you know what's right? There was something *you* liked, and there was something *she* liked, but who's to say it's the same thing? Chances are, you'll end up fixing something that was never wrong to begin with."

While Porla frowned in thought, Corlis cleared away their cups. "I hate to break up your seminar, but you've got about a minute before I turn in for the night."

"Then why don't you give us the last word, eh, Corlis?" Porla asked. "Which do you think is better, the first time or the second?"

Ladec chortled to himself. "Have you even had a first time?"

"A first time for what?" Corlis leaned on the counter before the Werrish. "You paying your whole tab instead of owing for three weeks in a row? Because that happens as often as my eyes point the same way."

"Hey now, you give Porla free drinks all the time!" Ladec spread his arms in indignation.

"And I get free rides in return. What do *you* do for me?"

Ladec puffed up his chest under the city guard uniform. "I help you sleep soundly at night."

"Like the family down the street, who got their house robbed clean not a month ago?" Corlis asked. "The only thing putting me to sleep is how bored I am with your excuses."

"Easy there." Porla raised her hand. "Just put in your two bits."

Corlis sucked his tooth. As much as he loathed to admit, Ladec was correct about his dearth of experience. Not that Corlis had ever been interested to begin with—he simply didn't like it when someone else was right.

"Whether the first, or second, or tenth one is best," he said at last, "all I'd say is that if you go into each time expecting it to feel exactly the same, you're only setting yourself up for disappointment."

Ladec and Porla hemmed in vague agreement, then dove into their purses to fish out the price of their drinks. While they did so, Corlis took out the box under the counter and turned out its contents.

"What kind of money is that?" asked Ladec, gesturing at the small mound of wooden chips.

"Beer tokens," Corlis replied, grouping them into stacks of ten. "There's construction in next lot over, and all the workers come here at lunchtime. The company gives them these to exchange for beer. I take them back in the morning for the price of the drinks and then some."

Ladec stroked his whiskers. "Is it worth it for them? The company, I mean."

"If the workers buy their own drinks, they buy wine or harder. I'd say it's worth it for the company not to have their men get sloshed in the middle of day, especially with summer around the corner. Wine and heat are as bad a mix at a construction site as any."

"Seems there's plenty to go around," Porla noted, as Corlis completed the fourth stack and began the fifth. "There's been a lot of work around these parts lately. Every other day, I'm driving some foreman or broker, looking at all the old unfinished buildings. At this rate, something might actually become of the Wall District."

"Wouldn't that be news and a half," Corlis muttered.

Some twenty-six years ago, shortly before Corlis was born, the council of New Montres had made massive plans to expand the city northwards between the railway and the Ryonne delta. The roads were all laid out and paved, and the lots sold like hotcakes. But then the last Werrish conflict broke out, and the Emperor of Ardonne halted all construction, as the men and materials were needed for the war effort. Peace was declared two years later, but only a fraction of the work picked up again.

For the most part, the formerly ambitious Wall District remained an empty shell, with half-finished skeletons of factories and apartment buildings on every other corner. There was a minor resurgence in interest a decade or so later— that was when Patrell Andassi decided to invest his modest inheritance in erecting The Lame Mare inn. Unfortunately for him and his family, the gamble didn't pay off. A year after opening, Patrell was killed in a bar fight. His widow Ulmira and their adopted son Corlis were left with the inn and, more importantly, the mountains of debt. Fourteen years after that,

Ulmira died as well after a protracted illness, leaving only Corlis.

Eight months had passed since then, and life had not become one bit easier. But it had become bearable. For a long time, that was all Corlis thought he could hope for. Now there was a promise of change, as the Wall District was on the verge of a third wind.

"Not all of us are thrilled about that." Ladec laid his coins on the bar and rose from his seat. "Out-of-town workers think they're in a whole other country where the laws don't apply. We're breaking up fights left and right all the time. Some days, I barely have time to think."

"Clearly." Corlis swept up the price for the numerous drinks Ladec had consumed during his discussion with Porla.

"Same time tomorrow?" Ladec asked.

"Right you are." Porla headed to the exit. "Anything you want me to tell Thessa?" she asked Corlis.

Corlis paused. He had not seen Thessa in weeks, but he knew she and Porla regularly met for lunch in the city. The thought stung him a little. He and Thessa had definitely not gotten off on the right foot when they first met, but after they narrowly escaped with their lives from the Imperial Paladins, they agreed to turn over a new leaf. Thessa settled down in New Montres and was a frequent visitor at The Lame Mare for a good while, calling on Corlis for help while she got used to life on her own. She was a quick study, though, and needed him less and less as time went on. Save for one bigger favor that Corlis had to do for her, she soon stopped relying on him. Once Porla helped her get a job at the Messengers' Guild, Corlis barely saw her at all.

He put the token box back under the counter and said, "Tell

her I sold the last of the pigs a week ago, so if she kills anyone again, she's on her own."

Porla and Ladec chuckled, then stepped out into the street, picking at the loose threads of their conversation as their voices faded into the distance. Corlis closed, bolted, and locked the door behind them before he gave the tavern one last check. Everything was clean and ready for Addie to open the next morning. He hung his apron on the peg next to the stairs, shut off all the oil lamps, and trotted up the back stairs to his room.

The Lame Mare was doing better than any time while Uncle Patrell had been alive. The previous month, for the first time since he could remember, Corlis made his payments to the creditor early. Addie had also done the numbers and found they could hire a cook again to serve proper food, not just roasted sausages and onions. She said they'd already break even if half the workers bought their lunch at the inn, and anything above that was pure profit. At the time, Corlis told her to wait another month, to make sure the construction didn't suddenly stop again.

But the truth was, he was afraid. Sure, most of him couldn't have been happier that he finally didn't have to scrape for every last copper while nursing a dying aunt. Moreover, the prospect of paying off his debts was closer than ever—barely a few more years, if that. He would finally become the sole and rightful owner of his home, free to do with as he wished.

And that was precisely what scared him—he had no idea what he wished. The Lame Mare had been Uncle Patrell's dream and legacy. Aunt Mira and Corlis had carried it after his death because they had no choice, and the one good thing about having no choice was that it required no thinking. Now, that comfort was threatening to fade. In a few years, Corlis would become wholly responsible for his own life.

He set the lamp next to the four-poster bed his adoptive parents used to sleep in, crawled under the covers and faced the window.

In the last few months, life had become bearable. Soon enough, Corlis would have to decide what else it could be.

Chapter 3

Thessa was already awake when the landlady's heavy knuckles banged on her door at six o'clock. She'd been up for almost a half hour, staring at what little she saw of the sky. Her cell-like room had two small windows, each of them one foot tall and two feet wide, right under the low ceiling. As Thessa lay in bed, the only thing that showed through them was the sparkling blue of the late spring morning. Looking at it, it would have been easy to think the world outside was nothing but light and beauty.

As she rolled over, the uneven crossbars under her worn-out mattress were quick to remind her of the opposite. Thessa pushed herself to a sitting position, slid her feet into a pair of house slippers, and prepared to face another day. In every practical way, it was a day like any other, promising the same drudgery and routine. But in one specific way—one that only meant anything to her—it was one of the most remarkable days of her life so far.

In the ridiculously complicated calendar that Ardonne insisted on using, the date was called *the second to the Wax of Shear*. In the simplified calendar used by the rest of the Ora Mara region, including Thessa's homeland of Sallis, it was the twenty-eighth day of the fifth month. And in the calendar of her own life, it was the first anniversary of her running away from home.

Her parents had intended to marry her into one of the most pious families of Sallis, which would have condemned Thessa to a life of service in a temple she could never leave. She begged and pleaded with them to find her another husband, and when they refused to do so, she saddled her horse and rode blindly into the night. It was an act of sheer desperation, in an attempt to regain control of her life.

A year had passed since then, and as Thessa sat in her squalid little room, she wondered how much control she had gained. She draped a thin cloth around her shoulders, grabbed the chipped pitcher from the floor, and stepped out to fetch water.

Outside, she was accosted by the smell of fish, garlic, and burnt oil. She made her way across the courtyard to the water pump, where she hurriedly filled her pitcher. Around her, the rest of the house was waking up as well. Mothers yelled after their children, husbands yelled after their wives, shopkeepers yelled after their customers. New Montres was either asleep or loud, with nothing in between.

After she washed and brushed herself, Thessa put on her uniform and her messenger's bag. Once out on the street, she normally would turn west and continue to the railcar stop, but not this morning.

"Over here!" Porla waved from atop her coach.

Thessa waved back and climbed up on the perch beside her. When she was up and seated, Porla took up the reins and started them off. They had been planning this meeting for weeks, but only had an hour or so before Thessa had to be at work. But it would be enough for what she had in mind.

"Today is the big day, eh?" Porla asked. "One year on your

own."

"One year," Thessa echoed.

"How's that feel? I'd wager you didn't think you'd end up here when you left."

Thessa shook her head. "When I was young, all I could think about was the places I'd travel to when I got married. New Montres was one of them, so I suppose that came true. Even if not exactly how I imagined."

"Do you ever think about your folks back home?"

"Hardly," Thessa said. "I've had more than enough of my own matters to think about, let alone theirs."

"What do you reckon they'd think of you?"

"My father disowned me the same night as I left to protect himself from the embarrassment. If anyone found out his daughter is now living a lowly commoner's life in New Montres, he might die."

As much as she joked about Papa's reaction, Thessa had to admit she had her own difficulties getting used to that same thought.

After she and Corlis barely got away from the Paladins, Thessa resolved to abandon her ways as a grifter and lead an honest life. As she was soon forced to learn, resolve and reality were markedly different things. Besides all the hassle that came with settling down in a strange city, there was a singular thought that was more bitter to swallow. That she, Thessalona Kalou, daughter of Lord Protector Xanthias Kalou, was now poor.

She had been hard up before, yes. The first days after she ran away were nothing short of a nightmare as she wandered the forest lost and hungry. Later too, as she traveled with Hanna, there were days when the money ran short, and they had to hole up in a shed or an attic for the night. At the time, it was never more than a temporary hitch, and the good life was only as far away as their next mark. But once Thessa gave up her old ways, every day was like those days.

With one last jerk, the coach stopped under them. A finely polished shingle in the shape of a delicate cup dangled on their left, below which a sign with flowery writing advertised The Pernilla Sisters' Coffee House. A tantalizing smell of freshly roasted beans surrounded the building.

"This is the one you meant, right?" Porla asked. "Have you been here before? Some of these places are mighty picky about who they let in."

"The sisters aren't like that," said Thessa. "I've been here many times, and I've seen all sorts of people here."

True enough, the guests inside were a colorful lot. The handful of small, round tables were occupied by lawyers, officers, and professors, as much as merchants and cooks— or indeed, coach drivers and messengers. Judging by their manners, it was easy enough to tell which of them were more accustomed to the place. Back in Sallis, Thessa drank coffee every day with her parents and sisters, but here in Ardonne, a single cup fetched the price of a decent dinner.

Despite being full, the coffee house was almost completely silent as everyone kept their voices barely above a whisper. It was quite dark too, with the only light coming from a handful of thaumaturgic quartz lights under stained-glass covers, further lending the place an air of luxury. The younger Pernilla came to seat them, and Thessa ordered two coffees.

"So, you've been here a lot, eh?" Porla asked. "If I'd known you lived so large, I would've had you treat me more often."

"I wasn't living large," Thessa replied. "I just didn't know how poor I was. But I wanted to celebrate this day with something special."

Learning to handle her money had not been a lesson that came cheaply to her. She did realize she would have to cut back on her spending, and for a while, she thought she did. She never bought anything expensive. A hairpin one day or a shawl the next. A book, a play, or indeed, a cup of coffee. None of those things were lavish, and yet, by the end of her first month, she was already forced to borrow so as not to be kicked out of her cheap room. She tried to rein in her money, but it was like water in her hand. The harder she grasped for it, the more it trickled between her fingers.

It had occurred to her that she should ask Corlis for advice, but she held back. She had relied on others her whole life— her parents at home, Hanna on the road, Corlis when she arrived to New Montres. She wanted to prove, most of all to herself, that she could stand on her own.

One day, as she stared longingly through the window of a jeweler, an elegantly dressed man approached her and struck up a conversation. When Thessa let slip that she couldn't afford the brooch on display, he revealed himself to be in the employment of a bank and offered a loan to her on generous conditions. Seeing as how Thessa used to make a living off of other people's gullibility, she was reserved at first. But when the man took her to his office and showed her a proper stamped contract, she put her concerns to rest and signed.

She soon learned what a mistake that was. The man showed up week after week and eventually demanded greater payments, citing all sorts of costs and interest. Before long, Thessa owed more than what she had borrowed. At last, suspicion prompted her to ask around about the bank she had supposedly struck a deal with, only to find it had gone out of business years before. When she confronted the man about it, his pleasant demeanor vanished. He threatened to send his "colleagues" to visit Thessa the next evening unless she paid in full.

The thought of the encounter terrified Thessa. Not because of what said colleagues might do to her, but because of what *she* might be forced to do. If those men threatened her, she could be compelled to transform. The last man who put her in that position ended up dead, and Thessa wasn't ready to face those consequences again.

That day, she finally did what she should have done weeks earlier.

She waited until The Lame Mare emptied out, so they could speak in private while Corlis and Addie were there. They listened to her without a word as the three of them sat around the table. By the time Thessa finished, she was fighting back tears of frustration. Not only over her situation, but her own self too—that she couldn't last a month without getting into trouble. She said so out loud, bracing herself for one of Corlis's vitriolic remarks that he was known for.

Instead, he only asked her the lender's name and what he looked like. Before he and Thessa met, Corlis had a long history of working for the underworld of New Montres, and though he cut most of those ties after the incident with the Paladins, he knew a few people who owed him a favor. One day later, the lender was back at Thessa's doorstep, apologized profusely for his miscalculation, and returned the whole amount she had paid over her original debt. It took him a little while to count out all the coins, as two fingers on his right hand were missing, and the rest were broken.

More than that, Addie taught Thessa how to make money last longer. Corlis may have been the owner of The Lame Mare, but Addie managed the coffers, and that girl could stretch a copper like fresh dough. She knew what everything should cost and where to get everything for the right price. She knew how to fix things and how to haggle when she had to pay someone else to do it. Not a single iron bit went unaccounted under her eye. When Thessa asked where she had learned all this, she only said, "You either pick these things up or starve."

The elder Pernilla brought the coffee to the table.

Porla waited for Thessa to put sugar in hers, then raised her cup. "Well, then, here's to you not starving for another year!"

Thessa took a careful sip, taking the time to savor every drop of the thick drink that coated her tongue. More so, she savored the chance to share it with a friend of her own, not just her parents or their guests.

"I wish Corlis could have come too," she said, "but he says even the smell of coffee gives him a bad taste in his mouth."

"Funny, that. Seeing how bitter he is all the time, you'd think he drinks nothing but." Porla took another sip. "I went up to see him yesterday, mind. Didn't mention it, but I'd wager he misses you."

"I know." Thessa tapped the side of her cup. "I want to visit more often, but there's so much more work than I imagined."

"How's that going?"

"They're running me on Ilvior Island in the mornings, but once that's done, I have to take deliveries all over the city. Most of them go to Montres or Crescent Bay, but rarely ever to the Wall District."

Even after the fraudulent lender was sorted out, Thessa's

problems were a long way from over. By that time, she'd been kicked out of one bar for slapping a guest, and the second one wasn't promising to last much longer, either. Shameless men were one front where not even Addie had much to offer in the way of advice—it was simply a part of the job. If she remained a server, Thessa would have loved to work at a coffee house, but such a position seemed to be more exclusive than the houses themselves.

That time, it was Porla who came to her rescue. Working as a rent-coach driver, she was familiar with a few people in the Messengers' Guild and got wind of an opening at one of their offices. By that time, Porla had known all about Thessa's past and that she was an avid rider. A messenger job was ideal for her—all she needed to do was learn the lay of the land around the city. Porla let her ride up on the perch with her, and Thessa committed all the streets, crossroads, and bridges to memory.

After a few weeks, she knew her way well enough to pass the tryouts and be accepted into the guild. From there, she spent all her days on horseback, running regular letters in the morning and special deliveries until the evening, blissfully removed from unwanted lustful hands. The money was barely any better, but coupled with all Thessa learned from Addie, it was good enough to get by—and to occasionally treat herself and a friend to a small indulgence.

"Right, then," Porla said. "I'd say we both better get going. Wouldn't want you to lose that plum job because I held you up!"

From the coffee house, Porla drove her all the way to the guild's offices in the Lower Court District. No sooner did Thessa land on the pavement than a haggard bureaucrat hailed

Porla down, and she was off again. Thessa called after her one last time, then hurried inside the building to pick up her morning load.

Life in New Montres had not started out easy, but little by little, it had become bearable. As much as Thessa wished to relish this simple fact, some part of her wished it could be more than that.

Chapter 4

The Wall District had never been the most illustrious borough of New Montres, but Corlis knew it well enough to find its tolerable spots. On the west, it was bordered by the Ryonne delta, which at that point was so wide that the other side was barely visible. The breadth of the river also diluted the water enough so that it didn't carry the same smell that permeated some of the inner city.

All the major dockyards were on the Wedge further up the river—out here, only a handful of small fishing ports dotted the bank every few hundred yards or so. Most of them featured a shabby little boathouse that sold freshly grilled fish for dirt cheap, with coarse bread and something pickled. Corlis and Thessa sat at the edge of a pier, finishing up their lunch while the sparks of midday light danced on the water before them.

"I remember seeing the river from your window, but I've never been down here," Thessa said. "It's so peaceful. Reminds me a little of Ilvior."

She was enjoying a day off from work, dressed in a plain linen dress instead of her uniform, and with her long black hair let down. The comfort clearly suited her, as she leaned back on her hands and turned her face toward the sun.

"Didn't you say Ilvior was boring?" Corlis asked. "I'd hate to think you're wasting your free time like this."

"Boring is good sometimes. I didn't realize how much. I spent twenty years being bored at home—at my parents' house. Then it was nothing but trouble until I came here, and it's been nothing but work since then. One boring day is a good change."

Corlis sniffed. "One year away from home, and you're already full of wisdom."

"And what are you full of?" Thessa shoved him on the shoulder.

"Right now, pickled melons and cod." Corlis tossed the sparse remains of his lunch into the river. "And my ears will be full of something else if I don't get back to Addie soon."

He clambered to a stand, and with a gentlemanly flourish, extended a hand to Thessa to help her up as well.

She shoved him again and got up on her own. "I'm sorry I didn't come sooner or more often. But in a few months, if I keep doing good work, they'll start running me in some of the inner boroughs. I'll try to ask for the Freighter District—that's not too busy and a lot closer."

"We're looking most forward for you to grace us with your presence," Corlis said with a bow. Then he added, "Don't fret it. I'm just glad you're doing all right."

They left the bank and wound their way back to the increasingly busy streets. The crowd and the noise grew around them, as carts full of crates and barrels clamored by on one side, freight trains thundered on the other, and workmen in dusty tunics ambled back to the dozens of construction sites. Watching the chaos, Corlis admitted to himself that a day of boredom wasn't too bad.

Which was, of course, why it couldn't last.

One block away from The Lame Mare, there came a high-pitched noise from around the corner.

"Is that Addie?" Thessa asked.

It was indeed. By the time they reached the crossroads, it became clear that Addie was screaming snakes and frogs at someone, and once they rounded the corner, it became clear why. Thessa covered her mouth. Corlis couldn't so much as open his.

The Lame Mare was in ruins. There was no other way to put it. Half of the roof was missing, as was a good chunk of the third floor and some of the second. Logs stuck out of what had once been the attic and lay haphazardly around the building. Piles of bricks heaped on one side, and the trashed remains of a pulley dangled next to a window. A faint cloud of dust lingered around the destruction.

As soon as the feeling came back into his legs, Corlis bolted toward the commotion in front of the inn. Pushing through the gaggle of onlookers, he forced his way to the epicenter, which consisted of three people. Addie was beet red and pausing only in her tirade to take a breath. The man across from her must have been some sort of foreman, middle-aged with a thick build and thicker hair on his forearms, doing his best to exude authority. In the middle was Ladec, keeping them apart, which mostly meant pushing Addie back. All three of them were Werrish, and so they shouted over each other in their native tongue.

"What happened?" Corlis asked.

Addie whipped her head toward him, smacking Ladec in the face with one of her straw-colored pigtails in the process. Without missing a beat, she went on in Ardonnese. "What happened is that these lowdown, scum-sucking sons of—"

The foreman crossed his arms. "Now, you listen, girlie—"

"Not another word from either of you," Ladec boomed, then said to Corlis, "There was an accident at the construction."

"I can see that much. What did you do?" Corlis addressed the foreman.

The man screwed up his nose. "What happened is that the rope holding one of the brick elevators in place seems to have come undone. The weight of the bricks tipped over the elevator and crashed into one of the scaffolds below, which then… fell over."

"Oh, it *seems* to have come undone?" Addie put her hands on her hips and opened her eyes wide in mockery. "And how did that happen? Is it because your men *seem* to have empty slop buckets where their brains should be?"

She yelled the last three words at the top of her lungs, and the flinging of Werrish insults resumed. Ladec stepped in once again and pulled them apart, sending each of them their own way. By the time the noise died down, Thessa had managed to catch up as well.

"The boys are already at the construction site, questioning the one who was in charge of those ropes," Ladec said eventually. "I only caught one look at him, but he was drunk as a skunk. We've got some witnesses too who can back it up. Once we've got everything written down, come by the guardhouse. I'll have everything signed and stamped, so you can have a better case in court."

"Is the city guard always so involved in accidents?" Corlis asked with some reservation.

Ladec stroked his horseshoe mustache. "Not usually, nah. Just figured I could help you sleep a little more soundly tonight."

Corlis swallowed. "Thanks, Ladec."

The guard scattered the remaining gawkers, then bid his goodbye.

Thessa rested her hand on Corlis's shoulder as they stood by what was left of the inn—what was left of Uncle Patrell's dream and legacy. Corlis's home for the past decade and a half. The place where, after ten years at the orphanage, he got a taste of what it was like to have a family. Even if that only lasted for a year, it left a mark on him that nothing could erase. He had never realized how much he equated that mark with The Lame Mare itself. Now, as the dust settled and the street emptied, Corlis watched both his past and future crumble away.

* * *

Corlis sat in the horridly uncomfortable chair across from the magistrate's desk, while she leafed meticulously through the stack of documents, despite having read them all multiple times before. Nonetheless, he held out waiting. It took two weeks just to get into this room and make his case, so he could spare a few more minutes. It wasn't like he was pressed to be anywhere else.

The magistrate's eyes jumped back and forth behind the brass-framed spectacles as they glided over row after row. At long last, she set down the papers, smoothed out her chalk-white robe, and brushed a single loose strand of mousy brown hair behind her ear.

"What are your aims with this case?" she asked, in a tone that took Corlis back to his school days.

"I was hoping you could give a firsthand assessment," he said. Corlis had accompanied both Uncle Patrell and Aunt Mira in legal matters a few times and was fully aware how long these processes could draw out. If he could get an early assessment in his definitive favor, he could try to negotiate damages out of court.

"Mm-hm." The magistrate picked out one of the statements with two bony fingers. "As far as direct culpability is concerned, there's no question. In his testimony, the worker in employment at the construction site has accepted full responsibility for his mistake."

"He did?"

The magistrate raised her eyebrows, as well as the document. "You haven't read this?"

Corlis indeed had not. As soon as Ladec handed over the pile of papers, he went straight to the Wall District courthouse to submit his case before closing time.

The woman read from the paper. "Upon questioning, the subject confirmed that his negligence had been the sole cause of the incident."

It made no sense. Corlis had heard plenty of workers talking at the inn, and if there was one rule they all agreed on, it was, "Always blame the tools." That way, if anything went sideways during work, the provider of the tools would be responsible for any damages caused—and it was always the employer's responsibility to provide the tools. Had this idiot been too drunk to remember this?

The magistrate continued, "The subject also admitted to being inebriated during work hours. By his recount, he consumed two cups of unwatered wine, which he purchased at The Lame Mare inn using a token provided by—"

Corlis's head fell back. *Son of a bitch.*

"Excuse me?" came the sharp voice across the desk, forcing him to realize he had spoken out loud.

"The men at the construction site got tokens they could exchange at my inn for beer," Corlis said, not bothering with an apology. "But only for beer, precisely to avoid an accident like this. I knew the rule, and so did my barmaid. There was no way Addie gave that man wine, especially unwatered."

The magistrate pursed her lips at the discourtesy, but turned back to the document. "Well, that puts you on much shakier ground. If the employer can argue that you or your barmaid broke the terms of your contract, they can contest the assessment and demand a formal trial."

"You mean they *will* argue, and they *will* contest." Corlis slammed the armrest of the chair.

It could only have been that damn foreman. Ladec had said the worker was obviously drunk, so the foreman told him to say he'd drank at The Lame Mare. Damn him and his whole lot to the dark depths.

The magistrate said, "Either way, you can prepare for a long process."

Long and expensive. More so than the repairs themselves. And unlike the repairs, there was no guarantee anything would come of it in the end. But even if Corlis's victory was set in stone, and he was sure to get all his damages compensated, it would take months to come to a ruling. The inn would stay in ruins until then.

There were no two ways about it. If he wanted to keep business going—and to make a living—he'd have to take out another loan. Just when he was close to getting out of it in a few short years, he'd have to get deeper in debt.

Just when life had become bearable, it found a way to screw Corlis over.

II

Part Two

Chapter 5

In the days before and after his appointment with the magistrate, Corlis went through a broader range of emotion than any point of his life before. Before the hearing, he was tense with anticipation. When the magistrate revealed the worker's lies, he flipped over into impotent fury. Fury then ebbed into frustration, tapered into resentment, and at last died out in resignation.

In some ways, it reminded him of losing Uncle Patrell. But at that time, there was also plenty of work at the inn to distract him and Aunt Mira, and give them some semblance of purpose. Without the inn, Corlis had nothing left but a numb emptiness, as if he had simply run out of things to feel.

But he kept working. If not *at* the inn, then *on* the inn.

The construction workers had quickly taken away the scaffolding logs, ropes, and whatever else belonged to them, but they touched nothing else. Ladec and some others had come by with wheelbarrows to help get rid of the debris. Addie also hung around to clean for a few days, but after a while, she had to take another job at an inn that had actual income. Thessa showed up whenever she could, though there wasn't much she or anyone else could do. The more Corlis tried to clean up the rubble, the more appeared out of nowhere.

Day after day rolled by in utter futility, and he kept working because there was nothing else. It was on the third week after the disaster that the sound of footsteps broke the monotone rustle of Corlis's broom while he emptied out one of the second-floor rooms.

"Is anyone here?" a male voice came from below.

Corlis trotted down the stairs, broom in hand. "In case the missing roof didn't make it clear enough, we're not open."

The visitor stood out in his surroundings like a silver coin in a slop heap. His impeccably fitted white shirt and green jacket pinned him as some sort of bureaucrat, likely the kind who thought his work was nothing less than the foundation of worldly order. His face complemented the impression, as he was younger than Corlis and almost as thin, with the kind of mouth that always looked like he'd just bitten into a lemon. "I'm hoping to find Corlis Andassi," he creaked.

"And if you found him?"

"Then I should like to introduce myself as Romer Calseus, a junior at Golden Lion Associates. I'm here to relay a message from one of our senior jurisconsults, Marello Fabreve."

He handed over a calling card exactly as pretentious as the name of the organization implied. On one side, a liberal rendition of a lion's head was printed in gold-colored ink, along with an inner city address. On the other side was the name Marello Fabreve, and under it the title *Vested Consult on Economic and Family Law*. The four corners of the card were marked with the words *Appointment*, *Return*, *Inquiry*, and *Other*.

"He should like you to pay him a visit at the office at your earliest convenience," the junior concluded.

Corlis handed the card back to him. "You can tell him not to bother wasting his time. I didn't take the case to court, and I'm not planning to. Unless he wants to come to me with an offer on damages, we have nothing to talk about."

Romer's mouth puckered further in his puzzlement. "Damages?"

"For the accident that turned my inn to ruin." Corlis gestured around the area and toward the stairs, most of which were buried under dirt and gravel.

"Oh." The junior looked around, as if he hadn't noticed the state of the building he stood in. "I think you misunderstand me. This isn't regarding any accident."

"Then what?"

"I haven't been made privy to the full extent of the details," said Romer, the way only a lawyer can take half a day to say he didn't know, "but I believe it concerns your parents."

The last word jerked the rug out from under Corlis. *Parents?* Patrell and Ulmira were both dead, with no legal loose ends that Corlis knew of. And if they had, Corlis would sooner have drank soap water for a month than believe they had anything to do with people like this Romer.

The junior didn't wait for a reaction from him. "Please make sure you have that on your person when you arrive." He ignored the card that Corlis held toward him and shot an unsubtle glance at his clothes. "So as to ensure you don't get held up at the entrance."

* * *

The office of Golden Lion Associates stood by Crescent Bay, alongside a number of civic and former imperial authorities, most of which Corlis had never heard of. At last, he found the building that had a line of green marble pillars at the front, with the capitals carved into lion heads and covered in gold leaf. The decoration made it obvious enough, but to be sure, he checked the spotless plaque by the entrance.

The solid red oak door opened almost before he knocked, and an elderly face like a bleached prune stuck through the crack. Corlis handed over Fabreve's calling card with the *Appointment* corner folded in. The porter bowed him in without another word, then asked for a minute of patience while he announced Corlis's arrival.

As a senior jurisconsult—whatever that was supposed to mean—Fabreve's office lay in the back of the building, at the end of a corridor that was wide enough for a cart and carpeted from end to end. The fifteen-foot walls were decorated with lacquered wood inlays on the bottom half and portraits of supposedly notable former associates on the top.

Fabreve himself sat in a room the size of a tavern, behind a desk that could have withstood a siege. He was dressed in a similar green jacket as Romer, except the buttons alone were probably worth more than the junior's whole outfit. His head, perched atop a pair of almost comically broad shoulders, was shaved clean from top to bottom, save for his graying mutton chops.

"Good afternoon," he said in a voice so smooth it was almost suffocating. "Corlis Andassi, as I have been told? Please do take a seat."

The porter helped Corlis into a carved mahogany chair, then backed out of the room.

Fabreve offered a drink from a crystal decanter, which Corlis declined. He had no idea who this man was or what his intentions were, so he wanted to stay as clear in the head as possible.

"I'm glad you could answer my call so soon," the lawyer said while he dug out a file from his drawer.

"I don't exactly have a lot to do." Corlis watched closely for a reaction, but Fabreve gave no hint that he knew what Corlis was referring to.

"Before we begin, there are a handful of questions I need to ask you. I apologize beforehand if some of these may sound indiscreet, but the matters we need to discuss are of the utmost confidentiality. Therefore, I must make sure there's been no mistake of your identity. Is it correct that you used to live in an orphanage?"

Off to a dubious start already, but Corlis decided to play along for now. "Yes."

"Can you please name this orphanage and the years you lived there? It's only to cross-check with what I have in my file." Fabreve held up one of the papers with a long list of notes.

Corlis replied, "The Seventh Street Home for Children in Need. Nine hundred and thirty to nine hundred and forty."

"In nine hundred and forty, you were legally adopted. Can you please name your adoptive parents?"

"Patrell and Ulmira Andassi."

Fabreve nodded along with the answers. "Are you able to name the exact date on which you were left at the orphanage? To your best knowledge."

"As far as the nurses told me, it was the Fore Wane of Thaw."

Another nod. "That is indeed what I have." He showed Corlis his own list of facts, which matched all of the answers. Impressive, but not terribly so. All of this was on public record. Fabreve, or anyone else for that matter, could have gathered this much on Corlis if they wanted. The real question was why they would want to.

"With that, I can now be confident I am talking to the right person." Fabreve clasped his hands. "But I would like to ask you one more thing. While at the orphanage, have you received any information about the identity of your birth parents?"

Indeed, Corlis had. Although, it wasn't exactly what he'd call information. He'd mostly describe it as a rumor—or, more likely, a joke. According to the nurse he once asked, a woman had brought him in the dead of night, clad in black from head to toe. The nurse couldn't see her face, only her hands. By her description, those hands had never known a day's work.

Corlis was six years old when he heard this story. For the next few days, he told all the others at the orphanage that he was the lost son of a foreign king, and that one day his parents would take him away to live in a palace. Eventually, one of the older boys said the nurse made up the whole thing because he heard her tell the other nurses about it. For the rest of the year, everyone called Corlis "Prince Gullible."

He buried that memory along with so many others and accepted the much more likely truth—that his mother was some maid or factory worker who couldn't afford to get rid of him before he was born. But every so often, when he had a few minutes of rest, he'd indulge in the daydream of being that lost son.

And now, one of the most obscenely expensive family lawyers in New Montres was asking if he knew anything about his birth parents.

"No," Corlis replied. "I don't recall anything worthwhile."

"That is understandable," said Fabreve. "Your birth was very much kept secret for a long time."

"I've been out and about in this city for the past twenty-five years. I think that's a pretty clear giveaway of my birth."

"You are right; I wasn't clear enough. Your birth was only a secret in a very select circle. Have you ever heard of the family Benuarte of Forterne?"

"Forterne, yes. Benuarte, no."

Forterne province lay in the northeast, on the foothills of the Lancum mountain range that separated Ardonne from Midorea. It was known for only one thing, but that one thing was enough to carry its fame not just across the country, but across half the world. The white wine of Forterne was known as "liquid gold" for its color, its quality, and above all, its price. Every so often, tales of some rich idiot trading a country house for a single cask of it would make the rounds among the common folk.

Corlis had never heard the family name, but if they were known as "the Benuartes of Forterne," that had to mean something.

Fabreve leaned forward. "My client, Hestor Benuarte, is the landlord of a village on Vertussi Hill. He has given me his full trust to give you the following recount of events, as it pertains to you.

"Twenty-six years ago, in nine hundred and twenty-nine, Lord Hestor stayed briefly in New Montres province. During that time, he met Lady Tinia Cuiliane, and the two of them became involved in what you may call a dalliance. Their affair was a clandestine one, as both of them were married at the time. Lord Hestor to his wife, Lady Wilhelma, and Lady Tinia to her husband, Lieutenant Carno Cuiliane.

"Lord Hestor returned home soon afterward. The next month, Lady Tinia found that she was with child, and she could not tell whether it was from her husband or, indeed, from Lord Hestor. Six months after that, as you may know, the last Werrish conflict broke out. Lieutenant Cuiliane was called away to serve in the Ardonnese legion, and as such was not present when Lady Tinia gave birth two months later, on the Fore Wane of Thaw.

"Lady Tinia saw immediately that the child had none of her husband's features, but was instead a spitting image of Lord Hestor. In her letter to the lieutenant, she wrote that the boy was stillborn. Then, that same night, she traveled to New Montres and left the boy at the Seventh Street Home for Children in Need."

Fabreve's words hung in the air. He took two small glasses from beside his crystal decanter, filled them both, and slid one tactfully forward. Corlis took it and sloshed it around under his nose. He had never so much as seen a bottle from afar, but he could tell it was Forterne wine, and unwatered at that. He set it back on the desk.

Having worked closely with the underbelly of New Montres for a decade, Corlis was familiar with a wide variety of frauds and schemes. Many of them revolved around long lost relatives or dying aristocrats in need of an heir. The ones that involved legal matters also required an air of credibility, such as stamped formal papers, or—in the case of Thessa's shady lender—someplace that can pass for an office. Corlis had also heard about plenty of con artists who would spend months planning, digging up secrets about their mark, and tailoring every bit of the story around them.

In those respects, this absurd circus reminded Corlis of a

whole number of scams. There was only one factor that he couldn't quite place. Scammers were willing to put effort into their work because the payoff would be more than worth it. That payoff, however, would have to come from the victim. If someone went to the trouble of getting an office like the Golden Lion involved, the money they'd be fishing after would be tens of thousands of silvers. Silvers which Corlis decidedly did not have.

In short, as far as he could measure, either Fabreve was telling the truth, or he was the world's dumbest scammer.

Corlis bought himself some time while he racked his brain in search of a third option. "Why is Lord Hestor making you tell me all of this right now?"

Fabreve set down his glass, which he had been comfortably sipping. "Lord Hestor was unaware of your existence until last year when Lieutenant Cuiliane died, and Lady Tinia felt she could now safely confess to Lord Hestor about their child together. She wrote a letter to him detailing when and where she left the boy, in case he wanted to find him."

"Why isn't it the lady who's looking for me?"

"As I understand, she and her husband moved overseas to Chalimn shortly after the lieutenant got back from the Werrish conflict."

"How convenient," Corlis said in a flat tone. "And is Lord Hestor not worried what his wife will think of his bastard son?"

"Lady Wilhelma passed in childbirth twenty years ago, as their youngest daughter arrived."

Corlis's eyebrows shot up. "Is that so? I have a good friend who's exactly twenty years old. She might be that daughter. She's Sallician, too. That should make for an even better story."

Fabreve remained unfazed. Credit where credit was due; if he was a scammer, he was decent at keeping an act. "I understand this may be quite unexpected. You may also wish to see this." He produced a rolled-up canvas from his drawer and smoothed it on the desk between them. "Lord Hestor sent it to me when he instructed our office to find you. It was commissioned a few years after your birth."

The man on the portrait was about five years older and twenty pounds heavier than Corlis, but the resemblance between the two of them was impossible to deny. The same coarse black hair framed the same deep-set eyes, above the same sharp pair of cheekbones, and the same thin lips. In the bottom-left corner was the painter's signature, and the year nine hundred and thirty-three.

"Supposing that this is all true," Corlis said, "what exactly is Lord Hestor's purpose with this whole farce—besides rubbing it in my face how rich I could have been growing up?"

Fabreve refilled his drink. "In a few weeks' time, there will be a gathering at the Benuarte villa on Vertussi Hill, where the family regularly convenes to celebrate the First of Summer. Lord Hestor decided it would be the ideal occasion for you to meet him, as well as the rest of your blood relatives.

"Naturally, he is aware of the limitations of your current standing. Should you accept this invitation, my associates have been tasked to arrange all preparations for you, including a suitable wardrobe and travel bookings to Forterne. The expenses are shouldered by the Benuarte estate, regardless of the outcome of your visit."

Silence settled between them once again, and Corlis picked up his glass at last. "You know," he said between sips, "up until that point, you almost had me convinced."

The lawyer's face remained as blank as ever, yet Corlis got the impression of a smile. "It's not my job to convince you of anything. I have simply been ordered to relay this message to you. Whether you accept, decline, or wish to discuss different conditions, I will forward your response to Lord Hestor."

Corlis swallowed the last of his drink and got up. He had just wasted his afternoon trekking through the city to this office and listening to Fabreve's drivel. He didn't have the time for this kind of nonsense—not when he had a ruined inn to get back to and a new loan to saddle himself with. At least he got some decent wine for his trouble.

Chapter 6

Thessa could not believe what she was hearing. Not only that Corlis was indeed the lost son of a wealthy aristocrat; or that he was now invited to this aristocrat's country villa; but, most of all, that Corlis had decided not to go.

"Why not?" she asked. "This sounds like the chance of a lifetime! You'd finally get to meet your real father, and he might ask you to live with the rest of the family! You wouldn't have to worry about the inn, or your loans, or anything anymore! Isn't that—"

"—too good to be true?" Corlis splashed his face with water. "Yes, it is."

They were at one of the baths on Ilvior Island, one that Thessa had discovered while delivering letters. It was a small and unremarkable establishment, tucked away in one of the side streets—but for that same reason, it was also blissfully quiet. All the other patrons were a good thirty years older than the two of them, and they mostly stayed in the tepid pool indoors. The cold pool was only a few yards on each side, but Thessa and Corlis had it practically to themselves, which was welcome as the days grew warmer.

"But it all adds up, doesn't it?" Thessa went on. "The day of your birth, the orphanage you were left at—even your father's face, from what you said."

"Listen, I don't know what's behind it, but I know it's a load of piss. Maybe they picked me because I look like the man in the painting. Maybe they picked me first and had the painting to match my face. Maybe Fabreve has dozens of portraits in his drawer."

"Why are you so set on not believing him? What do you have to lose?"

"I have a *lot* to lose. The Lame Mare may be in ruins, but I'm still a free man, and I'm still alive. Either of those can change very easily." He scrubbed himself with such vigor as if he was trying to wash off his very thoughts. "I might not even be the one they're trying to scam. I could just be a scapegoat. For all I know, they can hide contraband in my luggage to Forterne, or try to frame me for something else. They could do it because they know I have no money for a lawyer, and I'd be a hundred miles from anyone who can help me."

"Then I'll go with you," Thessa said.

Corlis thought it over at length. "You think they'll allow that?"

"If they want you to believe that Hestor Benuarte is a nobleman, then they have to. An open invitation from a lord always extends to one guest as well. It's common courtesy." Upon Corlis's expression, Thessa added, "Don't be so shocked! I grew up memorizing these kinds of things."

"In Sallis."

"Most of Ardonnese courtesy was copied from Sallis." Thessa wrung the water out of her hair as they prepared to get out of the pool. "I could help you with that, too. Learn how to behave in fine company, so you can fit in better."

"You really are making the best of this, aren't you," Corlis asked in his acerbic tone. "Trying to get back to your old life, now that you've had your fun being poor?"

That was a low blow, if anything. Particularly as he knew how hard it had been for Thessa to get on her own two feet. He hadn't made a petty jab like that since the two of them met all those months before, when they were always at each other's throats. Some part of Thessa wanted to walk away right there and leave Corlis to sort out his own problem by himself.

But she had learned a lot about him since they met and, in many ways, the two of them understood each other like no one else.

She sidled closer to him. "Corlis—what are you afraid of?"

Corlis stirred at the question, but didn't answer right away. The pool was empty around them, and the only sound came from a handful of seagulls that had ventured this far inland from the harbors.

"I was alone for ten years as an orphan," he said, staring ahead. "For one year, I had a family. Then I was alone together with Aunt Mira, and now she's gone too. It took me half a year to let go of her.

"If I meet him—this Lord Hestor, and all his children, and nephews, and nieces… all those people who grew up in a villa, who have spent their whole lives around other nobles"—he pointed at his misaligned eyes—"do you think they'll want *me* among them?"

His voice was low, almost in a whisper, struggling to get the words out. He let his head fall back. High above, the birds screeched and circled, racing one another to scraps of food on the street.

"I don't have it in me to lose another family," Corlis said at last.

Thessa wished she could offer some snappy bit of wisdom, the kind that Corlis and his aunt had always been so good at. But that had never been her strength. Instead, she simply put her arms around him. And although he didn't return the embrace, Thessa had learned to tell this was all he needed.

* * *

As Thessa had predicted, Fabreve agreed in Lord Hestor's name to her accompanying Corlis on the journey. In fact, not only did the invitation extend to her, but the arrangement of a wardrobe as well. Romer, the junior associate from the Golden Lion, showed up with a private carriage ten days before their planned departure and took them to be fitted for clothes suitable with the finest of Ardonnese society.

The Tailor District and Riverside District lay upstream on the Ryonne in the better part of town. The former offered dozens of workshops, where the cream of New Montres could buy the clothes to show off at the theaters and salons of the latter. The Golden Lion's carriage dropped them off before a spotlessly clean shop window arranged with the latest in Ardonnese fashion.

Inside, Corlis was escorted upstairs by Romer and a small army of tailors, while Thessa was left in the care of the head seamstress and her helpers. The seamstress was barely five feet tall and looked to be a hundred years old, but her hands moved quicker than any Thessa had seen before. Within a minute, Thessa stood on a stool surrounded by mirrors on all sides, while the women pinned an endless variety of dresses on her.

"What a pity it's on such short notice," sighed the ancient seamstress as she tightened a red silken gown around Thessa's waist. "I would have loved to make something special for you, but in under a week, I can only offer adjustments. Get me some belts for this, will you, darling?"

The last words were aimed at one of the helpers, who scurried off to fetch a whole box of waistbands in all fabrics and colors. Thessa wasn't in any place to complain about having to wear ready-made clothes, especially when all of them were this expensive and paid for by someone else. She and the seamstress also got along famously in questions of taste. In only a few hours, Thessa had multiple outfits for day wear, evening wear, leisure, and other occasions, all ready to be taken in.

Once the wardrobe was complete, Thessa changed back into her own clothes, thanked the women for their time, and snuck upstairs to see how Corlis got on. Much like her, he stood on a chair in a ring of mirrors, though he showed much less comfort in the situation. He was clad in only his undergarments and stared in silent frustration at a lanky, balding man holding up a pair of jackets in different colors.

"I'd pick the left one." Thessa stepped forward. "Indigo is a little old, but it suits the color of his cheeks better. And it goes well with gold trims, which are getting very popular now."

"Ah, indeed. Well spotted, my lady. Thank you." The tailor hurried away and disappeared behind a thick velvet curtain.

Corlis shook a measuring tape off his shoulder. "I knew guild jobs paid better than average, but I didn't think you were this familiar with inner city fashion."

"I don't dress in it; I only see it on the street when I ride across town." Thessa picked a loose bit of thread off of his shirt. "You'd see it too, if you ever went to a play. A bit of culture wouldn't kill you, either."

Before Corlis could answer, the tailor reemerged. This time, he had Romer on his side and a selection of embroidered fabrics stretched across his arms.

"Per specific request from the family," Romer said, "we've been asked to provide an equestrian drape as well."

Corlis glared at him. "Equestrian drape?"

"It's a traditional overgarment that is wrapped around the shoulders, not unlike a shawl," the tailor replied. "The equestrian classes wore it originally to protect their naked arms from the sun. It used to be a staple of men's formalwear, but it's been on the decline in recent years. For that reason, I'm afraid our stocks are limited, but I believe these will suffice."

The tailor held up the drapes as he spoke, but Thessa knew Corlis wasn't listening to the improvised history lecture. When Corlis didn't understand something, he would simply snap back, "What?" When he echoed something word for word, that meant he had clearly heard what was said and did not like it one bit.

"What is it about equestrian drapes?" Thessa whispered once the other two were out of sight again.

"I don't set foot in the Riverside District often"—Corlis stepped off the stool—"but I know that the only people who wear them today are the imperialists. Like our good friends the paladins from a while back. Aristocrats who are fighting tooth and nail to stop Ardonne from becoming a republic." He looked Thessa right in the eye. "And to keep people like me in the dirt where we belong."

Chapter 7

Ceci had seen more than her share of roadside inns, and all things considered, they could have done much worse. The floors may not have been clean enough to eat off of, but the tables were. That wasn't always something one could take for granted at these places. It was clear that Alendro and Lord Harmon had made this trip many times in the past and knew all the good spots to rest.

The food had been decent as well. There was a range of courses and multiple kinds of stew to choose from, each with recognizable ingredients. They even got a bowl of fresh fruits, once the plates had been cleared away. Ceci picked at a small cluster of grapes, occasionally reaching up to feed one to Alendro, who mostly preferred to drink rather than eat them. His second pitcher was already close to empty.

The other side of the table was occupied entirely by Lord Harmon and the ridiculously large pile of notebooks and ledgers he devoted his attention to. Since that evening back in Tarnecia, when Alendro announced his decision to take Ceci with him to the family gathering, the elder Benuarte finally gave up on constantly berating her, and instead, simply acted as if she wasn't there at all. As far as Ceci was concerned, this was better than if he had suddenly become friendly.

Alendro snapped his fingers at one of the serving maids. "More wine for you, Father?" he asked while the girl refilled for him.

"No, thank you," Lord Harmon replied, without looking up from his papers. "I'll make do with just the one pitcher for the evening."

Alendro let the comment fly past him without notice and took a cherry from the bowl. "How are the numbers shaping up? Do I need to start selling my boots?" He spat the pit on the floor.

The lord let out a sniff that made his jowls ripple. Though they shared most of the Benuarte features, from the piercing cheekbones to the bloodless lips, it was remarkable how unalike he and his son were. Alendro prided himself in his service in the Legion—as brief as it may have been—and made sure everyone knew that without him saying. Lord Harmon also expected people to know about his great deeds as a captain, but otherwise did not fit the bill at all. By his saggy rolls of fat and his thick fingers, Ceci would have pinned him as an accountant.

"I'm tempted to say yes, if only to knock some sense into you about your spending habits," said the lord. Even his voice was soft and oddly high-pitched. "Fortunately, we're a ways from that. But if you want to know how the estate's doing, you can always start paying a little attention."

"I can't focus during dinner." Alendro scowled. "Why are you doing this at the table, anyway?"

For the first time since they sat down, Lord Harmon reared his head. "Well, I can't do it in the coach, can I?"

He spoke as if Alendro and Ceci had conspired to force him into making the trip the most arduous way possible. The provinces of Tarnecia and Forterne lay in opposite corners of Ardonne—one in the west, the other in the northeast. A railway line between the two had been open for decades, which could have taken them to their destination in no more than two days, including an overnight stop midway. However, Lord Harmon Benuarte was the kind of person who believed that the world had reached perfection when he was a child, and everything that came after was a mistake. That included the widespread expansion of railways in the last fifty years.

It was for this reason and no other that he, Alendro, and Ceci had been on the road for two days and barely crossed two province borders. On distances like this, there was no coach comfortable enough.

"I have to agree," said Ceci and pouted at Alendro. "I couldn't do anything else in those cramped seats, either. They are dreadful to endure all those hours. Is it much longer to Vertussi Hill?"

"Three more days," replied Alendro. "Don't worry, it'll feel much easier when you come next year." The slight emphasis on the last two words elicited a disdainful scoff from Lord Harmon. Judging by the smirk in the corner of Alendro's mouth, that was exactly the reaction he hoped for.

Ceci knew she had to follow it up. "I can't wait to meet *everyone* in your family." Another scoff came from across the table. "Who's going to be there?"

"There's Uncle Hestor, the man of the house." Alendro poured another glass. "Father has never fully forgiven him for being born five minutes earlier. I'd also imagine we'll meet his eldest, Ernio, the famous former athlete—"

"—now a henpecked husband with a Mountain hag for a wife," muttered Lord Harmon. With a frown at his son, he added, "At least he has one, though."

Alendro went on unbothered. "Then there are my lovely girl cousins, the gifted Livia and the spirited Gretia." He dangled the end of the sentence like bait.

"Each more vapid than the other," his father bit as predicted.

"And I believe Aunt Dalma will be joining us as well."

Ceci had never heard the name before, but it was one that stirred a variety of emotions between Alendro and his father. The sound of it was enough to rile Lord Harmon into lifting his gaze from his notes again.

"What's that toad coming for?" he asked.

"Didn't you know?" Alendro asked in pure innocence. "Livia's been living with her in Callex for the past year."

The lord only huffed in indignation and attacked the ledger with his pen anew. Ceci had only known him for two months, but if she wanted to count the number of people Harmon Benuarte spoke highly of, she could have done so on one hand with fingers to spare. Most of the time, his opinion was one of dull contempt—the kind that Ceci herself had received at a steady pace throughout their acquaintance. Until that point, she had yet to see him respond to a person with open disgust.

Ceci pulled up her shoulders and twirled a lock of hair. "I have to say, it'll be a bit intimidating." She batted her eyes coyly at Alendro. "Being the only outsider in such a big family."

Alendro emptied his glass again. "Oh, you won't be alone. Uncle Hestor always invites Larence, our family advisor, as well. But, on top of that, I heard we're getting a new cousin. Corlis, his name was?" He looked at his father, but he may as well have spoken to a brick wall. "Uncle Hestor's long lost son. Grew up as a commoner in New Montres, and Uncle had him tracked down. It'll be the first time any of us see him."

"Sounds like something out of a play!" Ceci said dramatically.

"A farce, more like." Lord Harmon shut his ledger, his mood for numbers spoiled by all this talk of relatives he did not approve of. "I don't know what Hestor was thinking. Having a bastard out of wedlock is enough of a disgrace. It doesn't need to be brought into the family home for all the world to see."

"I think it'll be great fun," Alendro said. "Like when a friend takes in a stray dog, and you get to play with it."

His father did not respond to that, merely gathered up his stack of books and announced his intent to turn in for the night. He also reminded Alendro to do the same, as he did not wish to delay their departure the next morning just because they slept in. Then, making an ostensible effort to ignore Ceci, he headed up to his room.

A small burst of cheers came from across the room. The sound drew Alendro's attention, and his eyes glinted at the sight. "Seems like they've got a game going on."

The men at another table were passing a handful of dice around in a cup. Their ages ran the gamut from young to old, and they were all dressed in plain, sweat-stained work shirts. By the sound of it, one of them had just won the lot, which couldn't have been more than a dozen coppers or so.

Ceci didn't have to be a fortune teller to know what was going to happen next. Alendro would join them at the table, make outrageous bets they couldn't possibly match, and spend the rest of the game trying to get them into a fight over the money. An actual brawl wasn't likely, but Ceci had no desire to stick around for the shouting, either. Using Lord Harmon's instruction as an excuse, she kissed Alendro on the cheek and wished him a good time for the rest of the evening.

Once she got to her and Alendro's room, she only needed a few minutes to prepare the bag. A single change of clothes, a banknote with her emergency savings, and her documents—her *other* documents, that is. It was a bag she had prepared many times before over the years, when she planned to run away in the middle of the night. She had three more days to do it, but she was too excited. She needed to take this step. Her plans were coming together at last.

Ceci hid the bag among the rest of the luggage, then changed into her lace nightgown, stretched comfortably across the bed, and closed her eyes.

In one instant during that conversation, Alendro made her happier than with any of his lavish gifts before. After months of waiting, Ceci finally heard the name she'd been longing to hear all this time. The name that made everything worthwhile.

How would she do it? Stab him? Bludgeon him over the head? Push him out a window? Each one sounded more enticing than the last, but she'd have to leave that to when they got to the villa. Then she could decide on the easiest, and most satisfying solution.

The possibilities were endless, but they were in reach. Ceci turned on her side and waited for Alendro to come up.

Chapter 8

When the Andassis adopted Corlis, Uncle Patrell took him to buy some paintings for the inn, as well as their own rooms. One corner of the shop was dedicated entirely to pictures of the Forterne countryside: idyllic villages nestled between rolling hills, glittering lakes, and lush vineyards. Each frame was close to bursting at the seams with a cavalcade of vibrant greens and blues. Corlis, who had never left New Montres, refused to believe that such colors existed.

Looking out of the carriage as it wound its way between the real hills and vineyards of the real Forterne, he still refused to believe it.

To be fair, exhaustion likely played a part. In the capital, you had to get deliberately lost to take more than an hour to get anywhere. Compared to that, a six-hour ride to the province from dawn to midday was damn near unfathomable. And that was by train. How on earth did people tolerate traveling on foot all the time?

His nerves weren't much help, either. Fabreve had assured him and Thessa that the train booking was fully taken care of, but Corlis's instincts were far too deeply ingrained. He spent the first hour with a knot in his stomach, waiting for a guard—or whoever was in charge on trains—to show up and demand payment, then lead them away in chains when they couldn't make it.

As always with such matters, time was the only thing that helped. Two hours into the journey, his fear relented at last, and boredom set in soon after that. By the time they pulled into the station, he only wanted to be done with it.

The town where they stopped was Pont Lanca, supposedly the largest in Forterne, covering most of the southern slope of Vertussi Hill. It was barely the size of two districts in New Montres put together, but the surrounding emptiness made it seem bigger. It also didn't have the same mishmash of colors and building styles that the capital had built up over the centuries. Every house had the same red clay roof and white plaster walls, the latter of which were so clean they almost glowed in the midday sun.

At the station platform, a porter greeted Corlis by name and whistled two boys over to carry his and Thessa's luggage to the station exit. There, an open carriage awaited to take them up to the village of Doma Lanca, where the Benuarte family home stood. The carriage was every bit as opulent as Corlis had feared, with yellow plush seats, a lacquered dark green finish, and a golden emblem of two grapevines around an ornate letter B.

He took a front-facing seat and carefully smoothed out his jacket. His finished clothes had arrived the day before, and this was his first time wearing a complete outfit. Fortunately, the tailor had the foresight to include a sheet with detailed descriptions of which items to wear on what occasion. For the day of travel, he had a pair of light linen trousers, a simple fitted shirt, and a deep blue tunic with white decorative stitches. Each garment fit better than anything he'd ever worn before—yet, somehow, it was all uncomfortable.

Thessa, across from him, did not have the same problem. She too was dressed "simply" for the trip, in a light yellow sleeveless dress and matching ribbons woven into her hair. The ease with which she stretched her legs across the four-seater carriage, and her hands fiddled idly with her braid, reminded Corlis what a different world she had come from. No matter how much time she had spent living the common life, there was no question she was right where she belonged.

"Mmm!" She breathed deeply through her nose. "Can you smell this air?"

Corlis took a few vague sniffs. "No."

"That's right! No soot, no filth. It's just air. I've forgotten how good it is."

Now that he knew what he had to notice, Corlis smelled it too. His nose must have gone wholly numb over two and a half decades in the city, but the country air was different. It reminded him of the time the pipes under the orphanage had cracked, and they had to drink out of the cistern for a month. Water had never tasted so sweet as when they finally had it running from the taps again.

"And over there"—Thessa pointed—"that's Lake Forterne. I read about it in *The Travels of Darno Nevasses*. It's the biggest inland lake, not only in Ardonne, but the whole Ora Mara region."

Corlis had never seen any lakes before, inland or otherwise, but Lake Forterne was indeed massive. Their path ran well over a thousand feet higher than the water's surface, giving them almost a bird's eye view of the valley—yet the lake stretched all the way from one horizon to the other. It was so broad, the hills on the other side were barely more than a bluish haze. Corlis was already badly out of place, and all this empty space only made him feel smaller and more insignificant.

"You know," Thessa went on, "when I was traveling with Hanna—"

"As a robber, right."

Thessa made a face. "When I was traveling with Hanna, we talked a lot about which way we should go. I wanted to see New Montres because I heard so much about how it was the center of the world. But Hanna always wanted to come here. She said that if you only ever saw Forterne, you'd think there were no poor people in the world."

That was difficult to argue with. As the carriage rolled up the slopes at an unhurried pace, they passed one villa after another, each with its own vines, ponds, and stables. Occasionally, there would be small groups enjoying a drink and waving at them from their verandas. Whether this courtesy was aimed specifically at the Benuarte emblem or merely at someone they assumed to be a fellow noble, was one more of Corlis's uncertainties along this trip.

Finally, without any forewarning, the carriage stopped in front of a small, unmarked side gate. The driver opened the door on Thessa's side and said, "Lord Hestor is waiting for you in the garden, right up this path. I'll bring your luggage to the house."

Said path was a thin strip of gravel that veered sharply away from the gate and vanished among a grove of poplar trees. The foliage hid most everything behind it, letting only the vague outline of a house peer through.

Before Corlis could change his mind and order the two of

them to be taken straight back to the train station, the carriage clattered off. Corlis sighed. No turning back now.

Barely did the gravel crunch under their feet, when a series of uneven footsteps came from ahead. They were soon followed by an enthusiastic voice calling, "Corlis!"

During the days leading up to their journey, Corlis had spent a considerable amount of time imagining the day he'd meet his father. In his mind, it always played out in a grand, empty hall, where Lord Benuarte watched sternly from his seat atop a raised platform. The rest of the family—vague figures of varying age and size, with some combination of Corlis's features—lined up behind him and followed his every move in cold judgment.

The real Hestor Benuarte emerged from the trees in loose breeches and a plain white tunic under his red equestrian drape, hobbling along with a cane by his left side. He hurried as much as his gait and his sizable belly allowed, waving with his free hand the whole time. At last, he stopped a few steps before the two of them, and with a broad smile, he simply said, "There you are."

He was nothing like the looming figure Corlis had envisioned based on his portrait. Lord Hestor was barely as tall as him, with graying hair and large bags under his eyes. A childish pair of dimples deepened on his pudgy cheeks, which were flushed bright red from the short walk along the path.

He studied Corlis up and down and put a hand on his hip. "Drown me, it's like looking in a mirror." He giggled and added, "For me, I mean. A mirror that shows you from thirty years before. Not much of a sight for you, though, is it?"

Corlis had no idea what to say to that. He swallowed, and with a bow, he recited the greeting Thessa had taught him, "It is a pleasure and an honor to make your acq—"

Lord Hestor screwed up his face and cut him off with a flail of his hand. "Don't be ridiculous, dear boy. Come here." And without another word, he stepped forward and dragged Corlis into a hug.

More obligated than touched, Corlis awkwardly placed a hand on the lord's wide back. He figured it was Lord Hestor's privilege to decide when they separated, so he stood and waited while the lord rubbed his shoulder at length. The soft tunic under Corlis's palm was damp with sweat.

At last, Lord Hestor pulled back. "I'm so happy to have you here. And the young lady must be Thessa." He leaned forward and slowly said, "*Talakhe ypsoi ourophendos.*"

Corlis didn't know a word of Sallician, but he could tell Lord Hestor's accent was atrocious. Thessa didn't seem to mind. She curtsied and returned the greeting in her language.

"Right, we can leave it at that," Lord Hestor said. "Otherwise, I'll only embarrass myself. Come now, let's get you both a seat and a drink. You must be bored out of your wits after that ride." He led the way through the garden. "There's some wonderful wine punch chilling in the cellar. I had it brought up as soon as I heard the carriage come up the road."

"You heard us all the way from here?" Corlis asked.

"Sure, I did! I can imagine that's strange if you grew up in the city. With all that noise blaring in your ears all day, it's half a miracle you aren't deaf. You'll love how peaceful it is out here, you'll see. The nights get so quiet, you can hear the birds fart in their sleep."

Thessa's stifled chortle assured Corlis he wasn't the only one caught off guard by this choice of words. He wasn't going to complain about it. Lord Hestor may not have struck him as the mighty aristocrat he had pictured, but that was probably for the best.

When they emerged from the grove, the sight that greeted them was as unexpected as the lord's appearance. Instead of the sprawling marble monstrosity that existed in Corlis's mind, they now stood outside a two-story villa which, no matter how hard he tried, he couldn't describe in any way other than "charming." The walls were pale red, while the shutters and frames were green with vine motifs painted around them. Ivy twisted over large swaths of the wall, as well as the trellises over the patio that took up most of the yard.

It was on this patio where Lord Hestor took one of the cushioned wicker chairs and offered two others to Corlis and Thessa. A man appeared by his elbow and placed a glass decanter on a table, filled with wine and a variety of fruits on the bottom.

"You know, some figs would be lovely too," the lord said to him.

The man bowed and drew back into the house. Corlis only got a passing glance, but that was enough to note that the servants at the Benuarte villa were easily as well-dressed as him.

Lord Hestor poured out into the three glasses beside the decanter and toasted. "To health—and to family!"

The wine was everything wine should taste like and more. Peaches, lemons, elderflower, raisins, and a dozen other flavors Corlis wasn't refined enough to notice. Coupled with how welcome its chill was under the hot sun, it went down dangerously smooth.

"Nothing better in this weather." The lord let out a satisfied sigh and bit into one of the figs that the servant had left for them in the meantime.

"Mm," replied Corlis, having no idea how he was supposed to behave.

"Not a man of many words, are you?" Lord Hestor asked with a mouthful of fig. "Don't fret it. I remember what it was like meeting my late Wilhelma's family for the first time, so I can only wonder how tangled up your insides must be. Besides, I know you're not in your element. Fabreve wrote me his impression of you after your first meeting. He said that you possess—and I quote—'an exceptionally keen wit that is quick to make sharp insights, if perhaps overly focused on the worst.'" He recalled the words in an affected tone, miming flowery handwriting with his right hand.

"Couldn't have said it better myself!" Thessa laughed, and the lord laughed with her.

"You don't need to worry," Lord Hestor said in the end. "I told Fabreve to make sure you got here first. This is the perfect time for you to meet the family, and we can all get to know the both of you."

"Thank you," Corlis said.

"If I may ask," Thessa chimed in, "who else will be joining us?"

Lord Hestor leaned back in his chair and squinted pensively at the vines overhead as he counted. "For one, there's my brother Harmon. He and I are twins, you know, though not much alike, inside or out. He's bringing his son Alendro, along with some girl or other that the boy picked up a while ago.

"Then there are my children, of course. My firstborn, Ernio, should be coming later today. Used to be one of the finest athletes in Ardonne, until he fell for this Mountain girl,

Rosilla—lovely creature, if a bit trying at times. Her family has properties in Astercium, so that's where they settled. I've already taken to spoiling their first child, and the second one just came this year."

Even if he didn't say much about Ernio per se, Lord Hestor's tone left no question about how unshakably proud he was of his son. Corlis raised his glass to his mouth before his lips could hint at the twinge of envy that struck him.

"And then besides him are my daughters, Livia and Gretia. They're about your age." The lord motioned at Thessa.

"Have they married already, too?" Thessa asked back. Her voice was as light as before, but Corlis was well aware what a loaded question this was for her. She must have been relieved when Lord Hestor shook his head in response.

"Livia loves the harp more than she'll love any man. She dreams of being a professed musician, so last year she moved in with her aunt—my late wife's sister." The lord's tone soured. "Can't say I was happy about it, but I'm afraid she inherited every drop of stubbornness from both me and her mother, and that's not a little.

"Gretia lives at home with me. She doesn't have the same ambitions, but she's done plenty of reading over the years. As much as I can tell, the only way she'll get married is if someone breaks into her room and whisks her away in the dead of night."

"That sounds more like a crime than marriage," Corlis said.

"Well, in the books she reads, that sounds like true love." Lord Hestor spread his hands in resignation. "But she is a darling girl; you'll see for yourself. Speaking of which, we should make our way home if we want to have lunch. Don't know about you, but I'm starving!"

He picked up the cane from beside the chair, and with some effort, he pushed himself to a stand. "You two can finish your drinks. I'll need a bit of a head start, anyway," he said as he knocked the cane against the floor. "We can meet up in the carriage by the gate." He ambled back along the path.

Corlis was lost. *Home?* Weren't they already there…?

The patio door opened, and the man who had brought them the punch came out, asking if he heard correctly that Lord Hestor had left.

With a sudden sense of unease, and in a sharper tone than he meant, Corlis asked, "Do you work for Lord Hestor?"

The man furrowed his thinning eyebrows, and his face made it clear how little he appreciated the assumption. "Work for Lord Hestor? No. I pay my taxes to him, but I'm not in his employment."

"Why was he here, then?"

"To discuss those taxes. Specifically, to discuss raising them, given how good business has been lately. Lord Hestor is of the opinion that if we make more, we can give more."

"And you waited on him hand and foot while he was here?"

The man's eye twitched. "It's only good manners to be hospitable to one's landlord and his son when they visit." He clasped his hands. "Is there anything else I can do for the young lord?"

The last two words may as well have been dipped in venom. Corlis said no, thanked him for the drinks, and headed down the path beside Thessa, mulling over what he'd heard.

The fact in and of itself that nobles showed up at people's houses and ordered them around wouldn't have been news to him. If anything, it would have been strange to find otherwise. But that was when he thought he had nothing to do with those nobles.

The knot in his stomach was back with a vengeance. He could only hope the rest of his stay would be boring enough for it to go away again. Something told him he may as well hope to cross Lake Forterne on foot.

Chapter 9

Thessa would never have thought she'd be grateful for growing up in a loveless family. During the twenty years in her father's house, she had spent countless dinners where some of the people refused to speak to one another, while the rest of them were supposed to pretend nothing was wrong. It was torture at the time, but it taught her how to read a room and navigate a conversation like a ship around a stormy reef.

Compared to that, sitting in the carriage with the coldly tense Corlis and the jovial Lord Hestor was outright leisurely. All she had to do was keep the lord's attention and steer clear of any topics that might directly involve Corlis. The easiest way was to make the lord talk about himself as much as possible. And as someone who had spent years trying to get noblemen to fall in love with her, Thessa had plenty of experience making men talk about themselves.

They had just crested the hill when Lord Hestor finished an anecdote about him and his brother Harmon and asked, "How long have the two of you known each other?"

Corlis froze up at the question, but Thessa was quick to step in. "A little over half a year. I was newly arrived in New Montres and met a man who… was regrettably less of a gentleman than he wanted me to believe." She ran a hand over her hair. "He took me back to his inn, which turned out to be The Lame Mare. Corlis helped me get rid of him, and we've been friends ever since."

Strictly speaking, that was all true—she had only left out a few details. Such as how she had originally tried to rob that man, but ended up killing him by accident; or that Corlis's plan to get rid of his corpse was a ruse to frame an innocent man for murder; or that the three of them were then hounded by the Imperial Paladins, and the innocent man died a tragic death so that Thessa and Corlis could get away. Thessa had often wished she could leave those details out of her memory for good.

"How gallant of him!" Lord Hestor beamed at Corlis. "Glad to know you've grown up to be an upstanding young man."

Corlis took the oblivious compliment. Thessa searched her mind frantically for another topic to distract the lord with. To her relief, the carriage rounded a final bend, and the Benuarte villa came into view.

It stood at the very top of Vertussi Hill, with a splendid view overlooking the villages and the lake on one side, and a steep slope covered in dense forest on the other. The pale yellow walls had decorative patterns running along the bottom, as well as directly beneath the red clay roof.

Like most Ardonnese villas, it had two identical, two-story wings running parallel, connected at the middle and at the very back. The middle connection divided the space between the wings into an inner and an outer courtyard, and it was before the latter that the carriage pulled up.

The courtyard was paved with intricately arranged tiles of varying colors. A square pool stood in the middle, with a pure white fountain sculpted into the shape of a veiled woman, pouring water from the pitcher in her graceful hands.

Lord Hestor said, "Welcome to our home."

While the three of them clambered down from the carriage, a woman approached them through the yard. She was a short, plump thing of some fifty-odd years, clad in the traditional plain blue dress of household staff. Her gray hair was tucked under a bonnet, and a ring of keys on her apron rattled with each hurried step. She stopped before them and bowed. "Good afternoon, lord."

"Good afternoon," Lord Hestor greeted her back, then turned to Corlis and Thessa. "This is Donella, my cook and housekeeper. Since it's only myself and Gretia at home now, we've been running on something of a skeleton crew. But don't worry—between her and Nicki, you'll be in plenty good hands, and I can guarantee you'll never tire of Donella's cooking. Where is Nicki, anyhow?"

"She's on her way, lord," Donella said with a slight blush. "I sent her to the ice cellar when I heard you coming, in case the guests should like some in their rooms."

"Very good." Lord Hestor said. "You can show my son and his guest to their room, then. I'll go up to Gretia, and the lot of us can have lunch in a half hour or so. I thought it would be nice to eat in the yard today."

"As you like, lord." Donella bowed again and bade Corlis and Thessa to follow.

The trip to their room was a short one. The four guest rooms lay on the ground floor, two in each wing, opening directly onto the outer courtyard.

Donella led the way to one on the left hand side. "Lord Hestor said you'll not be wishing to sleep together, so we prepared one of the rooms with separate beds. We trust everything will be to your liking." She pushed the door open before them, then stepped aside.

The room, while not remarkably big, reflected every bit of the villa's decorum. The walls were painted in a warm coral tone, while the floor and the furniture were all carved and lacquered hardwood. The two large beds each had richly embroidered covers and mountains of velvet pillows. Quartz lights with heavy brass bottoms were on the nightstands next to both of them, and more quartzes were fitted into the chandelier above.

Thessa leaned out the wide double window. It opened onto the forested slope, which seemed to melt directly into the wall of the villa. The trees didn't start until a half dozen yards below, which left an unobstructed view of the hillside and the blue mountains of the Lancum range in the distance. It was a sight meant for painting.

Donella said from behind, "Nicki will be here presently. If there's anything you should need, she will be at your service at all times."

"Thank you, Donella," Thessa replied. "I think we'll be all right for now."

The housekeeper bowed out of the room. The door clicked behind her, and Thessa threw herself on the closest bed.

"I can't believe how much I missed this." She rolled back and forth. The broad, soft mattress didn't make the slightest sound under her. "I got so used to the bed in my room; it might be strange not to wake up with my back hurting."

Corlis didn't say anything. He stood in the middle of the room, dressed in his fine new clothes, all groomed and cleaned up, and hopelessly lost. He went to their luggage, which the driver had neatly piled up for them, pulled out a trunk, and proceeded to empty it onto his bed.

"What are you doing?" Thessa asked.

"I should put these away."

"You don't need to do that. We have a maid here."

"Yes, I do."

He continued to put his clothes into the chest and wardrobe on his side. He was about to get a second trunk, when the door opened again, and Nicki came in.

She was younger than Thessa—no more than seventeen, if that. She was dressed the same as Donella, except she had a cloth headband. Most surprising was her face, or rather her complexion, for it was an even deeper tan than Thessa's.

She gave Corlis a quick curtsy, careful not to drop the two heavy jugs in her hand. "Good afternoon, I'm Nicki. Donella sent me to get fresh ice for your room."

Upon hearing her accent, Thessa sprang up. "You're Sallician!"

Nicki blinked. "Yes, that's right, my lady."

Thessa rushed to her. "Here, let me help." She took one of the pitchers and set it on Corlis's nightstand.

"You don't need to do that; we have a maid here," he murmured into her ear as she passed him. Thessa knocked her leg against his shin.

"Thank you," said the girl. "Please let me know if there's anything I can do for you."

"Did you say your name is Nicki?" Thessa asked. "It's not one I ever heard in Sallis."

The maid was clearly not used to such questions, but Thessa couldn't help herself. Outside the province of Callex, which lay right on the border, Sallicians were a rare sight in

Ardonne. The thought of having someone from her home nearby excited her too much.

"My real name is Nykhe," the girl replied. "But Ardonnese people tend to have trouble pronouncing it, so they call me Nicki."

"That's not fair. It's not your fault they can't speak properly."

Behind her, Corlis cleared his throat, while he hung more of his clothes in the wardrobe. "I'm done with mine. Do you want me to get yours, too?"

"Oh, no, please," Nykhe said, almost frightened. "I apologize. I'll take care of your clothes. And Donella is ready for you with lunch in the inner courtyard. Lord Hestor and the young lady Gretia are there."

"Let's not keep them waiting, then," Corlis said and joined the two of them. "Good to meet you, Nicki. I'll do my best to learn your proper name."

Nykhe bowed again and waited for him and Thessa to leave the room, assuring them their things would be unpacked by the time the meal was over.

Their room was right next to the passage that connected the wings of the villa and separated the two courtyards. On the other side, a table was set up next to a similar pool as the one in the outer yard. It was surrounded by four recliners, two of which were already occupied by Lord Hestor and his daughter.

The sight of Gretia Benuarte was another surprise. The name Wilhelma made Thessa suspect that Lord Hestor's wife had been Werrish, but to see that heritage show so starkly in her daughter was almost off-putting. Gretia's skin was lighter than the typical Ardonnese olive, and her hair was a striking strawberry blonde. Barely any of the typical Benuarte features were discernible on her.

"Come, come." Lord Hestor beckoned. "Everything's ready. Corlis, I'd like you to meet your youngest sister, Gretia."

"It's lovely to meet you." Gretia got up from her recliner and kissed Corlis on the cheek. There was a girlishly sunny nature to her voice and her movements. Her cheeks were round, and her hair was done up in a simple knot that Thessa used to wear when she was a decade younger. Overall, she may have been twenty years old, but didn't give that impression.

Corlis muttered something in response.

"Haven't eased up yet?" Lord Hestor asked. "A good meal should help. Go on, no need to be shy. Is the room all right? Are Donella and Nicki taking good care of you?"

"Everything is perfect, thank you," Corlis said while he eyed the spread on the table.

Bowls of cheese, sausages, eggs, pickled cabbage and gherkins, and herbed beans stood around loaves of old-fashioned emmer bread. After a few bites, Thessa concluded that Donella's skill as a cook deserved every bit of the praise Lord Hestor leveled at her.

For a few minutes, all four of them were occupied with filling their plates. Once they settled on their recliners—Corlis across from his father and Thessa across from Gretia—she prepared herself for yet another stretch of conversation that she'd have to actively keep Corlis out of. Her concerns were quickly proven to be moot.

"Thessa," Gretia began, "You're from Sallis, aren't you? Who are your parents?"

"I've been wondering that myself," the lord added. "You were obviously raised in a good family, so how did you wind up in New Montres?"

The two-front question threw Thessa's balance, but she recovered. "You are right. My father was one of the eleven lords of the High Chamber in Sallis. Lord Protector Xanthias Kalou, in charge of keeping the Sallician borders safe."

"Lord Protector?" Lord Hestor echoed. "Drown me, girl—you outrank us all then!"

"Not any more, I'm afraid. My parents and I had differences about who I should marry, and it didn't end well."

"How did it end?" Gretia asked.

It was a risk telling them the truth, but Thessa counted on the lord's sanguine nature to take it well. "I ran away from home. Right on my engagement night. I got lost in the woods and had to be rescued by peasants. When they tried to take me home, I found out my father had disowned me. I was left alone, until I met this other woman named Hanna. The two of us traveled through Sallis and Ardonne. That's how I ended up in New Montres."

The tension in the air over the table was thick enough to cut with a knife. Gretia clasped her hands over her mouth. Lord Hestor sat dumbfounded, his hand frozen mid-motion dipping his bread into oil. Corlis kept his head down.

Thessa wondered if she had made a grave mistake. Then Gretia lowered her hands, and in a breathless voice said, "That is *wonderful.*"

If Corlis had been uncomfortable before, Thessa now got a taste of that. "It's not—"

Gretia cut her off. "How long were you alone in the woods? Was it terribly frightening?"

Thessa swallowed. "It was, yes. For about three days. I didn't know where I was or which way I was going."

"But you made it out safe and sound," Gretia said, more

absorbed in her vision of the story with each word. "And then you traveled all those months, wherever fortune took you! Braved the wrath of the elements and men alike! Lived the life of the common folk, with no coin and no cares!"

Lord Hestor leaned over to Thessa. "I told you about all those books she's been reading. I'd wager you've struck quite the chord with her."

Gretia paid them no mind. Her eyes were now fixed in the distance, and her mind more distant still. She rested her cheek in her hand and sighed deeply. "I wish I could be poor."

Clank. Corlis's plate, along with his cutlery, rattled loudly as he dropped them on the table. "Sorry," he said under his breath. "My hand slipped."

Refilling his wine glass, Lord Hestor replied to his daughter, "Poor is just what you might end up being if you keep refusing to give your hand to anyone. Half the men of Forterne are clamoring at my gates to see you. Should I tell them to bring ladders instead and try your window?"

"I want to marry for love, father," Gretia said. "Not for riches."

"I understand that, dear girl. What I don't understand is how you plan to fall in love if you never meet anyone."

Thankfully, the rest of the lunch went by in peace. Lord Hestor and Gretia spent most of the time chatting about their own family and others in the province. By the end, Corlis deigned to join in and talk about his years at the orphanage, further fanning the flames of Gretia's imagination. In the hour and a half they spent at the table, Thessa enjoyed herself more than at any meal in her childhood home.

Once they were finished, Lord Hestor gave them a tour of the villa, which took a lot longer than the size of the building warranted—not only due to his limp, but also because he insisted on recalling several anecdotes in each room. The ground floor had the four guest rooms on the outer side; the dining hall, kitchen, and bath on the inner side, and Lord Hestor's study in between. The inner courtyard also featured the staircase to the upper floor with the family's own chambers, as well as the long gallery at the back of the building. Much like the one Thessa and Corlis were staying in, none of the rooms were overly spacious, but every detail about them spoke of wealth and taste.

After the tour, Lord Hestor retreated to his study, but encouraged the two of them to make themselves at home until Ernio arrived later. Corlis chose to rest in their room, but Thessa took the lord up on his offer and went for a stroll around the building.

The Kalou manor in Sallis had a network of gardens with all manner of local and exotic plants. By contrast, the grounds around the Benuarte villa were entirely plain, yet it had more warmth to it than the meticulously kept flowerbeds and greenhouses. Outside of the gravel footpaths was nothing but the natural greenery of the hills. A sea of knee-high grass rustled in the breeze, speckled with tiny wildflowers.

Thessa hiked up her dress and rounded the building all the way to its backside, where the two wings connected. It was here that she made the most thrilling discovery yet, in the form of a smaller building tucked away behind the house. She had already spied it from the windows of the long gallery during the tour and now approached it with mounting anticipation.

The stables stood some dozen yards from the back wall, and the wind carried their familiar smell to Thessa. She could make out the outlines of four horses, as well as another shadow busying about inside. When she got closer, her excitement only grew.

The man tending to the horses was another Sallician, with a physique that was lean but strong. Thessa figured him to be a little older than Nykhe. His features were on the rough side, but in a way almost handsome, had it not been for a thin mustache that made him more childish than mature.

"Good afternoon," Thessa called to him in their mother tongue.

The boy turned around. "Good afternoon," he said in Sallician and hurriedly wiped his hands on his shirt. "Are you Lady Thessalona Kalou?"

"Thessa. Are you Nykhe's brother?" It was only a guess, but Thessa found it unlikely that two Sallicians would end up in northern Ardonne independently of one another.

"Yes, I'm Iolinos." The boy bowed stiffly. "Julian, they call me in the house. Is there something I can do for you? Please forgive my state; I was getting the horses ready for when we fetch Lord Ernio and his family in the evening."

"It's all right. I was only taking in the scenery." Thessa looked around. There were four sturdy mares fit for pulling carriages, but there was a fifth horse as well—a splendid, lean white gelding, off by itself in one of the corners.

"That's Avalanche," Iolinos said, noticing Thessa's interest. "Lord Hestor's horse. Used to be, rather. He doesn't ride any more since his ankle gave out a few months ago. We're going to sell him after the family gathering."

"What a shame." Thessa stroked Avalanche's neck. "Does no one ride him any more?"

"I take him out for a run now and then to keep him in shape,"

Iolinos said. "Do you ride, Lady Thessa?"

"Just Thessa," she repeated. "Yes, I do. I used to ride all the time at home, and now I work as a horseback messenger in New Montres."

"You must be outstanding, then," the boy said, with a tone of admiration.

"Do you think Lord Hestor would mind if I took him for a round? A half hour, no more, here on the grounds."

"I don't think it should be a problem. I can saddle him up right away, if you give me a few minutes."

Thessa stood back to let Iolinos work. Getting to ride such a magnificent horse freely across the countryside made her swell up inside. And to think she could do this every day while they were here—that did sound too good to be true.

She was playing with Avalanche's mane, when Iolinos stepped up and casually swatted a horsefly on the gelding's neck. The critter had been bulging fat with blood and left a smear of red on the spotless white hair.

The scent attacked Thessa's nose with a force like never before. It cut through the smell of hay and manure and spread itself over her palate. Her muscles gave a jolt, nearly making her double over as her veins caught fire. Under that fire, terror clawed into her like an ice-cold blade in every inch of her bones.

This was impossible. She couldn't transform in daylight!

Thessa stumbled back and leaned against a support beam, clutching one hand over her mouth. She did everything she could to slow her breathing. Her mind wrestled with her instincts in a desperate struggle to regain control over her body.

Slowly, by moment after agonizing moment, the fury inside

her ebbed.

"Thessa…?" Iolinos's voice came from beyond the haze. "Are you all right?"

She was not. Every fiber of her body trembled. Her mouth was drier than the Sallician desert, and her eyes were a dizzying kaleidoscope.

Iolinos carefully guided her to a stool and brought her a flask of water. Thessa drank to regain her voice and her thoughts.

"What's wrong? Should I get help?" the boy asked.

"No, please," Thessa protested and scrambled desperately after an explanation she could give him. "It's just… blood makes me sick."

Iolinos's mouth fell open. He stared in horror at the stain on Avalanche's neck and hurried to wipe it off with a rag. "I'm so terribly sorry. I should have been more careful."

"It's all right." Thessa took the half-full flask and emptied every drop. "But I think it's best if we put off the ride for now."

Chapter 10

The immaculately painted ceiling stretched above Corlis and occupied his view. In contrast to the warm shade of the walls, it was made to mimic the daytime sky, with feathery clouds against a backdrop of ethereal blue. In a way, it resembled the mural that Uncle Patrell had ordered to decorate the tavern of The Lame Mare. Except, evidently, the Benuartes could afford a craftsman who knew what he was doing.

Like back home, only better in every way.

Corlis shifted. No matter how tired he was from the trip, he couldn't sleep. It didn't make sense. Nothing about the last few days did.

He should like his new family. They were good people.

At least, they were *nice* people. To him.

He turned over on the bed. Thessa was out somewhere exploring the villa, most likely having a whale of a time, feeling right at home. She belonged here. Corlis didn't.

And yet, he couldn't be happy for her, either.

He shuffled up to a sitting position and rested his back against the headboard. Seeing through other people's bunk was an ability he had always prided himself upon, but he had never considered having to see through his own. And he had a whole cartload of it running through his head, turning his thoughts into mush.

The truth of the matter was that, over twenty-six years, Corlis had grown comfortable hating the rich—so much so that becoming one of them was more like a threat than an opportunity. He had run through his choices, and none of them were appealing. If he stayed with the Benuartes and blended in with them, he would become what he hated. On the other hand, if he stayed and tried to be different, he would risk becoming what *they* hated.

Then again, he could also thank them graciously for the invitation and go back to New Montres, where his ruined inn and a lifetime of poverty awaited. That way, he could be sure he'd stay true to himself. But as he sat there, and his hands ran along the brocade bed covers, that option fell further and further to the back.

Then the door flew open, and Thessa came in. Before Corlis could speak, she turned the lock behind her and rushed to his bed. "We have to talk."

Most days, Corlis would have leapt at the chance to comment on the grass on her dress and in her hair, but this was not one of them. Thessa's eyes were wide with fear. The last time Corlis saw her like this, she had just killed someone.

"What is it?" He slid closer.

Thessa looked around the empty and locked room before answering. "I almost transformed." She then gave a hurried recount of the events at the stable.

Corlis listened carefully. "Didn't you say you can only transform at night?"

"That's what I thought, too!" Thessa's whisper was hoarse with repression. "I had never been able to before. But as soon as I smelled that blood, I could barely hold myself back!"

"When was the last time you transformed?"

"When we broke into that gambling den all those months ago. Do you think it's because I haven't done it for so long? What if I can't control myself?" She took a few breaths in an effort to calm down. "Maybe I should go back to New Montres. Tell Lord Hestor and the others I got sick."

"If you leave, I won't last another day without you." It felt selfish to say, but it was true. Corlis didn't trust himself to stay in the Benuartes' company without her help.

"But if I stay, I can get you into trouble." Thessa twisted her braid nervously until the end came undone, and the yellow ribbons hung loose. "I got you into trouble before. I got both of us into trouble, and two people died, and—"

"Hey," Corlis cut her off before Thessa's mind careened off the slope. "That wasn't only you. *I* got us into trouble as well. And then the two of us got ourselves out of it." He put a hand on her shoulder, which was coarse with goosebumps. "Maybe we're overthinking this. It might only be the horse's blood that set you off like that. Have you smelled horse's blood since you became a werewolf?"

Thessa hesitated. "I don't think so."

"Either way," Corlis went on. He only needed to distract her long enough so she wouldn't panic. "We've been through worse before. We learned to trust each other. We learned it the hard way, but we did. And I still trust you."

It took a little while, but Thessa mustered enough strength to say, "I trust you too."

From what Corlis could tell, the worst of it was over. He went to the nightstand and poured her a large cup of water. He wished there was something stronger in the room. Maybe he should see to that.

"Besides that," he said while Thessa drank, "I haven't thanked you for all you've done today. But I do appreciate you helping me get on the family's good side. Or keeping me from getting on their bad side."

Thessa lowered the cup. She was shaken, but slowly getting back to her old self. "They do appear to like you. It makes me a little envious, to tell the truth." She ran her finger along the rim of the cup. "You should give them a chance."

"I know. But what could I talk to them about?"

"What would you talk with Uncle Patrell about, if he was with us?" Thessa added, "Besides complaining about the inn."

"Complain about Aunt Mira, probably."

"Do that, then. Tell them what it was like growing up with your aunt and uncle. People like those kinds of stories."

Corlis did not count himself among one of those people. He had never seen the use of talk like that. Then and there, he had to yield to Thessa's experience on that front. With a sigh, he straightened out his jacket, and like a man about to face his executioner, he set out to find his father for a chat.

* * *

Lord Hestor's study wasn't an actual room, but a furnished area in the passage that separated the inner and outer courtyards. An ornate desk stood in the middle, with everything else arranged around it. A long case of shelves held a hundred books, while a glossy cabinet held more documents. From a movable wall hung detailed maps of Forterne province, Ardonne, the Ora Mara region, and the whole world. A small seating area was outfitted with half a dozen chairs, a low table, and a glass cabinet.

When Corlis found him, Lord Hestor was going over some ledgers. At the sound of footsteps, he set down his pen and offered the seat across from the desk. "Any better?"

"Much better, yes." Corlis sat down. He fidgeted for a while, then decided it was best to get it out and over with. "I'm sorry if I've been acting cold. I want you to know I am grateful for your invitation. I'm just… struggling to accept this is happening after all these years."

Lord Hestor waved the apology away. "Nerves can always get the best of us. I know that too well. And as much as I can tell so far, you take strongly after your mother in your temperament. She wasn't quick to warm up to people, either."

It was as if he had read Corlis's mind. "Can you tell me about her?"

The lord leaned back in remembrance. "Tinia—She was a world apart from all the other women in New Montres. Distant and unknowable. Full of mystery. I remember seeing her in that grand hall, filled with the flashiest colors everyone could wrap around themselves, and she was almost like a statue. Draped in all whites and grays. She barely gave anyone the time of day, and I couldn't keep my eyes off of her.

"Make no mistake, I loved my Wilhelma with all my heart, and I do to this day. Around that time, we were on something of a rough patch. Our Ernio was five years old, and we'd been married for seven. We had fallen into a rut, and as they say, familiarity breeds contempt." Lord Hestor let out a bittersweet chuckle. "You might see that for yourself when you're married one day.

"During those months I spent in New Montres, away from my wife, Tinia was everything I thought I'd missed. The enticing thrill of the new. But, in truth, our dalliance never dampened my affection for Wilhelma. If anything, it made it stronger. Reminded me of how much I cherished her."

"Did you ever tell her about Tinia?"

"Oh, no." Lord Hestor said emphatically. "I loved her dearly, but I did have my wits about me."

Corlis smirked. He may have inherited his mother's temperament, but by the sound of it, his practicality was firmly rooted on his father's side. "I wonder about Ernio, too," he said after a bit. "You said he was already five years old when I was born and… well, I'm not sure if he might begrudge me for—"

"Begrudge?" Lord Hestor balked. "Dear boy, my Ernio hasn't got a mean bone in his body. Even if you were at fault in any way, he couldn't begrudge you if you burned down his house before him. Not that I'd ask you to try."

"You sound very proud of him."

"Of course I am. I'm proud of all my children." Lord Hestor clasped his hands. "I don't always understand them—but I'm proud of whatever they make of themselves."

Corlis thought over the words. Earlier, hearing the lord talk about Ernio had brought a bitter taste to his mouth. Maybe he was going about it wrong. If Ernio didn't blame Corlis for being proof of his father's infidelity, then maybe Corlis could not blame him for having the family he had missed.

"Now, enough about me already," Lord Hestor said. "Why don't you tell me about yourself?"

The question brought Corlis back to the room and reminded him of Thessa's advice. He took a deep breath and settled into a long afternoon of regaling Lord Hestor with tales of Aunt Ulmira's ill temper.

* * *

Before they knew it, evening had fallen. The carriage was sent down to the railway station to fetch Ernio and his family, and everyone, including Corlis and Thessa, went to meet them in the outer courtyard.

Like his youngest sister Gretia, Ernio took more after their Werrish mother. His hair was a warm shade of brown and continued down his cheeks in a short but thick beard. Corlis vaguely remembered hearing about a tradition that new fathers were supposed to keep their beards until their first child left for school at the age of seven. No one in New Montres kept this habit, but the countryside stayed comfortably behind by a few decades.

Ernio didn't wait for the driver to get to the door. He threw it open himself and leapt to the ground with a heavy thump. Corlis had noted that his head stuck out much higher than the other passengers, but only now did he fully take in his brother's size. Ernio was four inches over six feet, with shoulders to match. The body under the loose traveling shirt hinted at his past prowess as an athlete, but also at his more recent comforts in the family home.

Once on the ground, he reached back into the carriage to pick up what looked like a package from the seat. As he lifted it into the air and spun around in place, the series of delighted shrieks revealed that the package was in fact his four-year-old son Berto. After a few more throws, Ernio settled him on his shoulders and went to greet his father and sister.

Corlis waited his turn with a familiar dread. Being so close to someone so much bigger reminded him of being around the older kids at the orphanage—the kind whose idea of play involved someone else getting fistfuls of dirt in their face. Not to mention the number of Werrish thugs who used to visit him at the inn later in life, delivering dead bodies that needed to be disposed of.

However, like his father had insisted, Ernio was as harmless as he was large. The only way he threatened to hurt Corlis was by breaking his back in a hug—although he could do that with one arm while balancing a child around his neck.

"Berto, this is your new uncle Corlis," Ernio said, tilting his head up. "What do we say?"

Berto pointed down at Corlis with glee. "Your eyes are funny!"

"Come, now!" Ernio patted his son's knee. "That's not what I meant!"

It was nothing Corlis hadn't heard plenty of times growing up. He fixed one of his pale eyes on Berto's saucer-sized brown ones. "Yours are nicer. Can I have them?" He did soften his tone, compared to how he would say it back in the day.

Father and son both howled with laughter in response.

"Can't believe I've had a brother all along!" Ernio said. "I wouldn't have been outnumbered every time we decided where to go on a weekend. Don't make that face, Gretia!" He pointed at his sister. "You know you always voted with Liv! You two were the reason I had to suffer through all those concerts. We could have gone boating with Corlis here!"

Before Corlis was dragged into the middle of a quarrel between siblings he never had, Ernio's wife Rosilla came up. Lord Hestor had mentioned her parents were from the Mountain Kingdoms, and Corlis recognized some of the features he'd seen on Porla, mainly the freckled skin and reddish hair. The latter was barely held together by a strap, which also could have been said about Rosilla herself. Her otherwise exquisite white dress was rife with creases and had an elongated yellow stain just over breast height. She climbed out of the carriage with decidedly less enthusiasm and did a round of perfunctory greetings.

"I'm Corlis, pleased to meet you," Corlis said.

Rosilla leaned in, and not so much gave him a peck as she slammed her cheek into his. As their faces got closer, Corlis noticed a distinct set of crow's feet.

"You too," she replied, already addressing her husband. "Ernio, can you help with the bags? Millie's getting fussy; I want to get out a toy for her before it gets worse. It's in the one with the white straps. Show the driver where that is. It should be on top of your trunk, to the right. Be careful, there are bottles in there. Never mind, I'll just get it."

And with that, she was off.

The last one out of the carriage was another, younger Mountain girl. She was much more robustly built than Rosilla, much less elegantly dressed, and much more placid. She kept her attention entirely on the swaddled-up baby girl in her arms and cooed soothing nonsense at her.

"This is our wet nurse, Ogde." Ernio patted her on the shoulder. "She's been a lifesaver for Rosie."

Ogde nodded to Corlis, then turned back to Millie. Her face had a simple sort of quality—not dumb, merely unconcerned with whatever wasn't directly in front of it.

Once the greetings were out of the way, Lord Hestor instructed everyone to the dining hall, where Donella awaited them with Ernio's favorite, roast swan. Ernio clapped and hooted like a schoolboy at the news and led the way with a song.

Thessa fell in next to Corlis as they crossed the courtyard. "What do you think?"

"As far as first impressions go, I have more in common with my sister-in-law than my brother."

"Maybe you'll get along well with her."

"I'd say that's exactly why I wouldn't get along with her."

"And Ernio?"

Corlis thought for a while. Up in front, his brother took Berto off his own shoulders and put him on his father's instead. Lord Hestor pretended to teeter left and right while Berto squealed with joy, and Rosilla scolded them all for being reckless.

"He seems like a good man," Corlis said at last, as they were about to enter the dining hall. "I only wonder if he knows he's not the father of his son."

Thessa stopped dead in her tracks. "What do you mean?"

"It's only a guess, but Porla told me something a while back. In the Mountains, the easiest way to tell someone has foreign parents is if their eyes are brown. Mountain people's eyes are only ever blue or green. Rosilla's are blue, and Ernio's are green, but Berto's are brown."

"Maybe that rule only works for Mountain people," Thessa whispered. "If it's so obvious, don't you think they'd already know?"

"Maybe. Which is one reason why I'm not going to bring it up. But it does make me wonder."

III

Part Three

Chapter 11

Thessa was already awake when Nykhe knocked gently to call them to breakfast. She had risen before the early summer sun and sat on the bench by the open window. The night's sleep had dampened the memory of the events at the stable, but the weight of unease refused to leave her. Her mind kept coming back to the same questions. Was it only one time? Was it as bad as she thought? Could it happen again?

She picked up a small pair of scissors and pricked her finger with it, ready to jump out and tumble down the hill if she were unable to resist transforming.

A thin strand of blood trickled forward. Thessa picked up the scent, but it wasn't followed by the same rush. Bizarrely enough, that didn't reassure her, only left her with more concern. Perhaps her own blood didn't have the same effect. Perhaps Corlis had been right, and it was only horse's blood that set her off. Perhaps it was better if she never found out.

Thessa sucked on her finger until the bleeding stopped, then stayed on the bench until Nykhe's knock came. There was nothing else to do but face another day.

The dining hall lay in the far end of the building, under the long gallery that connected the two parallel wings. Much like Lord Hestor's study, it resembled a furnished arcade more than a room. A series of arches connected it directly to the inner courtyard, with three walls to separate it from the kitchen and the outside world.

As for the furnishings, the Benuarte villa upheld some of the oldest traditions that New Montres—and even Sallis— had long outgrown. Among these was the habit to eschew tables and chairs in favor of recliners arranged all over the room. Each was fitted with a comfortable mattress, as well as a sizable pillow at one end, so the diners may rest their elbow while picking freely from the dishes between them. Said dishes stood atop a number of low holders that crowded the mosaic-covered floor.

"Good morning!" Lord Hestor greeted them from the center. Ernio was on his right, along with Rosilla, who was in the middle of coaxing some honeyed porridge into her son. Gretia lay on the other side and called Thessa over.

"I was just asking Father if we could take the carriage down to the village for the morning. I'd love to show you the bookseller, and my friends would be thrilled to meet you too!"

Thessa politely thanked her for the invitation. She had her reservations about Gretia's friends, but the prospect of browsing new books enticed her.

Ernio joined in, "I'll take the other one. Do you like boating, Corlis?"

"I wouldn't know," Corlis replied, shifting around to get comfortable lying sideways. "I've never done it."

His brother gave him a look of utter bewilderment and asked his father, "Didn't you say he lived right by the river? A stone's throw from the Ryonne delta, only a few miles from the wide open sea—I'd imagine it would be teeming with boathouses!"

"It wasn't for a lack of boathouses," Corlis said, darkening in the face. "But mostly a lack of time. Or money."

Ernio's chipper mood remained unaffected. "Well, there's no better place to make up for it than Forterne." He reached over to his son and gently patted him on the head. "Berto's been obsessed with pirates ever since Ogde read a story to him, so I figured I'd take him down to the lake. You need to come with us. It's a crime not to sail on a day like this."

Corlis made no comment, either in favor or against. Thessa was aware how much he despised the Crescent Bay market in New Montres, which consisted entirely of moored boats connected with a web of planks. He claimed to get seasick merely crossing from one end to the other.

Berto, on the other hand, loudly agreed by waving his spoon like a cutlass, landing chunks of porridge on his mother's face and dress.

"You didn't tell me about this plan of yours," Rosilla said as she wiped herself.

"It's my gift to you. Berto and I will be out of your hair for most of the day," Ernio said, brushing his wife's reddish locks and picking out a clump of oats. "This way, you can have some time to yourself."

"Will you be taking Millie too?"

"I don't think she'd appreciate it. Especially if she needs to get changed in the middle of the lake. But I do need to take Ogde to keep an eye on Berto while I show Corlis the ropes."

"Mm-hm," came Rosilla's unenthused response as she concluded that she would be alone for the day with their infant daughter.

Thessa saw it best to step in. "What if you came with us to the village? We could help with Millie as well. I don't have much experience with babes, but I'm sure I can hold her for a while."

Gretia shared little of Thessa's willingness. "If you want to," she said tentatively to her sister-in-law. "We'll be walking around a lot, though."

"No, it's all right. You go have your fun." Rosilla shook the remaining crumbs off of herself and got up. "I'll go tell Ogde to bring Millie down to the yard when you leave."

She took Berto by the hand and left the dining hall, while Ernio continued with his breakfast, blissfully absorbed in his thoughts about their upcoming adventure.

Lord Hestor said to his children, "Make sure one of you gets back early after lunch. Livia's train is coming in at six, and I'll need to have them fetched on time."

The words pierced Ernio's unawareness. "*Them?*" he echoed. "Is Aunt Dalma coming too?"

"She is," came Lord Hestor's strangely curt answer.

Over the dishes, Ernio and Gretia shared a stiff glance of recognition, but said nothing. For the rest of the meal, it was as if the name had never come up.

* * *

The village of Doma Lanca was a small place that offered little distraction, but its charm was undeniable. All the houses were painted in the same blinding white that was customary around the province, with bright red clay roofs over colorful doors of blue and green. Along the narrow cobblestone streets that wound haphazardly down the hillside, wide shuttered windows broke the monotony of the walls, and chest-high bushes of herbs grew from stone troughs.

Gretia found her friends at one of the two inns by the main square, which was their usual gathering point. The girls were more or less the same age as her, all daughters of local families with mostly nominal titles and their own branded vineyards. They also shared her profound flair for the dramatic.

"And do you know, Thessa was *kidnapped* on her engagement night! Isn't that right? Oh, you have to hear it all from her!" Gretia implored Thessa over their plate of tiny fig cakes, only to tell most of the story herself anyway, in significantly more colorful detail than Thessa remembered.

The girls were happy to provide an audience, and Thessa had to wonder if she would have grown up to be like one of them if she had stayed at home—or if she already had been one before she ran away.

Around mid-afternoon, they said their farewells at the square and, figuring Ernio would take his sweet time on the lake, they got into the carriage to make it back as Lord Hestor had instructed. As they found out, their rush was unnecessary.

"We've been back for hours," Ernio greeted them in the yard. "Got off to a good enough start, but then a side wind came, and poor Corlis turned greener than the neighbor's grass. I couldn't go over the basic knots without him leaning out at every rock of the boat."

He said all this with a broad grin, while next to him, Corlis had the face of someone who'd been to war. If the lack of time or money had been his only reason not to go boating before, he now had a much more compelling one.

Later on, once Iolinos cleaned down the horses and the carriage, the driver headed off to Pont Lanca to fetch Livia and Aunt Dalma from the train station, while the rest of the family settled in for some time before dinner. Around seven o'clock, the clatter of hooves sounded from the road below, and Lord Hestor called them to the outer courtyard to greet the newcomers. Gretia didn't need to be told twice; she nearly tumbled down the stairs in the hurry to see her sister again.

Corlis and Thessa lined up beside the others and waited for the carriage to emerge around the bend. When it did, the atmosphere in the yard changed. There was only one person behind the driver. Judging from her age, she must have been Livia, and as the distance shrunk between them, Thessa only became more confident in her guess.

Lord Hestor's other two children took strongly after their Werrish mother's fair skin and light hair, but Livia was nearly as much of a spitting image of her father as Corlis. The unmistakable Benuarte cheekbones and bloodless lips adorned her heart-shaped face, framed by jet black hair in a crown of intricate braids. Her clothes were in a much more subdued dark blue, and she wore almost no jewelry, save for a few simple silver pieces. Sitting with her back immaculately straight as the carriage pulled up, Livia looked more of an aristocrat than any of her siblings, or indeed their father.

Once she reached the ground, Gretia jumped at her and kissed her on both cheeks. Livia hugged her back at length.

Lord Hestor waited patiently until they separated. "Welcome home, dear. How come you're alone? Has Dalma fallen ill so she couldn't join you?" he asked, not without a wishful tone in his voice.

What little joy had been on Livia's face was replaced with embarrassment. "No, Father. She's here." She spoke barely above a whisper.

Ernio put his hands on his hips. "If she was here, we'd definitely know that."

Livia's cheeks flashed pink. "She's in Pont Lanca. We drove by a dance hall on the way from the station, and when she heard the music, she got off, and"—she sounded almost afraid to finish the sentence—"told me to tell you to fetch her later."

"*Later?*" Lord Hestor gaped. "It's already past seven! The trip to town is near an hour, and then the same back! Where does she think she is, that we'll just drive her around in the dead of night? Larence is coming tomorrow, and I have heaps of ledgers to go through." He huffed. "That woman is impossible."

"We could leave her there," Ernio said. "She can spend the night in town."

Lord Hestor scoffed. "And then we'll never hear the end of it! No, someone will have to go back. Otherwise, she'll go on about what a bad host I was, sending nothing but an empty carriage for her after dark."

"I promised to watch Berto while Rosie gets some rest." Ernio put up his hands. "I'm duty-bound as a husband."

Corlis stepped forward. "I can go. If that's all right with you, that is. I don't mind making the trip, and I'm familiar enough with being out at this hour."

Thessa, who was about to make the same offer, joined by his side. "I'm happy to go along as well. I'd quite like to see the waterfront at night."

"Oh, dear boy." Lord Hestor patted Corlis on the shoulder. "I can't thank you enough. Do try not to get in trouble, if I may ask. She can be more than a handful."

He left them outside; Ernio mouthed a quick "Good luck", and followed after his father. Livia briefly welcomed Corlis into the family, then excused herself after an exhausting trip, with Gretia in tow. Before long, it was only Thessa and Corlis in the courtyard. Seeing no reason to wait around, they climbed into the carriage and gave the word to go.

*** *** ***

The sun had already set by the time they reached the town. When they arrived by train the day before, it was not long after noon. The streets at that time were largely empty, with mostly tradespeople and servants going about their business. But when Thessa and Corlis rolled in after eight o'clock, it was like a different town altogether. Everywhere was filled with lights and merrymaking, and the crowd in places was comparable to New Montres.

The dance hall Livia mentioned was barely a block away from the train station. Corlis stopped the carriage beside the entrance and asked Thessa to wait for him while he went in to get Aunt Dalma. He straightened every part of his outfit before he climbed down to the pavement, and with a final breath of determination, dove inside the building.

A minute passed, then two, then five, and ten more. Then, at long last, Corlis emerged—just as alone as he went in. He got back into the carriage, sat stiffly down in the seat, and in a stiffer voice said, "She's not here."

Thessa blinked. "*Was* she here?"

"She was. And now she isn't. A bunch of people remember her being here, and they remember her leaving, but none of them know where."

Any other onlooker would have thought Corlis unfazed, even bored by this revelation. Nothing in his tone hinted at the slightest of disturbance. But to Thessa, his expression told a wholly different tale. Behind the indomitable mask, Corlis was panicking.

The driver turned halfway back to them. "Will we be taking off, young lord?"

A thought struck Thessa. "Gercio," she addressed the driver, "have you driven Lady Dalma to town before?"

"That I have, my lady. Been a few years since she's been here, but I have."

"Do you remember what places she went to?"

"More than a few."

By now, Corlis had caught on. "Take us to every one you can remember. The fastest way you can get."

A sly smirk crept to the driver's plain face. "That'll be a long ride, young lord." And without waiting for a response, he took up the reins and led them off.

He wasn't joking. As they soon learned, Aunt Dalma was quite well versed in the nightlife of Pont Lanca. The carriage barely had to go from one corner to the next before they stopped again at an inn, salon, or private playhouse. Once, they slowed down by a brothel, but it was only to let another carriage pass. By that time, Thessa wouldn't have ruled out anything.

The night rolled on, and they made stop after stop on their wild goose chase. At each spot, Corlis went inside and interrogated any members of staff he could find, and each time, he emerged worse for wear. Besides his mounting frustration, he often came out with a lighter purse as he had to jog the servers' memory. At one point, he also got the front of his shirt covered in what smelled like wine that had already been drunk.

As the second hour crept by, they crisscrossed through the streets until a familiar sight greeted them anew. Gercio drove them past the back side of the train station and pulled up in front of the same dance hall they started at.

"That was the last one, young lord," he announced to Corlis. "'Fraid I'm out of ideas after that."

Corlis leaned forward and ran his hands through his hair. "It's over. I'm sunk. I had one thing to do, and I couldn't even do that."

"Don't worry." Thessa rubbed his back. "I'm sure it will be fine."

"How? We scoured the whole town." The panic he had kept under the surface was now seeping through the cracks. "Even if we haven't checked every single watering hole—if she's anything like the family says she is, *someone* would remember seeing her. What if she was kidnapped? What if she's dead?"

"This isn't New Montres," Thessa said, trying her best to sound reassuring.

"People are people everywhere. Just because most of them here are rich doesn't mean they're any better. If anything, they're worse." A sharpness crept into Corlis's voice, like he'd been waiting to say something this whole time. "Maybe this was the plan."

"What plan?"

"You heard how Lord Hestor and his son talked about Aunt Dalma. Both of them were all too eager to let us come get her. What if this is a setup? Dig up some nobody who can pass for a long lost son, invite him out here, then suddenly, the dear aunt goes missing. They all have their cover stories up in the villa, while I take the fall for it."

Thessa was agape. Who was this person sitting next to her,

and what had he done to her friend?

"Corlis, stop it." She grabbed him by the shoulder. "You're talking nonsense. This is what Fabreve said; you always assume the worst about people. There has to be a simpler answer."

"Like what? That the earth swallowed her?" He pointed at the dance hall. "Everyone said they saw her leave, so how—"

He bit his tongue and froze like a statue. So did Thessa. They sat locked eye to eye, as if time itself had come to a halt, while they both grasped the meaning of what Corlis had just said.

Then, on the same beat, they threw open the carriage doors on either side and leapt to the ground.

Corlis barged into the dance hall like a hunter out for blood. It was a single open space, with benches and tables lined along the walls and a small stage in the corner for the musicians. He counted the exits. One to the street, one to the kitchen, one to the privy—and one at the back. Corlis launched forward like an arrow, burrowing through the crowd with shoulder and elbow, Thessa following in his wake.

On the other side of the fourth door, in a closed-off area, a separate company held their own celebration. Over the ruckus of the music and dancing in the main hall, they faintly heard the inner crowd chanting, *"Dal-ma! Dal-ma! Dal-ma!"*

Before they could step through, a man the size of a boulder lurched in front of them. "Invitations only."

Corlis glared up at him. "I'm here to speak with the woman in there. The one who paid all you sorry lot to say she left."

The boulder's face twisted into a sneer at the realization. "Lady Dalma, you mean?" He crossed his arms and leered down at Corlis, letting his beady eyes linger on the prominent vomit stain. "And who's asking to speak with her, Lord Lizard?"

Thessa saw the flicker of doubt in Corlis. He may have been furious—and rightfully so—but he was also out of his element. Back in the Wall District, he could count on his reputation within the underworld to get him what he wanted. In Pont Lanca, the name of Corlis Andassi meant nothing.

"You mean you don't know?" Thessa stepped forward and raised her voice above the clamor. "This is Corlis Benuarte, second son of Lord Hestor Benuarte. Surely, you've heard of him?"

It was now the guard whose confidence faltered. "Lord Benuarte has only one son."

"And how do you know?" Corlis joined in, regaining his footing. "Are you a regular guest at his villa? Do you have a seat at his table? Because if you do, we can all hop right back into that cart, and pay him a visit."

He pointed through the open window at the carriage with the Benuarte emblem proudly emblazoned on the side. "Gercio!" He whistled to the driver. "Open the door, we have company!"

The guard watched the driver obediently come down from his perch at Corlis's order. At that, he bowed to the side. "Apologies, young lord. My lady. She's right in there."

They stormed past him without another word, except for Corlis muttering a low "Thanks" to Thessa.

"Please be careful in there," she said. "I don't want to risk smelling blood with so many people around."

The back room was barely a third the size of the main hall, but just as packed, if not more so. Men of all ages stood in a circle, singing and clapping along in a disjointed chorus. A handful of them held a chair high aloft over their heads, and in that chair sat a woman, basking in the undivided attention.

If Livia had been the picture of propriety, then Aunt Dalma was its antithesis. Her faded strawberry blonde hair may have started the day in a majestically towering bun, but now was a tangled mess of loose curls and dangling pins. Her emerald green dress was cut deeper than that of women a third her age, while a dozen bangles, armbands and necklaces rattled on her naked arms and shoulders. Her face was like a painter's used palette and flushed bright red in the cheeks, while she poured a goblet of wine from atop her throne into a man's open mouth.

Corlis called back to the guard, "Get her down from there!"

The human boulder, visibly torn between Aunt Dalma's and Corlis's instructions, sheepishly made his way to the middle of the room, where he begged the noble lady's pardon to announce that the Young Lord Benuarte was here to see her. The singing died off, and the men gingerly lowered the chair to the floor, casting wary looks at the two of them.

"Young Lord?" Aunt Dalma echoed in a voice hoarse from wine and cheering. "Ernio, is that you? Or Alendro, by some rare chance?"

"Corlis." He stepped forward. "Lord Hestor's other son. He might have told you about me."

The words had no visible effect at first, but eventually wound their way through the lady's drunken haze. Her glossy eyes lit up.

"Oh, my word! You're Hestor's lost little lamb, are you? What am I asking—who else could you be with those sunken cheeks? How *wonderful* to meet you, darling boy." She threw her arms open, letting the half-empty goblet fly loose from her limp fingers, and planted a loud kiss on each side of Corlis's face. She then swung to Thessa. "And who's the young lady?"

"I'm Thessalona Kalou, a friend of his."

"*Kalou!*" Aunt Dalma savored the name like an exotic treat. "What an *absolute* delight. I live and die for the Sallician arts. That's why I settled in Callex, I'm sure you know. Do you enjoy the theater? Oh, we must, *must* go see a piece! Is there a playhouse open?"

She directed the last question at the room, but before any of them could answer, Corlis cut off her rambling.

"We should go up to the villa. Lord Hestor and Livia are waiting for us with the rest of the family."

"Ah, yes. We mustn't keep the *esteemed* Lord Benuarte of Vertussi Hill waiting!" She made another dramatic gesture. "Come along, then, to the carriage. Family calls!"

She then flounced right out of the room, as naturally as if none of the evening's events were the slightest bit out of order. The revelers shuffled awkwardly behind her, careful to avoid Corlis, who was rooted to the spot. As always, whether he was plotting or panicking, his face remained pale and unmoved. But Thessa knew that he finally found something he held in common with his father, and that was a seething disdain for Lady Dalma Lazewic.

Chapter 12

It was well past midnight when they finally got back to the villa, and Corlis fell headfirst into bed. When Nykhe called them in the morning, he decided to allow himself an extra hour of sleep before he sought out the dining hall.

Most of breakfast had already been cleared away, but Donella was by his side the instant he crossed the threshold, ready to take his order. Blurting out the first thing that came to his exhausted mind, Corlis asked for fried blood and onions. He didn't know if such fare was customary in refined circles, but after the previous night's ordeal, he cared even less.

He had been vaguely aware that Lord Hestor was speaking with someone when he entered the room, but only when he got closer did he notice that it was an unfamiliar face. The man was a smidge under forty, with features that may as well have been carved out of stone with a sorely dulled chisel. Every part of his face was straight and sharp, from the narrow jawline, to the pointed nose, to the wide forehead. His already graying hair was combed back flat, which only accentuated the angular shapes of his skull. Though the cut of his white shirt and maroon tunic was outright plain, the fabrics were as fine as money could buy.

"Ah, there you are!" Lord Hestor said. "How are you, dear

boy? I heard about the runaround Dalma gave you. Did you get some rest?"

"Yes, thank you." Corlis mustered some basic manners and greeted the other man. "Good morning."

"This is Larence Maiesco," the lord said. "He's our family's advisor in all matters of finance."

"Very good to meet you, Corlis." Larence gave a small salute. His eyes were dark and naturally narrow, which made him look like he was constantly suspicious.

"I've been waiting to introduce you two," said Lord Hestor. "Larence here clawed his way up from less than nothing. His mother died early, and his father spent more time in chains than without, but today, some of the finest families in Ardonne seek his advice." He spoke with such pride as if Larence's accomplishments were his own.

"A few smart choices and lots of hard work." Larence bowed in obligate humility.

"Are you also with the Golden Lion?" Corlis asked.

"I'm not from the kind of stock they'd allow in," Larence said. "Truth be told, I don't mind. I prefer to pick for myself who I work for. I heard you're quite the enterprising young man yourself. Your father tells me you have your own inn, is that right?"

Corlis poured himself a drink. He was not used to being praised as a child, and it was not a habit that came easy to him as an adult. "My uncle—my adoptive father—built it with his inheritance and a mountain of debt. I only took over after he and his wife both died."

"Don't diminish your accomplishments." Larence pointed a finger at him like a schoolteacher. "Maybe you didn't build it, but you've been running it on your own, haven't you? That's no mean feat by itself, either."

"I have, up until a few weeks ago. There was an accident at a neighboring construction, and much of the inn is in ruins." Corlis drank. "Considering the state I left it in, I'd imagine it would be looted by now—if there was anything in there to loot."

Larence relented. "Well, what matters in the end is your wit, and I'm sure it'll be of great use to the family."

That put the topic to rest. Donella came out with Corlis's breakfast and set it down before him, along with copious slices of warm bread. At the orphanage, fried blood with onions was one of the staple foods that Corlis loathed with a passion, yet as an adult, he found himself craving it from time to time. Usually, when he was in a foul mood.

"Larence will be staying with us for the week as well," Lord Hestor said. "The summer festival is about the only time when myself, my brother, and Ernio are all together, so it's become something of a tradition to discuss the matters of the estate."

Corlis broke off a piece of bread and heaped onions onto it. "Did you arrive from Brasthe this morning?"

"He is a sharp one." Larence winked at Lord Hestor. "Most people take much longer to pick up on my accent."

"My aunt was from there," Corlis said. "She'd been living in Ardonne for decades by the time they adopted me, so her accent was mostly gone. It only came out when she was angry. She'd say *weet* instead of wait or *tine* instead of ten, and I'd get into more trouble because I didn't understand what she wanted."

Larence laughed. "Yes, occasionally I find my Brasthen slipping through as well. But I've lived in New Montres for years now. I came with the night train. The clacking always puts me to sleep, so I travel by night whenever I can to make the best of it."

That did sound like a good idea—definitely better than spending the first half of the day doing nothing and the second half being tired from all that nothing. Corlis would have to try that when he took the train back to New Montres. Which, in turn, struck a thought in his mind like a spike. When *would* he be going back to New Montres…?

Before he had any chance to mull over that, a series of footsteps came from behind him, and right away he knew it only could have been Aunt Dalma. It was remarkable how ostentatious she managed to sound, even when simply walking.

"Good morning, everyone!" She glided into the dining hall in a loose white dress and a billowing shawl that was long enough to hang a man with. Considering the binge she'd been on the night before, she was as spritely as if she'd woken from a whole week of sleep. Granted, given the amount of paint on her face, she may as well have been a corpse underneath, and no one would have been any the wiser.

"No need to make space for me." She waved benevolently. "I'll be having my breakfast in my room." She then proceeded to rattle off her order to an increasingly dismayed Donella. Corlis barely understood half the words, but from what he could gather, it consisted entirely of nuts, leaves, and a handful of prunes.

Once the cook bowed out, Aunt Dalma graced them with her attention. "Larence!" she breathed with a token effort at feigning shock. "How *fabulous* to see you." She smiled at him with more teeth than Corlis would have thought possible to fit inside a human mouth.

"My lady." Larence pushed himself up from the recliner and kissed Aunt Dalma's liver-spotted hand. "You grow younger each year."

"No need to feed her vanity," Lord Hestor grumbled.

"Come now, Hestor, allow *one* of your guests to be any fun," the lady scolded him. "Your house is always so *frightfully* dull. No wonder your daughter is such a shrinking violet! I'm almost embarrassed to introduce her to my acquaintances. Do you have any plans at all to entertain your guests, or will we be spending the whole First of Summer's week locked in our rooms?"

"The festivities will be in the village tomorrow. Today, I'm taking the children down to visit Wilhelma's grave." Lord Hestor glowered up at his sister-in-law. "I don't suppose you plan on showing her any respect?"

Aunt Dalma merely waved again. "Life is for the living, my dear. I see no point in wasting it over what's gone. When I'm laid to my final rest, I want it to be amidst song and dance!" She threw her hands up as if she already was at her own funeral. "But you go and mourn all you want. I'll be down in Pont Lanca; hopefully there's something worth seeing there. Oh, and will you please have the maid bring some proper candles to my room? I can't *bear* quartz light. It's so cold and bleak."

She flung her shawl over her shoulder and departed through the open arches. Not once did she so much as acknowledge Corlis's existence—and he found himself more than comfortable with that.

* * *

Thessa and Larence weren't invited to Lady Wilhelma's grave, so once breakfast time was over, the former went out for a ride in the woods, while the latter joined Aunt Dalma on the town. As the rest of the family got ready, Corlis went out to the inner courtyard to wait.

He was not the first one there. Livia sat on a bench next to Ogde, who had Millie in her lap. The two of them huddled in muted conversation, watching Berto wade intently around in the fountain pool.

The gravel crackled under Corlis's foot, and Livia looked up. "Corlis! I didn't see you there."

"Sorry," Corlis said. "I didn't mean to interrupt."

"That's all right. Come, sit." Livia slid closer to Ogde—needlessly, as the bench was long enough for five people.

Corlis joined them right when Berto slammed his hands into the water. "I got one!" he shrieked in excitement, splashing water everywhere as he danced in place.

"What's he after?" Corlis asked Livia while Ogde went up to the boy.

"Goldfish," Livia whispered back. "He's playing pirates."

"Pirates hunt goldfish?"

"Well, they are gold."

The nurse now stood over Berto's cupped hands, surveying his trophy. Then, with typical Mountain sobriety, she told him it was dead.

Upon being confronted with the fragility of life this way, the boy let out a soft "Oh," threw the deceased fish into a flowerbed, then proceeded to yank random clumps of grass in search of buried treasure.

Before he got too involved, Ogde took him upstairs to get some dry clothes on him, leaving only Corlis and Livia in the yard. With everyone else in their rooms, the only sound was the soft trickle of the fountain and the occasional chirp of the birds that flew down to peck between the stones.

"I'm sorry about Aunt Dalma last night," Livia said after a minute. "She can be… overwhelming."

"That's one word for it," Corlis replied, maybe with more of an edge than he meant to. As far as he could tell, Livia was the last person who needed to apologize. But he appreciated that someone did. "I guess I shouldn't complain, seeing as how I'm not the one living with her."

Livia kept her eyes down. "It's not always easy."

"Must be worth it."

"She's lived in Callex since before I was born, and she's famous for being a patron of the arts, especially music. Father once sent me to study the harp in New Montres, and even there, when people heard I was her niece, they asked me to put in a word with her."

Corlis followed along and concluded, "So you put up with her to get what you want."

Livia turned to him, equal parts taken aback, offended, and amused. "When you put it like that, it sounds awfully selfish."

"It's practical. Sounds like something I would do."

The girl's thin Benuarte lips curved into a smirk. "Do you put up with *us*, then?"

"Not with her, that's sure and a half."

Livia snickered. It was small and measured, barely above a sniff, but in many ways it was the most sincere response Corlis heard since he arrived. At once, the two of them were no longer strangers, but cohorts in on the same joke.

"I can only imagine how difficult this must be for you," she said. "To be uprooted all of a sudden. I've been living in Callex for a year, and I'm still not used to it. Aunt Dalma keeps inviting new people over before I could learn the names of all the last ones. It makes me feel so lost, like a fish out of water."

Corlis cocked one eyebrow and wordlessly shifted his gaze at the flowerbed where Berto's catch had landed. Once Livia figured out which eye she was supposed to follow, she smacked him on the back of his hand.

"You are *terrible*." She laughed. "Come now, let's see if the others are ready." She got up from the bench and left Corlis alone.

Well, not quite alone. He had a number of questions to keep him company. The first one was still whether something was amiss around Berto's parentage, and if Ernio knew about it. The second one was whether he had only imagined it, or if there truly was a shade of fright in Livia's voice when Corlis interrupted her conversation with Ogde. And if so, then the third question was what Ogde—who knew more about Ernio and Rosilla's marriage than anyone else—could have said that Livia was so scared to have Corlis overhear.

Chapter 13

Ceci had been in Forterne for less than a day, but she was already fed up with it. Everything was sickeningly peaceful and moved at a snail's pace. Even when they were only a few miles from their destination, it felt like they'd never get anywhere. But she had to hold out. She never believed the saying that good things come to those who wait—but she did know that good things often took time. As the carriage crept up the incline, so did Ceci inch closer to the fulfillment of her plans.

When they reached Pont Lanca, Lord Harmon sent a message up to the Benuarte villa, and the family's open carriage came down to fetch them. The lord took the front-facing seat by himself, with Alendro and Ceci across from him. If she only saw how he was dressed, Ceci would have imagined he was meeting the last emperor of Ardonne himself. Despite the warm summer evening, he wore not only a velvet tunic over his silk shirt, but also a gold-colored equestrian drape with all his war medals, each one polished to a blinding sheen.

Alendro stretched his legs comfortably across the passenger space and rested one foot on the cushioned seat. His clothes were much lighter, though he did also have his drape on. He bathed his face lazily in the setting sun with his eyes closed, as if he was being painted. One of his hands drummed on the side of the carriage, the other on the back of Ceci's neck.

Ceci brushed aside a branch from a fig tree beside the road right as they rounded the final curve, and the villa came into view. She sighed with relief and leaned on Alendro's shoulder.

A small group of people awaited them outside. At the forefront was an old man who could only have been Lord Hestor. Despite he and Lord Harmon being twins, they weren't much alike, beyond the overall family resemblance. While Lord Hestor's round face made him affable, Lord Harmon's cheeks puffed up like he was always about to spit. He also didn't so much as budge until the driver opened the carriage door before him, at which point he heaved himself out of the seat and climbed down the steps to dignify his brother with a curt hug.

Alendro then followed and helped Ceci out of the carriage before greeting his uncle. "Where's Ernio?" he asked with obvious disappointment. A little too obvious.

"He and Rosilla are tied up with the children." Lord Hestor motioned toward the house. "I asked them to meet us in the dining hall."

"Tied up?" Lord Harmon scoffed. "Your eldest should set a better example than this."

Lord Hestor replied with some indignation, resting both hands on his cane. "He'll be joining us later. It's not as if he ran off cavorting when he knew family was coming," he remarked at Alendro, then turned to Ceci. "And who do I have the pleasure of meeting in the young lady?"

"This is Cecina Virago," Alendro answered. "We met when Father and I were passing through New Montres and have been inseparable ever since." He punctuated the last sentence by pulling Ceci in by the waist.

Lord Hestor bowed courteously to her. "Welcome to our home, Cecina. Make yourself as comfortable as if it were yours."

"Perhaps not just yet," Lord Harmon muttered, in between accepting kisses on the cheek from Lord Hestor's daughters.

The girls greeted them mostly as a formality. Just as well, as Ceci could barely bother to listen to their names.

Finally, they came to the last two people in line.

"Ah, you." Lord Harmon sized the man up and down by way of greeting. "You must be the one Hestor mentioned. Corlis, was it?"

Ceci hadn't been sure what to expect when Alendro mentioned Lord Hestor's bastard son, but the sight underwhelmed her nonetheless. While Corlis had all the key Benuarte features, he got the worst possible version of them. His black hair was coarse, wiry, and stood in stark contrast to his pale skin. The bloodless lips reduced his mouth to barely more than a slit, and the prominent cheekbones only served to highlight his bulging eyes, which were a sickly greenish gray and pointed in two different directions.

Coupled with the fine clothes he obviously wasn't used to, his movements were just as awkward, as he stepped forward to bow. "It's a pleasure to make your acquaintance, Uncle Harmon."

Instead of replying, Lord Harmon addressed his twin. "You haven't given him our name yet, have you?"

"No, I haven't," Lord Hestor replied stiffly.

Lord Harmon said to Corlis, "Then for the time being, you will address me as Lord Harmon, like any other outsider."

"He's my son," Lord Hestor said, stressing the last word. "A blind man could tell that."

"He's not a Benuarte by law." Lord Harmon adjusted his drape. "You can be as lax with your manners as you like, but I will uphold the respect our name deserves." He started across the courtyard, medals rattling like a tambourine. No one tried to stop him.

Alendro took his father's place in front of Corlis and offered a hand. "Good to meet you, Cousin. Don't fret, you can simply call me Alendro. Even if you and Father don't see eye to eye, I trust the two of us can." His words weren't merely laden with mockery—they were laden with the knowledge that Corlis would realize that mockery and couldn't say a thing about it.

"Likewise." He accepted the handshake, showing no reaction to the vice grip that Alendro delighted in giving people. He then went on to introduce the woman next to him. "This is Thessalona Kalou, a close friend of mine."

Ceci regarded her with much greater interest. A Sallician in this part of Ardonne was enough of a curiosity, and the ease with which she carried herself among nobility made it all the more implausible that someone like her would be in Corlis's company. But there was something else to her. Ceci couldn't quite put her finger on it until Thessa greeted her.

"Lovely to meet you, Cecina." She clasped her hands before her thighs. "Your necklace is beautiful."

As with Alendro's comment to Corlis, there was a veiled message that Ceci picked up on. She was wearing all of the garish gold jewelry that Alendro had given her, and Thessa clearly knew where they had come from. Her compliment wasn't a simple jab. Rather, there was a familiar look upon her as she said it—a look that said, "Like knows like."

With the tedium of introductions out of the way, they were at last shown to their rooms. Ceci and Alendro were accommodated on the ground floor, while Lord Harmon settled into his old quarters upstairs. All the better to stay as far away from him as possible. Besides that, the guest rooms were placed around the outer courtyard, which would also give her a shorter escape route out of the villa later.

"It's exactly how I left it last year," Alendro said, observing the furniture. "I wonder if they've changed the sheets since."

"They'll certainly have to after our stay." Ceci simpered at him.

Alendro dragged her into a kiss. "So, how do you like it here?"

"Your uncle seems less appalled by my presence than your father. That's a welcome change."

"Yes, he and his son are about the two most pleasant people this world has ever seen. Two weeks of their company should last you until next summer." Alendro sneered. "I guess I should go find Ernio and ask if the rumors about him trying to compete again were true. That should be entertainment enough for the evening. Would you care to join?"

Ceci bit her lip. "I need a little more time to freshen up after the trip. But you go ahead, and I'll find you in the dining hall later."

Some part of Ceci was greatly relieved that the man she was going to kill wasn't in the welcoming party. If she had seen his face right away, the temptation to do it the same night could have overpowered her. That would have been foolish. She needed a plan first—to learn her way around the villa and find the time, place, and means to do it. The next day's feast would give her ample opportunity for that. After biding her time for years, she could wait one more day.

Alendro gave her one last squeeze on the thigh, then set out to find his cousin. Once he was gone, Ceci cased the room. The only other way out was the window, which opened onto a forested slope. Not too treacherous, but she would have to watch her step carefully if she were to climb out at night. The lamps on the nightstands and the chandelier were all quartz, so if she wanted to take a light with her when she snuck out, she'd have to get a candle from elsewhere. It would likely be safer to simply go without.

The covers on the double bed hung all the way to the floor, but the bed frame itself was high above the ground, leaving ample space to hide her secret bag underneath. After she dusted off her hands, her gaze fell on the writing desk—more precisely, what lay in the brass holder at the back of it.

It was a foot long end to end and weighed almost a pound as Ceci lifted it. The handle was made of smooth, carved bone, besmirched only by a small chip toward the end. The blade was the same brass as the holder and barely wider than her finger. It had no edge, but the point was sharp enough to skewer an ox.

Ceci turned it over in her hand. The maker may have intended it as a simple letter opener, but she would find a much better use for it.

Chapter 14

With the arrival of the remaining family members, the Benuarte villa was a far cry from when Thessa and Corlis first crossed the threshold. Where the walls used to echo with emptiness, nine bedrooms were now full. Besides the family's own two carriages, Lord Hestor had to hire a six-seater from Pont Lanca, so the fifteen of them could make their way down to the village on the First of Summer.

The festivities took up all of the main square and a small slope nearby with a view of the lake. Tall poles stood every few yards, with garlands of white and yellow flowers. Between them stretched braided ribbons, both in the blue and red of Ardonne, as well as the green and gold of Forterne. Colorful stalls offered flags, noisemakers, and all sorts of trinkets to the crowd that swarmed the streets. The air was laden with the smell of stews bubbling in massive cauldrons and spit roasts dripping with fat.

Once they arrived in the village, and Lord Hestor finished the obligatory round of greetings, the family was guided to a canopied platform with padded recliners and servers to keep their plates and cups full. This placement was reserved only for those who bore the Benuarte name, so Thessa had to remain on the square.

Corlis showed little enthusiasm at being on his own with the rest of the family, but she nudged him on. "You'll never get to know them if you're only ever around me."

Somewhat reluctantly, Corlis took his place among his siblings, and Thessa set out to explore the festival. She wandered aimlessly among the stalls, while around her, the villagers danced in flower crowns, threw wet rags at someone on a high chair for prizes, or watched a juggler keep five flaming sticks in the air at the same time. While nowhere near as big, it reminded her of the Crescent Bay market in New Montres and the sense of wonder during her first time there. It felt like a lifetime ago.

Eventually, her promenade led her to the lakeside slope, where the food was being prepared, including some delicacies from other lands besides the usual Ardonnese fare. One that aroused both her curiosity and her appetite was an old woman selling skewers of spiced meats in a traditional Brasthen style.

"You'll want to be careful with that," Larence's voice came as she handed over the copper. "Back home in Brasthe, we used to call it 'maidenmeat.'"

"Why so?" Thessa asked back.

Larence's narrow eyes flashed mischievously. "Because the only women who ate it were the ones who didn't have anyone to kiss."

Puzzled at the answer, Thessa bit off a piece of meat, and her mouth filled with a more pungent taste of garlic than she had ever imagined. In an effort to maintain good manners, she hastily swallowed. Larence passed her a small wooden cup of mead, which she gratefully accepted.

"Maidenmeat, you said?" she asked, almost afraid to speak.

"That's right." Larence replied from behind his own drink. "Or rather, as we said it, '*meedenmite.*'"

"It sounds very similar."

"Brasthen is more of an accent than a language. According to the Ardonnese, at least."

Thessa remembered something about that. Her parents had taught her precious little about the world outside Sallis, but the roadbooks and journals she stole from Papa's study told her that Brasthe used to be a part of Ardonne for centuries.

"How come you don't speak Brasthen now?" she asked while she cautiously picked off the next bit.

"In the circles that I work with, it's not an accent that commands much respect. When I moved to New Montres, I had to pay someone to help me get rid of it before people would talk to me, let alone make deals."

"Pay someone?"

"And quite handsomely, too. I spent a whole month practicing until I could say, 'The maid makes the bed and waits for men to lay'—instead of *'The meed meeks the bide and weets for mine to lee.'*"

"I think that sounds nicer," Thessa said. "Some of it sounds almost like Sallician, in fact."

"That's kind of you to say. At this point, speaking without an accent is more natural than with one."

They continued around the village, slowly making their way back to the square. They talked about their homes and their travels while they drank their mead, and Thessa slowly finished her skewer of maidenmeat. By the last one, she barely noticed the flavor and oddly found herself wanting more.

As they strolled deep in conversation, another memory floated back to Thessa—the memory of her and Lokenn's time together as newcomers in New Montres. She hadn't made that sort of connection with anyone since, but now that she thought of it, there was some of Lokenn in Larence as well. Not so much in his face, which was far too sharp and angular compared to the delicate Midorean features, but rather in the subtle pride with which he carried himself. His clothes were also after a simple fashion, but flawlessly cut and tailored. He may have been born a commoner, but he was in many ways the picture of refinement.

They emerged from between the stalls next to the family's platform. Corlis was up there with the others, in the blue jacket with the gold trimmings that Thessa had helped choose. The outfit was rounded out with an equestrian drape in the same wine red that the Benuarte men wore. It looked far too warm for summer, though the canopy fended off the sun.

Despite all that, Corlis's movements in his aristocratic garb were more comfortable by the day. As their eyes met, Thessa gave him another wave of encouragement, then tapped her shoulder. Corlis picked up on the hint and adjusted the pin that held his drape in place, then resumed his conversation with Livia.

They were now about to pass the square, where a band stood upon a smaller platform and played lively tunes for the dozens of couples dancing in the middle. Almost as if on cue as they approached, Aunt Dalma erupted from the crowd and sailed toward the two of them.

"Larence!" she cried over the ruckus of the festival. "My hero upon a white horse! Do come to my rescue, and save me from having to dance alone! None of these boys have been able to keep the pace. What has the vigor of youth come to?" She pouted at a small group of men, none of whom must have been older than twenty.

"It would be an honor, my lady," Larence replied. "I merely hope that you have two right feet, so that between us, we may have all the right parts for dancing."

The excuse did nothing to faze Aunt Dalma. "Darling man, I have all the right parts for any occasion. Come now, the music beckons!" And without waiting for another word, she dragged Larence off in her shawl.

Thessa had to admit, the atmosphere was infectious indeed. The musicians held nothing back, and neither did the dancers, transforming the square into a dizzying whirlwind of song and color. It didn't take long before one of the youths jilted by Aunt Dalma came to ask for her hand too. While her time as a barmaid had left Thessa somewhat wary of men caught in the haze of wine and music, her partner proved courteous enough that she joined him for the next piece as well.

The afternoon turned into evening, but the festivities showed little sign of slowing down. Alendro came down to dance with Ceci, and so did Ernio and Rosilla, acting the part of a couple for the first time since Thessa met them. It wasn't until a fair bit later that the band let up, and the mass of people in the square began to thin out. Many of them retreated to the long tables where beer and wine flowed aplenty, to gather their strength for the second wind once the sun set.

Thessa sat at one of these tables for a while, with Larence and the members of the family who had come by. Right as she considered calling Corlis down to join them, the music ceased with an abrupt cut, and an ear-splitting whistle blew from the bandstand.

"Ladies and gentlemen, friends and neighbors, and the *esteemed* family Benuarte!"

If the whistle hadn't grabbed Thessa, the voice did. Aunt Dalma stood next to the band leader with his whistle in hand, waving both arms in a flourish. The two lords regarded her with an expression that left no doubt as to how little they appreciated this interruption.

Once she commanded everyone's attention, Aunt Dalma continued. "Gather round one and all, for now that we've delighted our palates with food and our ears with music, it's time to delight our minds with a one-of-a-kind experience. The marvelous Pamur Gavennas and his talented colleagues have accepted my invitation to perform before us one of the great theatrical masterworks of our time!"

While she spoke, a group of men made their way to the middle of the square. Thessa recognized them from the back room at the dance hall, where her and Corlis's chase after Aunt Dalma had ended. Up on the platform, Corlis's face was as stiff as ever. Inwardly, Thessa would have bet good money he was swearing.

Blissfully unaware of the curses her nephew muttered at her, Aunt Dalma concluded her announcement. "Watch, listen, and let yourself be enthralled by this seminal play in one act. Ladies and gentlemen, I give you: *The Feast!*"

On the last word, she clapped enthusiastically, and the crowd followed suit. Pamur stepped forth to bask in the celebration. He was a heavy-set man of fifty or so, almost as tall as Ernio, with unusually long hair in an oiled braid. He raised one arm and, in a thundering voice, began to narrate the tale.

Thessa had seen her share of such performances in New Montres. Most of them occurred in small playhouses that couldn't attract quite the same audience as the proper theaters, and many more took place out on the open street. Pamur's troupe was evidently most used to these circumstances as well. The set consisted entirely of painted crates and sheets, which could serve as tables, walls, curtains, rivers, and whatever else was needed.

The Feast, as Pamur related, was the story of a small village beset by a petty and avaricious lord who was impossible to please. No matter how the villagers tried to meet his demands, he only took that as encouragement to come up with increasingly more absurd ones—such as that everyone must always stand on one leg, wear their shirts on their bottom, or count backward while eating. As the audience roared at the antics on stage, Thessa had to notice that the actor playing the lord was a portly man in a gray wig, clad in green and yellow that strongly resembled the Benuarte family colors.

By the look on Lord Harmon's face, this was tantamount to open mockery, but it was nothing compared to the play's final scene. After the unending humiliation, the villagers grew tired of the lord's ridiculous tyranny, stormed his house, then roasted him on a spit and ate him—while counting backward.

Amidst gales of laughter and applause from the crowd, chief among them Aunt Dalma herself, Pamur's troupe bowed over and over while clearing away the stage. A young boy went around with a box to collect whatever coins the spectators deigned to give them for the entertainment. He stopped in front of Thessa as well, but she judged it better to let him pass.

While the performance had elevated the mood on the square, the same could not be said for the platform. The two lords sat huddled in intense discussion, or rather, an intense one-sided tirade from Lord Harmon. Corlis and Livia kept themselves occupied in their own conversation off to the side. Ernio and Alendro opted to linger some more at the tables, to fraternize with the villagers, and to stay well outside of their fathers' earshot.

Alendro sat a few seats away from Thessa, with Ceci in his lap. She giggled and swooned over him, eating grapes out of his mouth and smothering him in kisses, determined to make them the envy of every man and woman around.

After their first meeting the day before, Thessa wasn't sure what to make of the girl. Not in terms of her relationship with Alendro—that was abundantly clear. Everything about Ceci spoke volumes, from the vinegar-bleached hair, to the plunging neckline, to the dark shadows around her eyes. Thessa had seen that sort of makeup plenty of times in the salons during her travels. "Troubled eyes," the women called it, as it was meant to make them appear sleepless, frail, and in desperate need of a man's arms. Thessa tried it once, but on her tan skin, it only made her look like a badger.

Ceci, on the other hand, had no difficulty using it to its full effect. The golden headband, necklace, bracelet, rings, and hairpins all stood in testimony of that. She knew exactly what she was doing, and she was good at it. Had she and Thessa met a year earlier, they would either have been the best of friends, or the most bitter rivals.

But something wasn't quite right. In the few minutes Thessa and Alendro had spoken, the Benuarte cousin made as strong an impression on her as Ceci did. Alendro was as vain and selfish as they came, but he was also much too clever to fall for base flattery and troubled eyes. He used Ceci as much as she used him, and it wasn't hard to see what for. The only thing more obvious than Lord Harmon's disdain for his son's sweetheart was how deliberately Alendro rubbed it in his face.

Thessa had watched this game plenty of times during gatherings in her own father's court. And while he was enjoying himself, Alendro must have been more calculating than to play solely for amusement.

As she sat and regarded Ceci, Larence leaned into Thessa's ear. "She acts more like Valinne Miatti on stage than Miatti herself does in person."

Thessa had her cup to her mouth, and it took all of her restraint not to spit out her mead at the comment.

"I take it you're familiar with her work, then?" Larence asked.

Valinne Miatti was one of the most infamously brazen actresses in New Montres, well known for playing heroines who fainted at least twice in each act. Thessa had only seen one of her performances from the cheapest gallery seat, but when Larence pointed it out, the resemblance was uncanny.

"Have you met Miatti in person, that you know what she's like?" she asked, once she regained composure.

"Only once, and purely by accident," Larence said. "I helped one of my clients organize a banquet to raise money for the Bluewater theater. Do you enjoy plays?"

"Oh, absolutely," Thessa answered in Ceci's affected tone, careful to keep her voice low.

"If you're back in New Montres after next week, I would love to share the experience. I don't know if any of the theaters there put on *The Feast,* but I'm sure we can manage with some other piece."

Thessa laughed again.

"For now, I think we should get ready to return to the villa," Larence said and cocked his head at the platform, where both of the lords shuffled toward the stairs at the side, talking between themselves. The sun was dipping below the horizon, and while the festivities were nowhere close to ending, the family was meant to conclude the celebration in their private home.

Seeing how that was an hour-long carriage ride away, and how she'd drunk through most of the afternoon, Thessa decided to relieve her needs one last time before departure.

The village's public privy stood some ways off from the square. It took her a little while to find and a little more to find her way back, as many of the stalls she used as landmarks before had been taken down. Inadvertently, she ended up on a detour that led her behind the platform, passing by a makeshift tent adorned with colorful flags.

"Pamur, my darling, you're looking at it all wrong!"

The voice came from inside, where some half a dozen people were gathered. The affected cadence was unmistakable, but it wasn't Aunt Dalma speaking—it was Pamur.

Thessa slowed her steps.

"Don't you see, this is an investment. You just played for the cream of Forterne! Everyone here will remember your name, and who knows whom they'll pass it on to? The seeds you planted today will bear fruit a hundredfold."

The accuracy with which he mimicked the lady was remarkable, but the viciousness in his tone made it anything but flattering.

His words hung in the air for near a minute, until one of his colleagues stated, "What a load of piss."

A boyish voice piped up, "Then what do we do?"

"What else?" Pamur responded in a voice that closer matched his mood. "We pack up and go."

"When you say 'we,'" the first colleague spoke again, "which ones of us do you mean? Because after all the food and board, we can afford the train ride for maybe half of us."

"I know someone who runs a playhouse in Somnevici," said the leader. "We can rent a wagon to take us there, and we'll do a few shows."

"We were supposed to be back in Comarnum by next week, not Somnevici. We'll miss the start of the season," said yet another one. It sounded less like a conversation and more of an interrogation from the group.

"Why don't you ask the lord?" the boy asked again. "It's his village, after all. He should be paying us for entertaining his people."

"Psch!" the older colleague spat. "Did you *see* his face? Or that other mossback next to him? That one would rather have us flogged, if he had his way."

Pamur snorted. "Listen, it's not my fault the old hag swindled us. We'll have to make the best of it, this way or that."

A chorus of disgruntled murmurs echoed from the tent, followed by the shuffle of someone rising to unsteady feet. Before she could be caught eavesdropping, Thessa backed off and hurried along on her way to the family.

Aunt Dalma hadn't made a favorable impression on her and Corlis, and she was obviously not on the best of terms with the lords, either. That being so, Thessa had believed she reserved her capricious behavior for the Benuartes. Now, it would appear she had as few friends outside the family as within.

Chapter 15

"This is an outrage. An outrage, I tell you. How could you allow this?"

The trip back home was markedly less cheerful. Ernio had opted to sit with his own family, relinquishing his seat in the front carriage to Corlis instead. As the lone silver lining of the situation, Alendro wasn't interested in making fun of him for the whole trip, being thoroughly amused by Lord Harmon's sputtering indignity.

"It was only a play." Lord Hestor kept his cane by his elbow and his eyes on his twin brother, with a withering stare that Corlis had last seen on Aunt Ulmira.

It did precious little to cool down Lord Harmon. "It's incitement!" He flailed a pudgy hand over the side of the carriage. "It's rabble-rousing! She's openly riling them against us, and what did you do? Lay there, and let her walk over you like that!"

"She isn't walking anywhere. She's trying to get under your skin, that's what she's doing. And succeeding famously."

"I don't know, Uncle," Alendro butted in. "We might need to stand some guards at the gates tonight. Who knows if they won't storm the villa and roast the lot of us?"

Lord Hestor shut him down. "Alendro, stop egging on your

father. You're no better than Dalma." He then said to his brother, "This is our village and has been for generations. I've been working tirelessly to build a good rapport with these people. We have no reason to fear them. Especially not after some farce by a bunch of Comarnian hacks."

"The only thing you're doing tirelessly is making excuses," Lord Harmon snapped back. "If this were my house, I'd have sent that toad packing already. Why is she even here?"

"She's here with my daughter, who's hoping to build a career with her help. I don't like the woman any more than you do, Harmon, but I know how to act civil for someone else's sake. Dalma is family, like it or not. You'll just have to bear it."

That put an end to the rant for the time being and enveloped the carriage in resentful silence instead. Some of it dissipated by the time they reached the villa, though not by a lot.

Once they all got out, they filed up the stairs to the gallery, which awaited them in much of the same festive splendor that the village was dressed in. Garlands and ribbons hung before all the windows and from the ceiling, beside a generous spread and plenty of wine. The First of Summer was one of the few occasions when the household staff got most of the day off, so once Donella, Nykhe, and Iolinos got everything ready, the family was left to conclude the celebration on their own.

Corlis had more food stuffed into him during the afternoon than his entire life, so he poured himself a glass of wine and thinned it down considerably. He'd only been drinking liquid gold for a few days, but it was dangerously easy to get used to.

After the first round, Lord Hestor clapped. "Everyone, please gather round! The time has come for a special treat from our very own Livia." He made a flourish at his daughter, who stepped forward with a modest bow. "For the past year, she's been living under Dalma's wing, who I trust has been taking good care of her talent."

"That I have indeed," Aunt Dalma said, reveling in the attention much as she did in the village. "She's seen all the greatest tutors in the city. Nothing but the very best for my darling niece!" She put one hand on Livia's back and toasted with her nearly empty glass.

"And now we are about to see all that hard work come to fruition." Lord Hestor motioned for his son. "Ernio, if you will?"

Ernio went to the back of the room and brought out Livia's harp. It wasn't extravagant as instruments went, but it was in immaculate condition and tended to with great care.

The family clapped as Livia went to take a seat on a small velvet stool. "The piece I'll be playing for you is *The Sun Rises from the Sea*. It was my favorite as a girl and the first piece I ever learned when I began on the harp. I'd like to dedicate it to Aunt Dalma and everything she's done for me."

With that, she raised her hands and began to play.

Corlis had little experience with music outside of the bawdy numbers, trite ballads, sea shanties, and other lowbrow fare that tavern lutists earned their keep with. Whether Livia's playing was any good, he could never tell. But what he could tell was the effect it had on Livia herself. Her eyes were closed the whole time, and her fingers glided effortlessly on the strings, as if on their own. Her face was a picture of transcendence, focused on nothing but the music.

The piece went on for a good ten minutes, during which no one said a word. Around the room, Corlis observed a variety of reactions from the family. Gretia stood next to her sister with her hands clasped, enchanted as if she was witnessing a dog give birth to a horse. Lord Hestor also listened intently, as did Aunt Dalma, Larence, and Thessa. Ernio and Rosilla's attention was more polite than interested. Alendro yawned openly, and Ceci too was finally in agreement over something with Lord Harmon, as they watched with overt boredom.

Once Livia finished, the family once again broke into applause of varying enthusiasm.

"Marvelous, darling," Aunt Dalma said. "Simply marvelous. We'll be seeing your name atop the grand halls of New Montres soon enough!"

Livia rose from the stool and was instantly locked into a tight embrace from Gretia. Ernio then came to put the harp away again, and everyone dispersed into small groups around the room.

Corlis sought out Thessa, but she was engrossed in conversation with Larence by a window. Down at the village, Corlis had watched them chatter through the festivities. It made him glad that she had someone she got along with, but it didn't help him feel less alone.

Then, from behind him came the voice he least wanted to hear. "How's your evening, Cousin?"

Corlis turned around to face Alendro. "Pleasant, so far," he replied.

"I didn't get a chance in the village to commend you on how smart you look. Especially in this." Alendro felt the fabric of Corlis's equestrian drape between his fingers. "It becomes you. Almost as if you grew up wearing one."

But I didn't, Corlis finished the thought. He hated this game. Life in the orphanage and at the inn had taught him to say what he meant and mean what he said. He had little patience to dance around unsaid insults and underhanded implications.

However, this was neither the orphanage nor the inn.

"Thank you," he replied and straightened the drape pin. "It's not what I'm used to, but you do what you must for the family's sake."

"That I'm sure of," said Alendro and punctuated it with a sip. "That you're not used to it, I mean. I'd imagine you prefer something more practical that doesn't get in the way while you work all day."

"You're good at imagining what it's like to work all day."

Alendro didn't skip a beat. "Only because I do it so often. I admire people like you, you know. Such honest, salt-of-the-earth folks are the bedrock of Ardonne. We need more of your kind and fewer useless nobles like us." He patted Corlis on the shoulder and left.

Aunt Dalma, who had been spectating from behind the nearby bowl of wine punch, stepped up to take his place.

"A valiant effort, dear." She handed Corlis a full glass. "Unfortunately, you can't shame the shameless."

Her of all people saying this made Corlis wonder if Aunt Dalma was oblivious to the irony or enjoyed it. His money was on the latter. "It's nothing worse than what I grew up with. And it's only for the rest of the week."

Aunt Dalma raised her glass to him. "Here's to your stomach, then—may it be strong."

"To health." Corlis drank with her, although she took significantly deeper swigs.

Having seen the number of glasses she'd had during the festivities at the village as well, Corlis suspected Aunt Dalma could easily drink most workers in the Wall District under the table. Possibly one after the other. Under the paint that may as well have been applied with a trowel, her cheeks glowed visibly.

"Will you not be staying long, then?" he asked.

"No, I'm taking the train back to Callex in two days." She swayed slightly as she repressed a hiccup. She could hold her drink, but it wasn't ineffectual. "The countryside bores me to tears, to say nothing of the company. There's only so much fun to be had needling Harmon about his shipwreck of a marriage."

Corlis listened intently, making a mental note about the crumbs Aunt Dalma was dropping. If he was going to last five more days alongside Alendro, he may as well arm himself with whatever barbs he could.

"I suppose Livia must be eager to get back to her studies, too," he added. "I've heard the others say she loved music, but I didn't realize how much until tonight."

He scanned the room in search of Livia, but she must have gone off somewhere else.

While earlier Aunt Dalma could hardly contain her enthusiasm for her niece, she now merely tutted in pitiful regret. "That poor girl."

"Livia?" Corlis asked. "Is something wrong with her?"

"Oh yes, most *tragically*." Aunt Dalma heaved a sigh. "She's delusional." She took another long swig of her drink. "Last year, when she asked to move in with me, I was overjoyed. A professed musician in the family! I placed in her all my dreams that someone might bring some much-needed culture into this house. Alas, when she arrived, and I heard her play, I was crushed.

"The girl has not an ounce of talent. Dedication, yes—more than enough. Too much, you could say. If music was merely a passing fancy for her, she could get married like a proper girl and pluck away at the strings now and then while she ran a quaint little household. But she insists on devoting her whole life to the art, and she simply doesn't have what it takes."

"I thought she played very nicely just now," Corlis said, but Aunt Dalma puckered her lips in dismissal.

"She's been practicing that melody since she was eight years old. No wonder she's good at it." She gave Corlis a condescending smile. "Grand orchestras don't play study pieces, dear. They play sweeping, magnificent concerts that embody the very essence of beauty and passion. They need musicians who can *feel* the music, not merely memorize it. And Livia—she's not one of them.

"I invited one tutor after another so that they might coax some hidden gift out of her, but none of them stayed longer than a month. I'm honestly amazed she hasn't caught on yet, and it only worries me all the more." She sighed again. "What am I to do? Each of my choices is crueler than the other: shatter the poor girl's lifelong dream, or let her continue living a lie?"

Seeking relief at the bottom of her wine glass, Aunt Dalma found with dismay that it was empty. "Salt into the wound! Oh, darling, would you mind? I am *utterly* parched."

She directed the last two sentences at Gretia, who had walked past them with a half-full glass in hand. When Aunt Dalma reached for it, she pulled it back.

"This isn't mine, it's Livia's." She put her hand over the rim. "I'm only holding it for her while she's getting changed."

"Changed? What for?"

Gretia went beet red. "I knocked into her and spilled my drink on her dress."

"Hah!" Aunt Dalma threw her head back. "Of course, only she would be so meek about it. Had you done that to me, I assure you everyone would know two villages over! I will admit, mind, I'm no stranger to spills myself." She turned back to Gretia, or rather the glass in her hand. "If that's Livia's, then you might as well give it here. That girl can sip on a thimble for a whole evening until it goes sour. It'll only go to waste."

She took the glass out of Gretia's hand, emptied it in three rather unladylike gulps, then handed it back to her. Gretia was taken aback, but moved on without another word, casting only a passing glance of disbelief at Corlis.

"I'm sorry to burden you with all this," Aunt Dalma said, nearly tripping in place as she stood. "I'm not usually one to gossip, you know. But, as they say"—she tipped her glass—"in wine, there's truth."

"Yes," Corlis replied. "That's why they keep it locked in cellars."

Aunt Dalma cackled. "Indeed! And the older it is, the more it burns!" After that, she went off to swoon some more over Larence.

There wasn't much else to the evening. Corlis stood by and listened for a while as the lords, Ernio, and Alendro compared horse breeds in different parts of the country. Thessa and Larence were now accompanied by Aunt Dalma and Gretia, discussing Sallician plays. Livia had since come back in a different dress and now stood off to the side, talking to Rosilla. And once again, Corlis couldn't tell if it was his mind playing tricks on him, or if there truly was an air of unease about

Livia when she talked to her brother's wife.

Aunt Dalma was the first to announce her intent to retire for the night—or rather, that she was exhausted enough to sleep until next summer. The rest of them then filed off two by two, wishing one another a bountiful harvest as per custom, knowing none of them would ever so much as pluck a single bunch of grapes from a vine.

Corlis stayed behind. After fifteen years at The Lame Mare, the habits of an innkeeper were so deeply ingrained in every fiber of his body, he was sure he'd be unable to sleep unless he collected all the scattered glasses. As he gathered them all up and took them to the center table, he noticed one that was already there. Or rather, it was *still* there. Still on the gilded tray, completely intact, not having seen a single drop of wine all night. He thought back to all the faces he'd seen in the past hour, and realized Ceci's wasn't one of them.

Chapter 16

The house was dark and quiet. The time was long past midnight, and the family was fast asleep. The servants had also returned from the village and gone to bed, ready to get back to work the next morning. Everyone had their eyes glued down by the copious amounts of wine they'd had all day. Everyone, except Ceci.

She was the first to leave the gallery, right after Livia finished her tedious performance. While the others were upstairs, she went back to her and Alendro's room and got out her secret bag. Besides the change of clothes, her documents, and the banknote, she stuffed in all the gold jewelry from Alendro as well. She hid the bag in the hallway, so she could pick it up after the deed was done and vanish into the night. Finally, she tucked the letter opener under her pillow, pretending to sleep until Alendro came to bed. He was snoring within minutes.

Everything was in place.

She crept along the edge of the outer courtyard, inch by inch. It would have been quicker to go straight across, but she didn't want to risk being seen out in the open. There was no room for mistakes. Not now. She had waited far too long to be caught at the last minute.

Her path took her along the wall, across the passage and Lord Hestor's study, all the way to the opposite side, where she started counting the doors. After a minute that stretched into an eternity, she came to the third one. With a trembling hand, she knocked just loud enough that it may be heard inside. There was no answer. A sigh of relief—but only a short one. Ceci wrapped her fingers on the handle, pushed it down as slowly as she could, and stepped into Larence's room.

The inside was as eerily hushed as the rest of the house. The window was slightly open, letting a single streak of light fall on the bed. Ceci tested each cautious step for any sign of a creaky floorboard, but the Benuarte villa's condition was as immaculate as ever. She snuck over to the bed without a sound.

This was it. Her palm was clammy around the handle of the letter opener as she raised it over Larence's chest. Her heartbeat resounded in her ears. She was so nervous not to wake him, she didn't notice she was holding her breath. And that was when the realization struck her.

She wasn't breathing. But neither was Larence.

Instinctively, she turned back to the door, as if he was about to step through it—but it was exactly as she had left it, open by an inch. Cold sweat ran down her back, and her insides turned into lead. Holding her weapon aloft, she stood like a statue and listened intently, desperate for the slightest noise from the bed below. But nothing came.

Despite all her better judgment, she stretched out one hand toward the nightstand. There, she felt out the base of the quartz light, found the knob, and twisted it. With a series of faint mechanical clicks, the brass petals of the top cover began to unfold. Slivers of cold, harsh light scattered along the walls and ceiling as the mechanism gradually uncovered the glowing crystal at its center. The petals slid further apart, and the light grew, until it hit the face on the pillow.

It was a small miracle Ceci managed to cover her mouth before she screamed the house down.

The cheeks were purple and swollen, woven across with wormlike tendrils of dark veins. A trail of sickening yellow ran across one of them, as it trickled from the opening between the blackened lips. The eyes, red in the corners and upturned in their sockets, fixed lifelessly upon the bedpost from under a mess of faded blonde hair.

It was Aunt Dalma.

The letter opener clattered on the floor, and Ceci landed right next to it. How much noise that made, she didn't care. Nothing mattered except backing away from the horrid sight.

What was going on? Why was Dalma here? What happened to her? Was this a trap?

Questions flooded Ceci's mind and sent her into sheer animal panic. She pushed herself until she hit a wall, then scuttled alongside until her back was against the corner, and there was nowhere left to go. She then pulled up her knees and clasped both hands over her face, as if she could disappear from the room and those haunting dead eyes.

But she didn't disappear. No matter how much she waited, and wished, and begged—in the end, she was there in the room.

Then, little by little, she gathered her composure. Her breathing slowed, and with each gulp of air came a new morsel of reason, until she regained enough of her senses to think straight. And the first thought that occurred to her was to get out before someone found her next to a dead body.

She pushed herself up to a stand and went to climb out the window. Her foot knocked against the letter opener, sending it spinning across the floor with a racket that sounded like a landslide to Ceci's ears. She picked it up and hid it under the cushion of the bench by the foot of the bed.

Larence's room was in the south wing, so the window opened onto the path that ran around the villa, and not on the same breakneck slope as Ceci and Alendro's room. Ceci hiked up her nightgown and threw her leg over the windowsill, landing among the thick oleander shrubs on the other side. From there, she rushed all the way around the wing and to the outer courtyard, keeping next to the wall. Once she reached the corner, she allowed herself to stop and listen for any signs that someone may have woken up. After a solid minute of waiting and no other way to go, Ceci made the call to cross the yard to her room.

The rasp of Alendro's snoring was like a beacon in a storm. Slowly, as if she'd only gone to the privy down the hall, Ceci climbed back into bed next to him. There, she buried her face in a pillow and shut her eyes, resolved never to open them again.

IV

Part Four

Chapter 17

Nykhe's screams shook the house awake. Corlis tore open the bedroom door to see her standing outside one of the guest rooms and covering her face. With Thessa at his side, he darted across the courtyard, barefoot and barely dressed in their nightwear. Larence emerged from the next room over, looking equally lost and covered in only a sheet.

"What is it?" Thessa asked the maid as they reached her. "Nykhe, what's wrong?"

In place of an answer, the girl pointed hysterically inside the room. Lacking any better option, Corlis, Larence, and Thessa took a cautious step inside. When they saw the bed, they all exclaimed in shock.

By this time, Iolinos had arrived from the back of the house and was now comforting his sister outside. Meanwhile, a storm of footsteps and confused shouting sounded from upstairs. Ernio was the first to get down from the top floor, along with Rosilla, more bedraggled than usual. The voices of Livia and Gretia followed close behind.

"No!" Ernio yelled and held up a hand. "Liv, don't come in!"

He was too late. The Benuarte girls rushed in before he could stop them. Gretia shrieked, and Livia fainted at the sight. Ernio managed to catch her before she bashed her head on the sideboard.

With each passing moment and each new person inside, the chaos in the room grew tenfold.

"Is she dead?"

"Aunt Dalma's dead!"

"What happened?"

"Did Nicki find her?"

"Livia, wake up!"

"Where's Father?"

"Call a physician!"

"Will someone finally tell me what in the deep dark is going on in there?"

Lord Hestor came hobbling as fast as his ankle allowed, as did his brother Harmon. The two of them shoved their way to the bed, where everyone else was gathered. Once his father was in the room, Ernio picked up Livia in his arms and went to take her back to bed, with Gretia in tow. As they left, in came Alendro, strolling half naked at a leisurely pace.

Corlis stood by the nightstand, and his gaze swept across the faces in the room. Everyone was pale and wide-eyed, standing stiffly or trotting in place. The only exception was his cousin, who took a comfortable seat on the bedside bench, rested his elbow on the footboard, and regarded his aunt's corpse with lukewarm interest.

Lord Hestor pounded on the floor with his cane. His voice, which was normally as mild as his demeanor, now boomed over all others. "Everyone, settle down. I want to hear exactly what happened. Who was first in the room?"

All were now focused on Nykhe, who cowered next to the wall, held on either side by Thessa and Iolinos. She trembled before her employer in sheer terror, as though she was being accused of murder.

The lord's expression softened. "It's all right, Nicki. Just tell me how you found her."

Thessa patted the girl's shoulder and said something in Sallician. Corlis didn't understand what it was, but the soothing tone did the trick. Choking on the first few words, Nykhe slowly began to recount what happened.

"I was making the usual morning rounds, checking all the halls were clean after last night. I found a bag next to one of the urns"—she gestured outside the room—"beside the wall. I couldn't tell who it belonged to, so I thought I'd go around and ask if someone missed it. I came to this room first and saw the door was open. I knocked, but there was no answer, so I came in to see if anyone was inside and—"

Her voice broke off with a sob, but the rest of the story was straightforward enough.

Lord Hestor looked around. "Wait a minute. This isn't Dalma's room!" He pointed at Larence. "It's yours!"

Larence stood by the far corner of the bed, now smacking his lips in embarrassment. "That's right. Her room is the next one." He adjusted the sheet around his waist. "I can assure you, nothing distasteful was afoot. Lady Dalma and I merely switched rooms for the night."

"Switched?" asked Lord Hestor. "What for?"

"I didn't want to mention this, for the sake of her dignity, but"—Larence's angled brow deepened—"after we all left the gallery, she pulled me aside and said the wine had gotten to her. She was feeling nauseous, so she asked to have my room, since it has a direct connection to the privy." He indicated the side door near the bed.

So, even Aunt Dalma had her limits.

For a little while, everyone stood awkwardly around as their minds grappled with the situation at hand. It was a lot to take in. Off in the corner, Thessa poured Nykhe a cup of water.

Ernio returned at this point. "Gretia's upstairs in Livia's room." He joined the rest of the family by the bed, standing between Lord Hestor and Larence. Despite his immense stature and thick beard, he was like a frightened boy trying to find comfort next to his father. "Did she die in her sleep?"

"Suffocated, by the looks of it," said Alendro from the bench, picking at his nails.

"Suffocated?" Rosilla asked. "Did—did someone strangle her?" Her hand moved up to her throat, and she took a step back, as if any of them might jump her then and there.

Corlis stepped to the bed. "No, they didn't. Strangling leaves clear marks." He raised Aunt Dalma's chin with the back of his hand to show her turkey-like but otherwise pristine neck.

"How are *you* so sure?" Lord Harmon sounded almost indignant that Corlis might know something.

"I grew up in a bad part of town," Corlis replied offhand, keeping his explanation as terse as possible. This was probably not the time to reveal to his newfound family that he used to help criminals dispose of dead bodies.

"Then what happened?" Larence asked.

Corlis leaned closer to the purple, distorted face. Through the slight opening between the lips, he saw something inside.

"What are you—" Lord Harmon began, but was cut off by the disgusted noises that erupted from the onlookers when Corlis stuck two fingers inside Aunt Dalma's mouth. He made a scooping motion, and pulled them back out to reveal the crumbling, yellowish chunks.

With a resigned sigh, he wiped his hand on the bedsheet. "She choked on her own vomit. Probably passed out and didn't realize what was happening before it was too late." He'd seen this in the streets a few times. Ugly way to go.

"Are you now a coroner, too?" Alendro asked, immensely amused. "My, my, Cousin. You might just be interesting after all. Pity it took a death in the family to see that."

"All right, that's enough." Lord Hestor knocked with his cane again, then proceeded to hand out instructions, one by one. "Ernio—go fetch the physician. Tell her we need help both with Dalma and Livia. Rosilla—if you could be a dear and check on my daughters; I'm not sure how well Gretia can handle this on her own. Harmon—you and I will wait for the physician in my study. Alendro—go get a clean sheet from your room. Cover Dalma, then lock up here, and bring me the key."

All of them hurried out, except Alendro, who did not appreciate the order. "Why am I doing *her* job?" He cocked his head toward Nykhe.

"Because I told *you*, not her," Lord Hestor snapped back. "Now get up, and make yourself useful." He watched his nephew leave with a petulant scowl, then addressed the remaining people. "Corlis, Thessa, Larence—I am so sorry you had to witness all of this. Please, go back to your rooms, and get some rest. I and the family will take care of everything. Larence, I'll have to ask you to stay in Dalma's room until she's taken away. If all goes well, we can get this behind us by the end of the day."

Larence assured the lord of his understanding and bowed out as well. Iolinos had already left together with Ernio, but

Nykhe and Thessa remained.

"If it's all right, Lord Hestor," Thessa said, "I'd like to take Nykhe to the kitchen and give her some brandy for her nerves. Maybe Donella and I could take a glass each to the rest of the family, too."

Lord Hestor sighed. "Normally, I'd fire any servant I caught drinking this early in the morning, but I think we could all use it right now. Thank you, dear."

He then limped out of the room, with Thessa and Nykhe behind him, and lastly, Corlis. As the last to leave, he closed the door, sealing away Aunt Dalma and the secret about Livia that she had taken with her to the grave.

Chapter 18

After seeing to Nykhe, Thessa set out to make good on her word and take drinks to the rest of the house. While she had some experience carrying trays as a barmaid, she appreciated that Donella picked one for her with a tall rim and handles on both sides. They loaded it with glasses of dark pomace brandy, and she headed out on her round.

She started with the lords Hestor and Harmon in the study, then went out into the courtyard and knocked on Aunt Dalma's room, where Larence was forced to stay for the time being. Just then, Alendro came out of the other room where he had covered the body with a sheet, according to his uncle's instructions.

"Larence is in the privy," he said, locking the door. "Knowing him, you're better off serving the rest of the house before you try again. Maybe the village, too." He took two of the glasses. "I'll gladly lighten your load with these."

"Thank you," Thessa replied. "How is Ceci? I haven't seen her all morning."

"She didn't sleep well last night, and now she's got a splitting headache."

"If that's true, brandy might not be a good idea."

"Then we're about to find out if it's true or not," Alendro said and went on his way.

Heeding his advice, Thessa took the stairs from the inner courtyard to the second floor. Ernio was in the village with Iolinos, so she went to Livia's room.

Besides the gallery, the only rooms upstairs were the bedrooms belonging to the family members who actually lived in the villa. All of these were double rooms, where the entrance from the hallway opened into a small drawing room, which in turn had an opening to the bedroom proper. Save for some guest chairs, shelves, and other essential furniture, Livia's room was almost completely empty. She must have taken most of her personal belongings with her to Aunt Dalma's home in Callex—the home that she would soon be forced to leave, along with her dreams of becoming a great musician. The thought made Thessa's stomach clench. She could only imagine what Livia must have been going through.

She called into the bedroom in a hushed voice before entering. Livia lay in the huge canopied bed, with Gretia and Rosilla sitting by either side, both of them in their nightgowns like Thessa. She handed each of them a glass.

"Thank you." Gretia took the brandy without moving her gaze from her sister. She drank a small sip, then set about to wet the cloth on Livia's forehead in the basin of iced water by her chair.

"Will she be all right?" Thessa asked. "She didn't hurt herself falling, did she?"

"No, she's fine," Rosilla said. "It's happened before, and it'll happen again."

"That she fainted, you mean?"

Rosilla nodded. "She has a weak heart, and she's prone to

melancholy."

"She's not weak," said Gretia while she wrung the cloth. "She's passionate."

"I didn't say she was, only her heart," Rosilla replied. Her tone suggested that, like Livia's fainting, this conversation wasn't a first, either. "Anyway, the physician should be arriving soon. It's best you leave it to her. I should go and tend to my *own* children." She thanked Thessa for the drink and left the room.

Gretia huffed. "I know exactly what the physician's going to say. Peppermint, lavender, turmeric, and fading lancetip. I could have gone down to the village with Ernio and bought everything at the apothecary, if he had bothered to tell me he was going."

Thessa took a seat on the edge of the bed, careful not to sit on Livia's leg or spill the remaining glasses on her tray. She could tell Gretia needed a bit of company.

"I know what everyone in the family thinks of me," she continued, eyes fixed on Livia. "You probably think it too. I'm just the silly little sister who reads silly books, and that's all she does. Father never took me seriously, and neither did Ernio. She's the only one who ever listened."

Guilt pricked Thessa at the words. She had indeed formed a similar image of Gretia when they first met and hadn't cared much to dig deeper. What made it worse was that Thessa had known well enough what it was like to be overlooked and underestimated, especially by those who were meant to be close to her.

"She came a year before me," Gretia said, "but it always felt more like I was the older sister. She's so fragile and delicate. When she told us she was moving away, I was scared for her. I wanted her to find her dreams, but I was afraid it would take a toll on her health. And now, with Aunt Dalma dead"—she wiped her nose—"I don't know what'll become of her."

"I'm sure she'll be fine," Thessa said. "She will have other chances, I've no doubt about it."

Gretia muttered some indistinct acknowledgment, but didn't react beyond that. After a few more minutes, Thessa rose from the bed and left the two sisters alone.

Alendro had been right—by the time she got back downstairs, Larence still wasn't finished with his business. It was a good opportunity for her to get dressed, so she put the tray on an end table and went back to her and Corlis's room. Since Corlis was away somewhere in the house, she afforded herself some time to wash her face and braid her hair in peace.

The whole situation made her uneasy. At first, Thessa thought it was only because of how sudden Aunt Dalma's death was, but something else lurked behind it as well. Something about the rest of the family. All of them were shocked—but none of them seemed to be sorry. None except Gretia, and she was more concerned about Livia's future than anything.

Then again, the morsels Thessa had overheard outside Pamur Gavennas's tent spoke little in Aunt Dalma's favor, either.

She threw the completed braid over her shoulder and shook off the thought. This wasn't her family, and it wasn't her place to judge them. All she could do was try and help keep everyone's spirits up, for Corlis's sake. Of all people, he needed this the least. Thessa went back out into the courtyard, picked up the last full glass from her tray, and took it to Larence.

He was dressed in his same evening best as the day before, since the rest of his clothes were all locked away in his own room with Aunt Dalma's body. He beckoned Thessa inside and offered her a seat.

Although it was only a guest room, it had Aunt Dalma's presence all over it. Clothes lay strewn across the furniture, there was a pair of shoes on the dressing table, and half-used candles stood in every corner and on every surface. Thessa recalled her mentioning how much she hated quartz light.

"Have you already had one?" Larence asked, tipping the drink in his hand.

"I had some lemon water in the kitchen. I can't stomach anything stronger than wine, and even that, only if it's thinned down."

"This is all so hard to believe." Larence sighed. "One minute, she's talking the world—the next, she's gone like that. Such a shame, too. The family didn't like her much, but she was a clever and resourceful woman."

"If you don't mind me asking," Thessa said, "why do you think that was? That they didn't like her, I mean. Was it only because of her temperament?"

Larence didn't reply immediately, but his narrow eyes hinted at the answer ahead of time. "I'd say each of them had their own reasons. Aunt Dalma was never one to compromise, and—well, it's the nature of family that, sooner or later, you'll have to deal with one another."

He didn't need to tell her that twice. Thessa may have taken a drastic way out of that trap a year earlier, but the Benuartes showed a stronger bond than that. Had she only been that fortunate as a girl.

"I got the impression she had a soft spot for you," she said.

"I suppose she did. I never paid it much mind, to tell the truth. Back in New Montres, there are plenty of lonely widows and lonelier wives among the people I work with. Most of them like to play sweet, but it's only a formality."

"Do you think that's what it was to her, too?"

"It didn't come across as more than that. I guess we'll never know now. One thing's for certain— I will think twice about how much I drink after today." Larence swirled his remaining brandy. "What an awful death. I can't bear to imagine how she might have suffered."

He emptied the glass with a last swig, then went out to go talk to the lords. Thessa was once again left alone with her thoughts, and they weren't any more pleasant than before.

Larence may not have wanted to imagine how Aunt Dalma had spent her final moments in this world, but once he said it, the idea took root in Thessa's mind and grew from there. As she reached the courtyard, she couldn't help putting herself in the aunt's place, picturing her struggle again and again. She strained to keep the image away, but it only came back that much clearer.

Then, at once, she stopped—both in her tracks through the yard, and in her attempts to fight off the scene. She allowed herself to play it out, and as it did, a sinking feeling weighed in her stomach with each passing detail.

She had to find Corlis right away.

Chapter 19

Since Thessa had gone directly to the kitchen with Nykhe, Corlis only had the tailor's notes to help him pick an outfit, and none of the examples listed there included a sudden death in the family. Given the circumstances, he trusted that most of the others wouldn't pay much mind to how he clad himself, and Alendro would find something to be a prick about no matter what. He opened his wardrobe and picked out some pieces listed on the paper under "simple daytime wear, no particular occasion."

Aunt Dalma was dead.

She hadn't exactly endeared herself to Corlis, yet he couldn't help but respect her enduring spirit. As little as he knew about her past, being a childless spinster in noble circles mustn't have attracted a lot of favorable attention. In some ways, she reminded Corlis of Aunt Mira, who had also refused to let life get the best of her, no matter the twists and turns it took. Granted, Aunt Dalma never had to struggle with poverty on top of her other woes, which must have taken a lot off of her shoulders.

He stepped out of the room just in time to catch Alendro entering his own, with two glasses of brandy in hand. He ran his eyes up and down Corlis, smirked, then cordially bowed his head. As per usual.

Corlis proceeded across the outer courtyard to Lord Hestor's study, but stopped when he noticed Harmon was there with him. Unfortunately, Lord Hestor spotted him and called him over before he could turn around.

"Come," he said. "Have a seat. You missed Thessa with the brandy, I'm afraid, but there's wine over there if you wish to help yourself."

Corlis wished. While he poured himself a glass, Lord Harmon's voice sounded behind him. "Where's your drape, boy?"

Both lords had their equestrian drapes on—as did Alendro, now that Corlis remembered from a minute before, suddenly understanding his cousin's grin. Of course that prick wouldn't think to say anything.

"I was told the drape is for public appearances and social events," he said, setting down the decanter.

"The equestrian drape is a sign of respect *and* respectability," Lord Harmon said, as if reciting a passage from a compendium on courtesy. "Clearly, you're displaying neither."

Lord Hestor tutted. "Harmon, leave him. He doesn't know any better, that's all."

"I can go fetch it, if it would please you more," Corlis replied, using every ounce of restraint to keep the edge out of his tone.

"There's no point now. You've already shown how much respect you have for a family tragedy." Lord Harmon took a sip of his brandy. As if he was in any position to lecture anyone about respecting family.

"That's enough of that," Lord Hestor said. "Corlis, come sit. We can all talk like adults here."

"I have to write some letters," Lord Harmon replied sullenly.

He pushed himself out of his seat and trotted off toward the stairs, not dignifying Corlis with any further remark.

Corlis took one of the remaining chairs and sat down with his wine, which he had left unwatered. This wasn't going to be a short day.

"Don't mind him," said Lord Hestor. "Harmon likes to think that because he wasted his youth learning every minute custom, everyone else should be condemned to the same fate."

"I suspect there's more to it than that," Corlis said. If there was any time to breach the subject of his uncle's open disdain for him, this might as well be it.

"I can assure you there isn't. My wife used to call Harmon the most even-handed man she'd ever met, because he treats each person as abysmally as the last. Except maybe her sister."

"Why is that? I realize Aunt Dalma was difficult, but it didn't look like Harmon had to bear the brunt of her personality," Corlis said.

"Ha!" Lord Hestor guffawed. "Oh, dear boy, trust me—as far as Harmon is concerned, Dalma did him worse than anyone in the family, or the whole world, for that matter. She was the one who introduced him to his wife."

"The wife who gave him Alendro?" Corlis would certainly have considered that worthy of a lifelong grudge.

The lord leaned forward and hushed his voice, as if to divulge some sevenfold sealed secret. "The wife who *divorced* him." Picking up on Corlis's puzzlement, he added, "To a man like my brother, there is no greater insult than to have his marriage end on someone else's terms. Especially if that someone doesn't remarry until years later."

Corlis tried to work out the reasoning why that would be so egregious. "Because it meant she didn't leave him for another man—she left to get away from him."

Lord Hestor winked. "Now you get it."

Corlis had to admit that helped put a few things into perspective, such as why Aunt Dalma was so keen on needling Lord Harmon about his marriage. The divorce might have been the only time anyone had the backbone to throw his deplorable personality in his face. Wherever this mysterious wife was, Corlis had to admire her then and there. For all he knew, she could have been just as insufferable as her husband or the woman who introduced them.

* * *

About an hour later, Ernio came back from the village. As he explained, the physician was swamped with patients after the previous night's binge, so she sent her aide in her place. The man somehow managed to appear both five years younger and ten years older than Corlis at the same time, with flapping ears, knobby fingers, and a massive forehead that jutted forward by half an inch.

"Good morning, Lord Hestor," he said with a bow. "The master expresses her deepest regret that she could not come herself, but she has given me full permission to act on her behalf. I understand Lady Dalma Lazewic passed in her sleep?"

The whole time he spoke in his nasally voice, the aide kept adjusting his black robe with self-important tugs. It was already grating on Corlis's nerves.

"That's right," Lord Hestor replied. "She's over here."

Ernio left them to join his wife upstairs, so it was only Lord Hestor, Corlis, and the aide who went over to Larence's room.

164

Lord Hestor unlocked it and ushered them inside, where the body was exactly where they had left it. The only difference was the white sheet that Alendro had thrown over the bed with little care.

The aide pulled it back to Aunt Dalma's waist and leaned closer to the swollen, purple face. "Was this how you found her?" he asked.

"Yes," said the lord, then added, "Corlis here has already looked a bit closer. He suspects she got sick and choked on her vomit."

"Has he?" The aide raised a skeptical eyebrow at Corlis. "While I applaud the young lord's enthusiasm for the medical sciences, I should ask him to refrain from tampering with bodies until a professed physician has examined them."

Corlis crossed his arms. "I'll keep that in mind for next time."

The aide turned back to the corpse without further comment and proceeded to fiddle around it for a few minutes. While Corlis wasn't a professed physician, it was remarkably like he was buying time before finally opening Aunt Dalma's mouth and scraping out some of the same yellow debris that Corlis had.

"Hm, well," he said reluctantly, "I suppose the signs are there indeed. Both airways are fully clogged. If you may pardon the question, Lord Hestor—was the lady perhaps inebriated?"

Corlis saw the struggle it took Lord Hestor to simply say, "That she very much was."

"Then I don't think I have any more questions." The aide covered up Aunt Dalma again. "I do regret to inconvenience you, my lord, but I'll have to ask you to accompany me to the physician's office, so we may take care of administrative matters. I did call for the hearse before we left, so it should be arriving presently. Will someone be here to lead the pallbearers to the body in your absence?"

"Yes, my brother Harmon. I'll give him the key to the room before we leave."

The three of them parted ways in the courtyard. Lord Hestor proceeded upstairs, while the aide left to wait outside by the carriage. Corlis went straight toward his room, but before he reached it, Thessa rushed up to him out of nowhere and grabbed him by the arm.

"I need to talk to you," she whispered frantically. "Away from everyone. It's about Aunt Dalma."

Corlis instinctively hunched his shoulders and looked around the empty yard. "What is it?"

"I don't think she got sick. I think she was poisoned."

Chapter 20

Thessa dragged Corlis into their room and bolted the door, after checking one last time that no one was outside who might have seen them.

"Poisoned?" he asked in disbelief. "How? When?"

"I don't know," Thessa said. "Not exactly. But I'm almost sure she was. And it was someone in this house."

Corlis gave her a long, slow stare. "Remind me again what Fabreve said about me always assuming the worst?"

"No, listen!" Thessa hissed. "It's Larence. I mean, not that he poisoned her. It's just what he said that made me think about it." She knew she was rambling, but she could barely keep her own thoughts on track. "He said he didn't want to imagine what it was like for her to die that way, but it put the idea in my head, and I couldn't help but imagine it."

"Imagine what?"

"How she died!"

"She got sick, threw up, and choked," Corlis said, in the same flat tone as he always did when he thought someone around him was being stupid. "There's not a lot to imagine."

"Yes, there is!" Thessa said. "Think about it! What would it be like to wake up in the middle of the night and realize you couldn't breathe? I would be terrified! Scratching at my throat, throwing myself around in bed, trying to reach for a cup of water!"

She flailed about wildly with her arms, in an effort to convey the image to Corlis. At first, he listened to indulge her, but as she gave more and more details, his demeanor changed.

"You'd make a right mess of everything around you," he muttered and stepped to his own bed, moving his hand in the air like he was tracing the outline of a body in it. "Whereas Aunt Dalma lay there like she'd just gone to sleep." His brow furrowed. "But does that mean she didn't choke? There was vomit in her throat—the physician's aide said that too."

"No, she did choke," Thessa replied. "I think she was too weak to do anything by then." She took a deep breath. They were getting to the point she was trying to make, but it wasn't something she was eager to discuss. "When I was traveling with Hanna—"

"As a robber, right."

"Yes, as a robber," Thessa snapped. "Usually, we tried to get the men drunk enough that they passed out, and we could tie them up without them waking. But if they weren't drinking that much, we gave them sleeping drops. Very rarely, because they were expensive and dangerous. If we put too much in their drink, they could get sick while they slept and—"

"They'd be too weak to get up," Corlis finished for her. "That makes a frightening amount of sense."

He leaned on the nightstand while he mulled it over. As much as Thessa was scared by the prospect they were discussing, it was a relief to know he was on her side. She sat down on the bed and waited for him to gather his thoughts.

"Could she have taken the drops herself?" he asked.

"I shouldn't think so. Do you remember, she was the first

to go to bed. She said she was ready to sleep until next year."

"And she asked Larence to switch rooms because she was ill, even though she could famously hold her drink. Which could mean she was already under the effect of the drug." Corlis tapped the wood with his fingers. "How long does it take to put you to sleep?"

"No more than a half hour."

"Then she must have taken them while we were upstairs. The question is still—when and how?"

Thessa closed her eyes while she recreated the scene of the previous night. "It couldn't have been the food. We all ate it right from the platter."

"But it couldn't have been her drink, either. She had that glass in her hand all evening and never set it down. Except—" Corlis broke off mid-sentence. When he spoke again, his voice was hoarse with dread. "Livia."

"*Livia* poisoned her?" Thessa asked, bewildered.

He shook his head. "Aunt Dalma's glass ran out while she was talking to me, so she grabbed another one out of Gretia's hand. Gretia said she was holding it for Livia while she got changed."

The blood drained from Thessa's face. "Then Aunt Dalma wasn't the one meant to be poisoned?"

Corlis rubbed his temples. "This is all blind guessing. We don't know if any of it is true, including the poisoning. Is there any way to tell for sure someone took sleeping drops?"

"There might be," said Thessa. "When Hanna and I bought them, the apothecary warned that we should stop taking them immediately if we noticed a rash on our back. That means we had too much in a short time."

"So, all we need to do is sneak a quick peek at Aunt Dalma's back." Corlis sucked his tooth. "Not going to be easy, since the room is locked, and Hestor gave the key to his brother. I don't think any excuse in the world would be good enough to convince him to let me in."

"Couldn't we tell him what we suspect?"

"And accuse one of his relatives of murder, right to his face? Not even Hestor would take that kindly. Not without proof. But from what I remember, the shutters were open in Larence's room."

They went out into the courtyard and rushed through the entry passage, so that they may go around the outside of the building to find the window. Right as they stepped out on the gravel walkway, hoofbeats and the rattle of wheels came from a short way down the hill.

"The hearse," said Corlis.

Thessa turned to the road, where the cart had already rounded the last bend before the stretch that led to the villa. They'd be up in less than a minute—not nearly enough time for Corlis to get in and out unnoticed.

"I'll hold them up," Thessa said and pushed him by the arm. "But it'll only be a few minutes. Be quick!"

Corlis gave her one last look, then disappeared around the corner of the house.

As inconspicuously as she could, Thessa walked back into the outer courtyard. Behind her, the hearse came to a stop, and Lord Harmon was on his way to meet them outside. Perfect.

Thessa found the tray she had used to take the brandy to the family and put on all the glasses left in Lord Hestor's study. Staying out of sight, she slunk around the edge of the yard and stopped right before the corner of the entryway. There, she pressed her back against the wall, listening intently to the footsteps as they approached. They were about twenty feet away… then ten… then five…

Holding her breath, as well as the tray, Thessa swung around the corner and crashed directly into Lord Harmon's large body. She shrieked and tipped her load onto him, smashing the glasses on the floor, and spilling leftover wine on the lord's delicate clothes. He and the two men behind him all stopped in their tracks and shouted in confusion.

"Oh, no!" Thessa cried. "Lord Harmon, I am so sorry!"

She reached down as if to sweep the shards of glass out of the way and pressed one of them deep into her thumb. Then, she pulled out her handkerchief and proceeded to wipe the wine off of Lord Harmon's tunic, while he sputtered in protest and indignity.

"I was collecting the glasses around the house," Thessa babbled, rubbing her bleeding thumb all over the fine fabric. "I didn't see you coming and—"

She trailed off, pretending to only now notice the huge stain and wide streaks of red dripping from her hand. Finally, she rolled her eyes up with a gasp, and in a manner that Valinne Miatti might have envied, collapsed onto Lord Harmon.

It was fortunate that her own blood didn't send her into a frenzy, but she was forced to trust the men would be careful enough not to cut themselves too. Otherwise, this innocent scene could take a dreadful turn.

Once she was feigning unconsciousness, she could only rely on her hearing to tell how the others reacted.

Lord Harmon was the first to speak. "I swear, this is why we leave serving to the servants. They know how to stay out of everyone's way." He addressed the pallbearers. "Well, don't just stand there—get her up! There's a chair over there."

A rough pair of hands reached under Thessa's back and lifted her gingerly off the ground.

"We have smelling salts in the hearse, if it please the lord," the other one said. "It's a rare thing that we don't see someone faint when we're around."

"Yes, yes, all right," Lord Harmon grumbled. "We've got women dropping left and right today. But don't take long. I don't plan on spending my whole day here."

After setting Thessa down, the pallbearer strolled back to the cart in what sounded like a comfortable pace. She silently thanked him for his dispassionate attitude and stayed motionless in anticipation. After a few minutes, there was the small pop of a cork, and the acrid stink of ammonia bit her nose.

Thessa held out for a few breaths before fluttering her eyes open. She was greeted by a scruffy, sunburned face that was as rough as the hands that had carried her.

"It's all right, young lady. You had a bit of a spell there, is all. Best not look at your little hand for a while before you get to wash it."

"Indeed," Thessa panted, trying to get a quick view of the yard. Corlis wasn't back yet. "I get so ill if I see blood; I simply can't help myself. Iolinos swatted a horsefly when I was in the stables, and even that almost made me swoon." She put a hand on the pallbearer's arm. "Thank you, you're most gallant. Could I trouble you for some water too?"

The man turned to Lord Harmon, who grunted his permission and directed him at the jug in the study. Thessa took her sweet time emptying the cup, pausing after every few gulps to fan herself. At last, when she was nearly done, Corlis came walking through the far end of the entry passage.

"Oh, I'll be fine now," she said, pretending to realize that everyone was waiting for her. "Please, don't worry about me. I should go and lie down for a minute."

She got to her feet and sauntered off to her room, where Corlis waited for her beside the bed.

"You weren't joking about that distraction," he commented. "Anyway, I think you were right. I barely pulled down Aunt Dalma's nightgown, and her lower back was covered in hives. I searched the room as quickly as I could, but I didn't find any medicine bottles. Only this." He raised a small leather bag.

"What's in it?" Thessa asked.

"We're about to find out," said Corlis as he undid the buckles. "Nykhe said she found it in the hallway last night, but we've all been settled into our rooms for days. I shouldn't think any of us would have stray luggage lying around."

He pulled the bag open and dumped its contents onto the bed. A simple dress, a pair of shoes, some papers—and a handful of very familiar jewelry.

"These are Ceci's," Thessa said, picking up the gold and quartz necklace she'd seen on her when they arrived with Alendro.

"And how about this?" Corlis unfolded one of the papers. "Travel documents for"—he leaned closer to read the name—"Nina Baior, from Brasthe. Five feet and five inches, light brown hair, hazel eyes. Notable features: two birthmarks behind the left ear."

"I don't know about that, but the rest fits her description," Thessa replied.

"The question is, which one is her real name—Ceci or Nina? Either way, it's clear she wasn't planning to stay after last night."

"But would Ceci want to poison Livia? They've never met before."

They sat on the bed with the small pile in between, helpless to make any sense of it. Why would any of this happen, and why now? What grudge would Ceci have against Livia? And most importantly—if someone had tried to murder Livia and failed, would they try again? The questions flooded Thessa's mind in an overwhelming torrent.

Corlis wasn't any more convinced, either. "This is far too much. We have to tell Hestor as soon as he gets back from the physician's office. He can decide what to do."

Thessa agreed, albeit she wasn't comfortable with the idea. Something about the whole situation refused to add up. She could tell Corlis knew it too, but as far as either of them could tell, it was their best choice.

For lack of anything better to do, she decided to go check on Nykhe. Corlis told her to go on ahead, and he would join her after he packed everything away. Thessa left him alone in the room and continued to the kitchen with uneasy steps.

Nothing felt right. Over the course of their acquaintance, Livia had struck Thessa as one of the kindest people she had ever met. She couldn't think of any reason why anyone would want to hurt her. That meant someone in the family was capable of killing innocent people—and in that case, who was to say it couldn't be her or Corlis next?

Chapter 21

Ceci had never cursed as much as she did that morning. The things that she wished upon Aunt Dalma, the maid Nicki, Lord Hestor, Alendro, and Corlis were as numerous as they were unspeakable. Most of all—and most galling—she cursed her own stupid, careless self.

And it was all about that damn bag.

After she found Aunt Dalma's dead body in Larence's bed—*curse her for asking to switch rooms*—she panicked so badly that the only thing on her mind was to get out of there. In doing so, she utterly forgot to fetch her bag from the hall where she had left it.

Sure enough, the maid found it in the morning and—*curse her for not minding her business*—decided to ask around who it belonged to. And she just had to start in Larence's room and drop the bag in terror when she saw the corpse.

When she screamed the house down, Ceci knew exactly what was going on, and she had not the slightest desire to set foot in that room. She told Alendro that she had a terrible headache and let him go alone. She planned to sneak out later and get her lost belongings, but Lord Hestor—*curse him for his meddling*—ordered the room to be locked.

The only choice this left Ceci with was to try and get into the room through the window, once the coast was clear. But then Alendro—*curse him for his insufferable cockiness*— came back with glasses of brandy and insisted to spend the rest of the morning in bed to "take care" of that headache of hers.

When at long last they were finished, and Alendro sodded off somewhere, she was free to put her sandals on and go around the house unnoticed. At this point, she should have known that something else would go sideways. As soon as she found Larence's window, there were footsteps around the corner.

Ceci barely had time to hide among the oleander shrubs that grew along the wall. From there, she watched with a boiling mixture of horror and rage as Corlis climbed in through the exact window she had intended to and—*curse him and everyone he loved to the coldest, darkest depths*—emerged a minute later with her bag.

She figured the thieving lizard would take it back to his room, so she went around the back of the villa to his window. The wall on that side joined directly into the steep slope of the hill, forcing Ceci to crawl inch by inch so as not to lose her footing and tumble down into the woods below. As if she needed another reason to despise the world and everything in it.

The lone bit of solace she got was that Corlis and Thessa's window was also unlocked. There, she hunched down to eavesdrop out of sight. She couldn't quite make out any of their hushed words, but the noises that accompanied them—especially the rattling of Ceci's jewelry—left little to the imagination.

Counting the agonizing minutes, she waited for them to get

out of there. Thessa was the first to leave, and Corlis followed a few minutes after. As soon as he was out, Ceci straightened up and pushed herself over the windowsill. She had no idea how much time she had, so she got to searching the room before either of them got back.

She got down on her hands and feet to peek under the bed, and her heart leapt when she saw the bag right there, barely a foot away from her. With a swift motion, she reached in and grabbed it—but she knew right away that something was off. There was an ever so slight resistance as she pulled the bag out, which came from a string that was tied to it. Her eyes followed that string to the back, up along the bedpost, to a tray on the nightstand with half a dozen copper cups on it. As the string pulled taut, the tray tipped over, and the cups went tumbling, bouncing and clattering all over in a deafening racket.

The next sound after that was the creak of the door and Corlis's voice from behind her. "That didn't take long."

Rot in the deep dark, you fish-faced son of a bitch.

Ceci stood. "This is mine," she said, holding up the bag.

"Yes, we figured that out quickly enough. We were only curious why it was out in the hallway on the same night there was a murder in this house."

"I had nothing to do with it."

"You'll have to do better than that." Corlis stepped closer. "I do have to give you credit for your accent. I couldn't tell you were from Brasthe—if you *are* from Brasthe, Nina."

"I'm Ceci Virago and always have been," she insisted. "Those documents and everything else in here are only a safety net. I've had more than enough experience with men like Alendro to know I should always be ready to get out."

The bloodless streaks that Corlis called his lips twisted into something almost like a smile. "You're giving me cards by the handful here. Not only were you suspiciously prepared for Aunt Dalma's death, I wonder what your dashing prince or his loving father would have to say about your double life."

Ceci's cheeks ran hot. If this spineless white snake thought he could corner her, he had another thing coming. "Whatever happened to the old hag, I had no part in it. I couldn't have, because I wasn't there with the rest of you! I left as soon as that doe-eyed little wretch finished her plucking, and Alendro will tell you I was here with him when he got back. Besides, if I killed her, why would I stick around? I would have run for it as soon as auntie keeled over last night.

"You, on the other hand, were there the whole time. Not to mention, I saw you sneak into Larence's room. You're as suspicious as I am and just as much of an outsider. You think anyone in this family will take your side if you say one of them's a killer? Try and rat me out; I'm taking you with me. That's a promise."

Corlis stood in deep thought, with that blank face of his that barely ever moved. After a while, he crossed his arms and said, "Then I guess both of us have a reason to keep quiet for the time being."

Ceci smirked in triumph. She grabbed the end of the string to untie it, but Corlis put his bony hand on her wrist.

"The bag stays," he said. "Aunt Dalma's death might not have been your doing, but I know you were up to something. This is to remind you to watch your step. You can take me down with you, but you'll be going down nonetheless."

There was no dissuading him, Ceci could tell that much. *Curse him and his pigheaded ways.*

"What if I was planning to kill Alendro?" she asked with a scowl. "Would you try to stop that, too?"

"I wouldn't care who you kill. All that would matter is you're a killer, and I'm one reason away from being your next target. And trust me, I know well enough how good killers are at finding a reason."

"You're giving me plenty of reasons right now."

"Maybe. But I have a friend here to watch my back." Corlis slithered up to her until he was inches away from her face. "Do you?"

Ceci didn't answer. She only shot him one last glare and left the room, cursing to herself.

Things had not gone in her favor. But if she'd been the kind who gave up that easily, she wouldn't have made it so far. This was only a temporary setback. Her bag may have been in Corlis's grubby paws, but it was safe and had all her things—and whether or not Corlis realized it, he had given her the advice to wrest it back.

* * *

From Corlis's room, Ceci went directly to her and Alendro's, where she sat down before the dressing table to clean her hands after scraping around in the dirt. Alendro entered some minutes later.

"Grooming again?" he asked. "It's like you barely get up from that mirror."

She batted her eyes at him. "I only ever want to look my best for you."

"You've got too many clothes on for that."

From the mirror, Ceci watched Alendro throw himself on

the bed and take out the small stack he had under his arm.

"Bring me the letter opener, won't you?" he asked while examining the envelope on the top. "It should be over there on the writing desk."

The nail file almost fell out of Ceci's hand at the mention. In all her scrambling for the bag, she had entirely neglected her makeshift weapon, resting under the cushions of the bedside bench in Larence's room. It wasn't direct evidence of anything, but it would raise some eyebrows if anyone found it so oddly misplaced.

No matter. It was out of sight. She would have any number of chances to get it back unnoticed. Regaining her composure, Ceci put down the file and went over to the desk, preparing herself to feign confusion.

When she got there, no acting was necessary. Right on the desk, resting neatly in its holder, was the exact letter opener she had lost the night before. She picked it up. There was no question it was the same—the handle was chipped at the precise spot she remembered.

She turned around and passed it to Alendro, who took it without looking up from the envelope. "Thank you, darling."

Ceci sat back at the dressing table and finished cleaning her nails. Every so often, she glanced up at Alendro in the mirror, but he took no notice. He was fully engrossed in the paper he had in one hand, while the other one rested on the bed, playing absentmindedly with the knife.

V

Part Five

Chapter 22

Although no one in the family outside of Livia was particularly mournful, the day of Aunt Dalma's death went by uneventfully as everyone kept to their rooms. Usually, this would have bothered Thessa, but on this occasion, it was a boon. She and Corlis had a lot to discuss.

Whatever Ceci was up to, whether it was simple theft or cold-blooded murder, they needed to keep an eye on her, especially since she now had a reason to plot against the two of them. They had to find any excuse to separate her from Alendro, who would otherwise keep Ceci and himself behind closed doors. After some deliberation, they settled on a plan.

At breakfast the following morning, when Livia was once again strong enough to join them, Thessa proposed that the women take a day trip to the lakeside to lift their spirits. Gretia and Rosilla agreed with enough enthusiasm to decide the matter before Ceci could object. And to make sure her lover couldn't give her an excuse to stay home, Corlis suggested that Lord Hestor take the men on a tour of the wineries in Doma Lanca. The lord would never sleep on an opportunity to show off the most prized goods of his village, and so the carriages were ready within the hour.

The women rode in the hired six-seater where, per Corlis's

advice, Thessa quickly sat in the back so Ceci couldn't sit behind her.

"Even if she isn't likely to pull a dagger on anyone during the ride," Corlis had said, "it's best not to let her out of sight—if for nothing else than to make her remember she's under watch."

There was one more person in the carriage that Corlis wanted Thessa to watch out for, and that was Rosilla. He held on to the suspicion that not everything added up around Berto's parentage. If Livia had stumbled upon something, whether or not she meant to, her sister-in-law might try to make sure she never got to tell anyone. While Thessa wasn't as convinced about that, she had to admit that Rosilla was as good of a suspect as anyone else.

Suspect. The word sat uneasy in Thessa's stomach. She had been a suspect once, less than a year before, alongside Corlis and an innocent man. That time, the three of them were forced to investigate a crime in order to clear their own names, and of all people, the least deserving one was killed in the process. Now here she was, rushing headlong into another investigation. While her own life wasn't at stake—as of yet—there was no one to say it wouldn't end in another tragedy.

In an attempt to allow her concerned mind some rest, Thessa took in the scenery around them as they approached Lake Forterne. Nominally, the waterfront was an extension of Pont Lanca, although it lay several miles away with no real streets to speak of in between. As they got out of the carriage and onto the boardwalk, it wasn't difficult to see why the town would want to exert ownership over this narrow stretch of land.

Hanna had said that anyone who only saw Forterne would think there was no poverty in this world, and nowhere was that more apparent than on the shore. From what Thessa could tell, nobody *lived* on the waterfront. Every door led to a store, an inn or a salon, each striving to outdo its neighbors with their gaily colored facades. All had elaborate shingles boasting decades of business, yet none of them looked like they had been built more than a week earlier.

It was by one of these stores that something distracted her from the matters of Aunt Dalma's death and the rest of the family's secrets, though it wasn't an entirely welcome relief. They passed a window laden with all manner of jewels, trinkets, and novelties, when Gretia stopped to admire a bracelet in one of the displays. It was a delicate work of engraved silver, inlaid with a row of semi-precious stones sanded into small globes.

Gretia gazed through the glass with a longing that took Thessa back to that day when she had been captivated by a brooch. But, unlike Thessa, who was subsequently tricked into unending debt, Gretia was pulled away by her sister, who said, "Come now, don't you have enough already?"

It happened all so briefly, but to Thessa, it was almost cruel as a reminder of the difference in their standing. The silvers in her purse, given generously by Lord Hestor to spend at her own leisure, were now like alms to a beggar. A passing gift that could be taken away as easily as it was handed out. A symbol that Thessa was as much on borrowed time as on borrowed money.

Luckily, the grim thought only clouded her mind for a minute, and the next few steps soon replaced with it a new sense of wonder. Once again, it was Gretia who called their attention to a window, this time that of a confectioner. The signage above the entrance named it as the family Suilestre's sugar manufacture, established nearly a century before in the year eight hundred and seventy-one.

The left-hand side of the display consisted of a single rack of glass shelves, overflowing with a variety of treats. Each row was of a different kind, no larger than a bite, with candied fruits and works of spun sugar that defied all limits of human craftsmanship. This array alone would have been stunning enough, but it was the right-hand side that attracted the most attention.

That side had no shelves, but a single massive cylinder of glass. At its center stood another, slenderer one, which in turn encased a nearly foot-long piece of quartz that emitted a faint glow of greenish-blue light. The space around the quartz, between the inner and outer cylinders, was filled with gallons of brightly colored slush, mixed continuously by a pair of curved paddles. The mechanism was driven by a plump young man, who beamed at the group from behind the window while he turned the crank at a measured pace.

"Look!" Gretia exclaimed. "They started the water ice! We must get some!"

Even the usually reserved Livia showed excitement at the idea, and the two girls led the way inside.

"Are they using thaumaturgy to freeze the water?" Thessa asked aloud, marveling at the contraption.

"Yes," Rosilla was quick to reply. "It's called a *borea*."

"I've never seen one like this."

"They were only discovered a few years ago and needed lots of refinement before the technique could be released into practice," Rosilla explained. "Once the quartz is imbued, it must be handled very carefully. The first thaumaturge to make one ended up losing two of his fingertips, after he picked up the crystal with his bare hand, and they froze irrevocably to it."

Thessa shuddered. "A painful price for knowledge."

"They're already saying that *boreas* will change everything about how we store food," Rosilla said. "With the money he makes on the patent, he'll be able to buy solid gold fingers."

Upon reaching the counter, they placed their order for the water ice, a sample tray of confectioneries and, to Thessa's delight, a round of coffee. Gretia and Livia lingered to chat with the owner, who was a good friend of the Benuartes. Thessa, Ceci, and Rosilla took the only vacant table in a corner. Despite the hefty price of the goods on offer, the store was packed with well-dressed customers in chattering groups.

"I had no idea you knew so much about thaumaturgy," Thessa said.

"My brother studies in Midorea, and he always sends me clippings from the Academy's papers," Rosilla replied. "At least, the ones that are written in Ardonnese. I never got far enough into the language to make heads or tails of a real publication."

"You studied Midorean?" Ceci chimed in. It was the first time she spoke since they got out of the carriage, but her tone showed sincere amazement.

Thessa had to share the sentiment. Midorean was widely known to be unlike any other language in the region and dreadfully difficult for any foreigner to learn. "Have you been there, too?"

"I was going to." Rosilla's tone changed, and the shadows under her eyes deepened. "I wanted to take after my brother and become a thaumaturge as well. He helped me write my letter of application and prepare for the entrance trials. I already had my train booked for Namahil."

"Then what happened?"

Rosilla sighed. "I got morning sickness."

Thessa fell back in her seat. Behind her, the sisters giggled along with some anecdote that Suilestre was telling.

Rosilla bit her lip before continuing. "It was only meant to be a dalliance. Ernio was at the peak of his career, having won his third laurel that same year. He was tall, strong, and charming, and every girl swooned over him. I felt so lucky to be in his sights. But neither of us meant anything by it.

"I'll never forget how relieved my parents were," she said bitterly. "They didn't approve of my plans, but my brother was making enough money on his fellowship to cover my expenses, and they held no sway over him. He offered to"—Rosilla hesitated—"to set me up with someone, if you understand."

"I do," Thessa replied. She had met women who had to make that choice before.

Ceci pursed her lips. "But, let me guess—Ernio stepped up to do the right thing."

"He didn't ask me, of course," Rosilla said. "He asked my parents, and they agreed before he finished the question. Everyone praised him for how selflessly he gave up a bright future, and I was expected to be nothing but grateful."

She broke off while a server set a pot of coffee and five cups on the table. At the counter, the sisters bid their farewells to the owner and made their way through the crowded floor.

"I love my children. I truly do. I only wish they'd come five years later. And now, Ernio started training to compete again, while I'm at home raising them and running the estate."

"The estate that he so selflessly married into." Ceci scoffed. "Having his cake and eating it, too."

"Are the cakes here?" Gretia's voice came from behind. She and Livia joined the three of them at the table and relayed the story they'd just heard. Someone in town had paid a fortune for overseas fruit, only to have it all spoil during the trip. Rosilla listened along with Thessa and Ceci, without any mention of how a *borea* might have saved the precious cargo.

* * *

Once they left the confectionery and finished their stroll along the main street, the company made their way down to their destination for the rest of the afternoon.

For the most part, the shores of Lake Forterne were so steep as if the hills around it didn't rise upward, but rather it had been the water that pulled the earth down like a wet cloth. There were few places where the lake smoothed gently into the ground, and only one where the gravel on that ground was almost as fine as sand, instead of sharp and uneven pebbles. Like all good things in Forterne, this rare stretch of the strand was fenced off for the enjoyment of the select few.

After paying the entry fee at the gate, Thessa and the others spent a few minutes in search of a resting spot, until they settled by one of the colorful parasols that stood in orderly lines along the water. A uniformed attendant swiftly procured some canvas chairs for them to recline in and pointed them at the strand's many conveniences: the refreshment counter where they could get wine punch and other chilled drinks; the beauty stand where attendants would see to any make-up spoiled by the water; and a row of wooden baths where they could partake in the rejuvenating properties of the lake's mud.

Rosilla immediately headed off to the latter, as did Ceci. Shortly after they left, some of Gretia's friends from the village came over and invited the sisters and Thessa to a game of ball. When Livia said she'd rather stay under the parasol to read, Gretia insisted that she stay with her as well. She was evidently still worried about her and didn't want to let her out of sight—a notion that elicited both affection and annoyance from Livia at the same time.

"I'm not going to faint from holding a book," she told Gretia. "You don't have to fuss around me all the time."

Thessa leapt at the opportunity. "I'm not very good at ball games, anyway. I'd rather sit here too."

Livia picked up on the hint. "See, I'll be safe under Thessa's watch. Go on, enjoy yourself."

With some reluctance, Gretia waded off into the water alongside her friends, leaving the two of them alone.

Over twenty years in her father's court, Thessa had gotten plenty of practice in coaxing secrets out of people. Back then, it was only petty gossip, not potential reasons to commit murder. But she didn't have many options.

After a bit of empty small talk, she reached back, pretending to fiddle with her braid. While she did, she loosened the ribbons that held it together.

"Oh no," she pouted, brushing her loose hair over her shoulder. "Just when I was thinking about going into the water, too. Now it'll all get soaked."

"Would you like me to fix it?" Livia asked, setting down her book.

"Could you? That would be wonderful."

From the first day she arrived, Livia always had her hair in the most elaborately regal braids. In Thessa's experience, people were always more talkative when they were in a better mood, and people were always in a better mood when they did something they were good at.

"I've been so envious of your hair," Thessa said while Livia got to work behind her. "You have such a fine hand. It's no wonder you play the harp so well."

"Thank you," Livia said with an audible blush. "I suppose one does help with the other."

"I'm glad you're better after yesterday. Are you fully recovered?"

"Yes, I am. I have mostly Gretia to thank for it."

"She never moved from your side. I envied you a little for that, too. Not your condition," Thessa hastily added. "I meant that none of my sisters would have done such a thing. They only would have made fun of me."

"I'm sorry to hear that," Livia replied. "It must have been difficult, growing up in a family like that. Did you have friends outside?"

"None." Thessa shook her head slightly, so as not to disturb Livia in her braiding. "I only met people when my father hosted a dinner or a gathering, and they didn't strike me as much happier, either. I used to think all families were like that. But your father speaks so highly of you all, and the three of you take such good care of each other. It's nearly impossible to imagine you'd ever fight."

"I can assure you that's not true," Livia said.

"Oh, I'm sure you disagree sometimes," Thessa pressed on carefully. "But nothing to make you run away like I did."

Livia paused before answering, "There was one time when

I almost wanted to."

"I'm sorry. I didn't mean to bring up something hurtful," Thessa said. She trusted that Livia would feel pressured to fill the gap, and to prove that it wasn't hurtful by revealing exactly what it was.

"It doesn't matter much now. Just that, Father was very much against letting me move in with Aunt Dalma. When I first brought the idea to him, he outright said it's out of the question. I had to fight tooth and nail to make him consider. I even called him heartless once." Her voice trailed off. "I'm ashamed of that to this day. But he had to understand how much it meant to me."

"Of course." Thessa did her best to sound compassionate; meanwhile, she tensed up on the inside. Was she about to stumble on something? "But you can hardly blame him. It must have scared him to think of you leaving the home."

"No, it wasn't only that," Livia's answer came immediately. "He expressly said he didn't want me living with Aunt Dalma. He offered to rent me a townhouse in New Montres and pay for my tutors there. I had to explain over and over that I needed Aunt Dalma's help to meet the right people."

"Why was he so against that?"

"He didn't want her 'filling my head' with some ideas. I can't imagine what he meant. He already knew I never wanted to get married and accepted that."

The words echoed in Thessa's mind. *Filling her head with ideas?* Was there some secret Aunt Dalma held about the family? She had known the Benuartes for decades, ever since her sister married Lord Hestor. If she had found out something that wasn't meant to be known, that would go a long way to explain the lords' disdain for her.

Beyond all that, there was another question which chilled Thessa to the bone. If Livia had been the intended victim of the poison that killed Aunt Dalma—could Lord Harmon or even Lord Hestor have gone that far?

Before she could follow that trail any further, Gretia showed up with her friends and Ceci in tow, announcing that they needed one more player to balance out the teams. Livia preferred to stay under the parasol, and so, Thessa had little choice but to join.

She was assigned to a team with Ceci and one of Gretia's friends, taking their places in a triangular arrangement. The knee-deep water made them all clumsy and slow, leading to plenty of loud splashes and louder bouts of laughter on both sides. Thessa's teammate repeatedly blamed her loose sandal for getting in her way, and the opposing team goaded her into taking it off.

Shortly after the fourth round began, the girl let out a yelp of pain. "Ah! Curse these nasty rocks all over!" she complained, balancing on one leg while she pulled her foot out of the water. The pebble had cut deep into her sole, and from her wound ran a distinct stream of blood.

The scent attacked Thessa worse than the horsefly in the stables had. Before she could do anything about it, she was doubled over in a struggle. She clutched both hands over her nose and mouth, but it was no use. The scent crept through her nostril and her palate, flooding her brain and clouding her senses. Worst of all, her own horror only aggravated the effect further, as her heart pumped scorching hot blood into every crevice of her body.

Her awareness of the world around her diminished rapidly. There was a hand on her shoulder and a voice in her ear.

It might have been Ceci's—Thessa couldn't tell. When she was transformed, everything always sounded like she was underwater. Drawing one last desperate idea from the thought, she plunged herself into the lake and inhaled deeply.

The water burned her nose and lungs, but it did the trick. The onslaught of violent coughing wiped her mind clean and stopped the transformation before it could take hold. Thessa burst out of the lake, heaving and gagging, but human.

By the time she regained her sight, Livia was beside her too. Apparently, the rest of the girls had guided Thessa to the edge of the water.

"I'm so sorry!" Gretia wrung her hands. "I forgot how sensitive your stomach is to blood! I should have told them earlier."

"We should call someone over," one of the girls said. "I think there's a nurse on duty at the strand."

"No, please," Thessa replied quickly. She hadn't transformed, but she didn't want to risk anyone looking closely too soon. "Don't worry about me. I had a bit of a spell, that's all." She tried to sound carefree as she quoted the pallbearer from the day before. "I'll be all right in a minute."

The girls continued their game. Ceci dropped out to balance the teams again and offered to bring everyone drinks from the refreshment counter. As Thessa sat shivering on the ground, too weak to accompany her, she could only trust Ceci would have the good sense not to try and poison anyone then and there.

Chapter 23

Corlis had to admit that, all things considered, there were worse ways to investigate a murder than by drinking his way down Vertussi Hill. Once the women set out on their excursion to the lake, the remaining men—the lords, their sons, as well as Corlis and Larence— took the two carriages marked with the Benuarte emblem and started off the serpentine road to the south.

As they wound their way down, Lord Hestor would call for a stop at some house or another, where the owners would graciously invite them under the veranda and offer the best of their cellar or whatever the gentlemen preferred. Corlis had to wonder how much of this neighborliness stemmed from genuine hospitality. He could barely stand waiting on people when he was getting paid for it, and Lord Harmon or his prick of a son rivaled the worst drunk dockhands in their obnoxiousness.

Their final destination was a guest-house near the foot of the hill. Instead of a square, multi-storied building that was common in Ardonne, it was in more of a Werrish style, long and narrow with a thatched roof. The inside was entirely a single room, with massive legs of dry-cured ham and strings of sausages hanging from the crossbeams. As Lord Hestor explained, his late wife Wilhelma used to be fond of it because it reminded her of home.

The keeper of the guest-house—a stocky old man with the unmistakable Werrish handlebar mustache—greeted Lord Hestor with ridiculously elated gestures. He hastily moved a company of twelve to an eight-seat table, so that the lord and his illustrious company could sit at the best places in the middle. Around them, the hall resounded with a gale of song and chatter from wall to wall.

Lord Hestor ordered a tasting of the house's entire selection. Corlis braced himself for the brunt of the drinking journey, especially when the servers came forward and set three empty buckets on the table between them. As he found out, these weren't for what he initially imagined, but rather to spit each mouthful of wine into after savoring it. So much for refined table manners.

On the upside, it meant Corlis wouldn't have to worry about losing his focus. Regardless of the circumstances, one of the five men around him might be a killer. While that had also been true most days in the Wall District, especially while he and Aunt Mira ran their side business, Corlis still would have deemed that less dangerous. He was far from home now, in more ways than one. But his aunt hadn't raised him to give up easily.

When he and Thessa discovered that Aunt Dalma's death was likely premeditated, there had been a part of Corlis which urged him to pack up and bid farewell to the Benuarte villa before evening fell. He could have gone home to New Montres and the ruined Lame Mare, to pick up the pieces of his old life where he had left them. It would have both been easier and safer to choose that route if he wanted to.

But he didn't. Because loath as he was to admit it, he *liked* being rich. He liked not having to get up at dawn, not having to deal with unruly drunks and crooked sellers, not having to worry about what might happen the next day. While he was poor, he would daydream about all the indulgences of luxury, from fine clothes to finer foods—but now that he had all that, what he appreciated the most was getting a good night's sleep.

Money couldn't buy happiness, as the old saying held, but it could buy peace of mind. As someone who had grown up with little in the way of choice, Corlis knew how to settle for second best. And now that he had it, he wasn't going to let go without a fight.

Round after round came to the table with a different vintage of Forterne's finest. Corlis sampled each one along with the others, relishing their scents and aromas, all the while keeping his eyes open and his mind on track. If there was ever a time when too much was at stake to get drunk, this was it.

On his left, Ernio wiped his beard and set his glass back on the server's tray. "Say, Corlis"—he bumped him on the shoulder—"you've been with us about a week now, right? How do you like country life?"

Corlis had his mouth full with a six-year-old semi-sweet. He emptied it into the middle bucket, then replied, "The quiet needs some getting used to, but I'll take the smell of grass over slop any day."

"See, I knew it would grow on you," said Lord Hestor. "You'll feel at home here before long. It might even become your home." He took a small swig of his own glass. "What do you think? Could you see yourself taking on the responsibilities of a lord?"

Across the table, Lord Harmon croaked and hacked in his

revulsion at the idea. Alendro's grin was so wide it all but split his head in two. If only.

Lord Hestor's question sounded more of a jest than anything, but it did raise something Corlis had been wondering about. "What are those responsibilities, exactly?"

"Dear boy," Lord Hestor said, spreading his hands. "We do the most important job of all—collecting the taxes!" He snickered. "Not personally, of course. But we make sure everyone pays what they should be paying, for their own sake. The more taxes we collect, the more votes our province gets in the general assembly, so the laws are passed to our benefit."

"Like keeping the price of coffee good and high," Ernio butted in and nudged Corlis again. "Father's favorite hobby horse."

"Cheap coffee is a death sentence to wineries." Lord Hestor raised his finger.

Larence weighed in from Corlis's right. "He's not entirely wrong. Some producers in Brasthe say that ever since Sallis relaxed their tariffs on that border, a number of taverns have converted into coffee houses within the year."

Corlis was aware how prohibitively expensive the drink was in Ardonne, as Thessa used to complain. The same way Forterne wine was called "liquid gold", coffee held the moniker of "black gold". Nonetheless, as far as he could imagine, the makers of wine that sold for a silver per glass wouldn't have much concern about cheap coffee ruining their business.

Lord Hestor, however, was set in his position. "So, you see, it's vital for us to protect our interests, and that's what we're here to do. We set the rates, organize the census, and funnel the money to the imperial treasury."

"*National* treasury, Uncle," Alendro said from across Corlis. "Do keep up with the times."

"Don't start, boy," Lord Harmon grunted into his wine. As far as anyone was concerned, the tasting was now over and gave way to plebeian drinking. The servers picked up on this and replaced the spit buckets with filled pitchers.

"Those usurpers will be naming everything after themselves before long," Lord Harmon added.

If anything, Corlis was amazed it had taken a week for this subject to rear its head. While Lord Hestor's archenemy was the trainloads of roasted beans from the south, most of the Ardonnese aristocracy—chief of them the likes of Lord Harmon—were focused on preventing the senate from officially declaring the Republic of Ardonne later that same year.

"They have the power to do it," Ernio said with a resigned shrug.

"Because no one had the guts to stop them." Lord Harmon smacked his pudgy fingers against the table. "No one stood up to them, though it's treason, plain and simple."

Alendro's eyes shone with the glee of a child about to receive a present. "But Father, how could they betray an emperor that isn't there?"

His father took the bait, hook, line, and sinker. "They betrayed the empire itself. The families that made this country what it is. Me and my men flew the colors of the Empire of Ardonne on the *Stormwind*. That's what we risked our lives for at the Morusov Straits—not some *republic*." He spat the word like a curse. "If it were up to me, the lot of them would hang."

Corlis listened carefully from behind his glass. He had heard a rant like this before, from a bloodthirsty and thoroughly corrupt paladin general. At that time, he was preoccupied with not getting his head blown off by a thaumaturgic collar to pay much mind to the words, but this was a horse of a different color.

Beyond the occasional moaning about streets being re-named, people in the Wall District cared precious little about the goings-on in the palace of Jade Hill. Corlis used to readily count himself among them and only knew about the impending upheaval through Ladec and the other city guards. Over the seven years of "temporary governance" by the senate, he never considered to have any skin in their game.

In the most direct sense, he still didn't. But it was an undeniable fact that Lord Harmon was a man who intensely disliked change, especially if it threatened to diminish his personal standing. Lord Hestor could say all he wanted about how his brother was equally disdainful of everyone—to Corlis, it was clear his uncle would fight to his last breath to keep a commoner out of the family.

After Lord Harmon capped off his monologue, Ernio took up the thread.

"You would think a senate of the people would work for the people, but I was sorely disappointed. They had a chance to overturn the plumbing ordinance years ago, and they didn't so much as put it on the docket."

That one Corlis had heard of. Eight years earlier, an outbreak of cholera decimated both the Upper and Lower Court Districts of New Montres and crept dangerously close to the good parts of the city. Eventually, the physicians traced the origins of the epidemic to the sanitary conditions— or rather, the lack thereof—in apartment houses. The last emperor then issued an order of unprecedented strictness: that all buildings, new or old, must provide clean running water *on every floor.*

Larence smirked in response. "There was good money to be made on those works, that much is beyond a doubt."

"You don't need to tell me that," Ernio said bitterly and explained to Corlis, "Rosie's family has houses in Astercium, and we inherited a few when we got married. The ordinance gutted us badly. We had to almost double the rent to make the costs back, which made it twice as hard to get tenants. Went a whole year without profits."

Corlis did his best to sympathize with his half-brother, but the talk of sanitation only made him remember how much he needed to tend to his own fundamental needs. On that note, he excused himself from the table and sought out the small room of the teeming hall.

* * *

Stepping into the privy, Corlis was greeted with yet another reminder of the time difference between New Montres and the province. Instead of the individual stalls that had been the norm in the capital for decades, the guest-house kept the quaint tradition of communal experiences. A continuous bench ran along three of the four walls, with a dozen or so holes spaced far enough to give each user their own elbow room, but close enough to let them speak. The fountain in the middle provided a means for washing hands and a constant trickling sound for encouragement.

Given the throng of heavy drinkers in the main hall, most of the seats were occupied—some of them headfirst. Corlis took one by a corner, under a colorful mosaic that depicted a trio of merrymakers guzzling what he assumed to be white wine. No sooner had he dropped his trousers than the door swung open again, and Alendro strode in.

He went up to the pudgy, curly-haired youth on Corlis's right. "Move."

The boy, no older than sixteen, blinked stupidly up at him. "I'm not done."

"Then be careful not to soil anything on the way. This is a reputable establishment."

"Why can't you sit somewhere else?"

Alendro leaned forward and squeezed the boy's chin. "Because the dashing young man next to you"—he cocked his head toward Corlis—"is my cousin, and I'd like to enjoy his company. Surely, you're not so heartless as to separate kin from kin?"

The youth shook his head as much as Alendro's grip allowed, pulled his trousers up to his knees, and waddled awkwardly over to his newly appointed seat. A few of the nearby men watched, but none of them wanted or dared to comment.

"I hope my father's words haven't upset you too much." Alendro sat and leaned on his knees. "That's just how country aristocrats are, I'm afraid. Outmoded, stick-in-the-mud imperialists, the lot of them."

Even if Corlis had cared about politics, he knew better than to assume whatever his cousin said to him to be anything but mockery. But it gave Corlis an opening.

"I'm not the one who had to grow up with him," he said.

"Me neither. He didn't care to spend much time in the family home, so as long as I wasn't *too* much of a disgrace, I had free rein."

"What about your mother? Hestor said she and Harmon didn't part on the best of terms."

Alendro laughed. "There it is. Oh Cousin, you give your hand away so easily." He patted Corlis on the arm. "After being with us for a week and barely following along with everyone else, you and your lady friend suddenly come forward with plans for the whole family. Plans that split us up neatly for the two of you to divide and conquer."

Son of a bitch. Was Corlis's plan that transparent?

"You know, the others don't give you enough credit." Alendro went on and pressed a forefinger against the bridge of Corlis's nose. "But I see behind those glossy eyes of yours. Maybe not both at the same time, but I see it. You're a schemer, through and through. Picking up the scraps others so carelessly drop and scraping for whatever dirt you can." He wiggled his fingers as if to mime some critter scurrying along the ground. "I keep saying it—it's almost like you were noble your whole life. Almost."

Besides being upset over how easily the smug prick saw through him, Alendro's little monologue raised a dozen other questions in Corlis. No doubt it took a schemer to know one, but did Alendro suspect *why* Corlis asked what he asked? Had Ceci told him anything? Did he have his own irons in the fire—and was that the same fire as Corlis's?

All of them were pressing matters, but they'd all have to wait. First, the discussion at hand had to be settled.

"That's a lot to read into a simple question," Corlis said. "I heard something, and I thought it's best to clear it up with the person involved, instead of relying on rumors and gossip. But if I'm prying too much, you don't have to answer."

"That would be awfully rude of me, wouldn't it?" Alendro

tutted. "To rebuff such an earnest effort at understanding. No, I must oblige."

He picked up one of the clean sponge-sticks from a nearby bucket and proceeded to clean himself while he elaborated.

"Mother had any number of reasons to leave, most of them having to do with Father's deplorable personality. That did not bother him one bit. He knows what everyone thinks of him and wears it like a badge of honor. In his mind, being despised means you stand for something.

"Obviously, Mother didn't meet him on their wedding day. She knew full well who she was marrying and figured the title and fortune were worth it. Lord Harmon Benuarte, famed captain of the *Stormwind*, who won the last Werrish conflict. Any woman would have put up with him for that kind of prestige." He dropped the soiled stick in another pail filled with scalding soap water. "Unless it all proved to be a lie."

Corlis listened intently. The privy around them had emptied out in the meantime, leaving only the babbling of the fountain in the background and the muffled noises from the great hall outside.

"That decisive battle was not a battle," Alendro went on. "It was an ambush on Werrish ships in retreat. Werhen had already decided to yield and started calling back all forces that weren't engaged in battle, in preparation for the peace talks.

"The Morusov Straits was not a strategic point. Neither Werhen nor Ardonne cared about it. The top brass appointed Father to it simply to make sure he wouldn't meddle elsewhere in the battles that actually mattered. He was aware of this, and it did nothing to help his pride.

"When they saw the Werrish ships headed back north,

he knew what was going on. He was furious that the war was going to end without him getting his chance at glory. Knowing the olive branch had not officially reached Ardonne yet, he seized the opportunity and ordered an attack.

"The Werrish ships were caught off guard. Most of the men weren't in armor when the *Stormwind* ambushed them—they thought they were going home in peace. Father had all of them sunk within the hour, but they did manage to put up something of a fight. A good fifth of his own men died."

Alendro stood up to buckle his belt again. Corlis followed him to the fountain. It felt stupid and demeaning to surrender so obviously to him, but it would have felt much more so to miss the rest of the story.

"After the war," Alendro concluded, "Father saw to it that his officers were 'retired' with ample merits and small tracts of land, scattered as far across the country as possible. None of us in the family knew the truth about his glorious battle—until Mother went to visit her good friend Dalma in Callex, who happened to be entertaining Father's former junior as a guest. Isn't it funny how small the world is sometimes?"

He shook the water off of his hands. Despite the nature of the story, he had the same carefree tone as if he was telling a barside anecdote about someone accidentally sleeping with a dog.

"There you have it, Cousin." Alendro stepped in front of Corlis. "The sordid truth behind my parents' divorce, known to no one but themselves, the late Aunt Dalma—and now, you."

Corlis met his gaze. "I'm flattered that you trust me with it."

"I don't trust you." Alendro scoffed and put his hands on

Corlis's shoulders. "You're just not a threat. You wouldn't have clawed your way this far if you didn't have your wits about you. Surely, you know better than to rock the boat in this family." His hands crept closer inward and tightened. "And if you breathe a word of this to anyone, I will snap your scrawny neck like a twig."

Then, as always, he patted Corlis cordially on the arm and took his leave.

In wine, there's truth—that's why they keep it locked in cellars.

Corlis took a minute to wash his hands and think about what he had heard. Chief among them, whether it was true. Not the story itself, but Alendro's claim that no one else in the family knew about it. After all, Livia had lived with her aunt for a whole year. There was no telling what she might have overheard. Aunt Dalma may have been wily enough to know what to keep to herself, but Livia didn't have her experience. Corlis had to wonder if that could cost her life—or someone else's.

* * *

Back in the main hall, Corlis shuffled ponderously amidst the crowd on his way back to Lord Hestor and his company. Between the noise of drinkers around him, as well as the hurricane of questions inside his head, he was about ready to go deaf.

"Right on time," Lord Hestor said as he rejoined them. "I was in the middle of telling everyone that you should join us in my study tomorrow for the annual reckoning. It's the perfect chance for you to get familiar with the estate."

"You were saying no such thing," Lord Harmon said, jowls

206

wobbling. "If you had, I would have told you it's out of the question."

"Well, I'm saying it now," Lord Hestor replied, losing patience with his brother. "If Corlis is to join the family, he should know what he's getting himself into. It's not as if we're hiding skeletons under the floorboards."

Maybe not under the floorboards, but under the water, Corlis thought. Alendro's tale had definitely done a number on his mind.

"I think it would be good, too," Ernio said. "Uncle Harmon and I both have our own affairs to run in Tarnecia and Astercium. Father could use the help, and Corlis has a mind for business."

"He can mind his own," Lord Harmon replied.

Corlis waited in case anyone intended to ask him if he wanted to be present to begin with. After that didn't happen, he said, "If you do take me into the family, I'll still have my own business to mind. The Lame Mare. Although, it's currently not much in shape."

"Ah yes, good that you bring it up." Lord Hestor said to Larence, "Remind me tomorrow to go over our options with that."

"Options?" Corlis asked.

Alendro rushed to his help. "To take it off your hands. It's simply not becoming an aristocrat to be running a wayside inn in the unwashed outskirts of the city."

"Your wits will finally be put to the use they deserve," Lord Hestor said. "And, if you'd prefer to stay in that line of business, we might invest in some of the inns or wineries around here. Maybe this very guest-house!" He waved his glass around the hall. "Your experience could be a great asset to expand the family's interests."

He beamed with what he must have thought was encouragement, but it only compounded Corlis's trouble. There was a potential murderer in the family, Alendro was toying with his mind, and foul secrets crept out of every nook and crevice. Now, Lord Hestor was blithely suggesting that Corlis give up the one legacy he had from his past life. Once again, part of him wanted to turn around and leave the whole lot of them.

Instead, he adjusted his equestrian drape and said, "I'll think about it."

Chapter 24

Thessa's worst fear had been proven right. What happened at the stables was not a one-time incident, and it wasn't only horse's blood that set her off. Truthfully, she never believed Corlis when he suggested any of those explanations—she only wanted to convince herself. Now, the reality of it was undeniable. Her werewolf instincts grew stronger and more dangerous by the day.

What should she do?

The first answer was to run. Much like she had done a year earlier, when her parents planned to condemn her to a lifetime of servitude, Thessa wanted to saddle up the first horse she found and ride it as fast as it went.

The thought of Corlis only made that urge stronger. Even if she didn't hurt him, he could get into trouble merely by being associated with her. She couldn't let that happen. Corlis had a chance at finding a family here, and she would not take that away from him. He had faced death by Thessa's side and trusted her when no one else did. As much as she'd miss him as a friend, she'd sooner abandon him than risk his happiness.

Except, whether or not she might spare Corlis, she wouldn't have anywhere to go. That was the most horrific realization of all—that she would remain a threat to others, no matter where she went. Sooner or later, the wolf in her would force itself out, and there was no telling what would happen then. All she knew was that she had killed before.

It was under this dark cloud that Thessa reached the villa in the afternoon. Once the six-seater pulled up to the entrance, Rosilla, Ceci, and the Benuarte sisters all dispersed to their rooms for some rest before dinnertime. Thessa had already decided on other plans. Instead of going into the courtyard with the rest of them, she took the path that led around the house and to the back, all the way to the stables.

Iolinos was finishing up his work with the horses that had drawn the Benuarte carriages, which had returned about an hour before. He leaned out from behind the brown mare he was brushing down, and his face lit up. Thessa couldn't have told him how much this welcome meant to her.

"Good evening," Iolinos greeted her in Sallician. "How are you, Thessa? Have you and the ladies had a good time by the lake?"

"Yes, thank you," Thessa replied. "Although, I'm afraid I had another mishap. One of Gretia's friends cut herself, and I was right next to her to see it."

"I'm so sorry to hear that," Iolinos said. "Are you all right now?"

"I survived." *And so did everyone else, for now.*

"Would you like me to saddle up a horse for you? It'll be a while before dinner. And Avalanche is right here." The boy pointed at Lord Hestor's white gelding. "Larence Maiesco is out riding too, but he took one of the carriage horses."

"You've read my mind," Thessa said.

Iolinos brought forward the tack from the storage shed, led Avalanche out of his stall, and tied him to a post. Thessa stood by and watched, admiring both the horse's beauty and Iolinos's skilled work.

"How's Nykhe been?" she asked. "Has she gotten over her shock?"

"Mostly," Iolinos said, his brow darkening somewhat. "It helps her to keep busy during the day." He fastened the girth under the saddle. "I've been meaning to thank you for taking care of her. I should have been there."

"Lord Hestor gave you an order. You can't blame yourself for that."

The stablehand made a half-hearted sound of agreement and continued with his work. In a few minutes, Avalanche was ready.

As much as Thessa's mind was burdened by the mystery of Aunt Dalma and her own treacherous condition, climbing onto the horse's back was like she'd emerged into clear air from under a torrent of murky waters. She took the reins from Iolinos and darted off.

The gelding yielded to her eagerly, seemingly encouraging Thessa to spur him faster and faster. He picked up on her slightest movements, turning and changing speed almost before she gave the command. It had been a long time since Thessa had been so free.

The east side of the hill had the mildest slope and was overgrown with tall grass. They sped between rustling waves of green, until they reached the forest that dominated the rest of the landscape. Here, Thessa circled back and did a few laps along the edge of the trees, then stopped at last on a small crest that overlooked the south. The view from there stretched all the way down to Lake Forterne—and at the lake's edge, almost in a straight line from her, spread the town of

Pont Lanca.

Temptation crept upon Thessa at the sight. If she rode through the woods instead of the lazily winding road, she could reach the town in no more than a half hour. With the coins she had gotten from Lord Hestor for the day, she could take a night train and be back in New Montres before dawn. She could be a grifter again, skipping from one town to the next; not only to avoid getting caught, but also to avoid endangering anyone, especially her friends.

And yet, that path felt more selfish to consider. Corlis was in a precarious situation. There could be a murderer among his relatives, and Ceci was definitely up to something. He needed someone he could count on.

Thessa directed Avalanche back to the villa. She had to stay until she knew Corlis would be safe. After that, she would figure something out.

She was a good three hundred yards from the house when Larence emerged from the trees in front of her, astride one of the brown mares. He waved and waited for her to catch up.

"Good evening! I see we have yet another fondness in common," he said and patted Avalanche's neck. "Although, I must admit you are a great deal more daring."

"Do you think Lord Hestor will mind?" Thessa asked.

"No, never. I only meant that I don't have the courage to ride a steed like that. I grew up with plow horses, so anything over a trot feels like courting death to me."

Thessa laughed. "You'd be right at home as a messenger, then. Everyone says we'd be faster on foot."

"Is that what you did in New Montres?"

"I still do. They only gave me a short leave to come here. I'll have to go back in a few days."

"You will?"

"If I want to keep my job."

Larence gave her an askance look. "Do you?"

"I don't have a choice. Without it, I can only be a barmaid again, and I hated that. It's the only thing I can do well. And"—she played with a lock of her hair—"It was a difficult job to get. I worked hard to prepare for it. I'm a little proud of that, even if it's not much to be proud of."

"Hard work is the only thing any of us can be proud of," Larence said. "It's what got me where I am today. Hard work and a few smart choices."

"What kinds of choices?"

"Seeing an opportunity and seizing it." He pulled his horse closer to hers. "You're a bright young woman, Thessa. I'd hate to think of you wasting your best years trawling the streets of the city. I understand how much it means to you, but I know it's only the beginning."

He didn't need to tell her that twice. Buried under all her other worries—as if those weren't enough—there lay the one she had brought with herself, like one more piece of luggage alongside her borrowed gowns and dresses. The question of what promise the future held for her, if any. Not only when she returned to New Montres, but a year, or two years, or ten years afterward. She had a life there that was bearable, but not much else.

Yes, she was proud of her job and how she accomplished it. But pride did little to fix a ripped mattress or buy food that was more flavorsome than stewed offal.

"What opportunity do I have?" she asked aloud. "Corlis may become part of the family, but I won't. Not unless I want to be his kept woman."

"The Benuartes aren't the only ones who can help," Larence said. "Like you, I'll soon be back in New Montres. Most of my clients are there—aristocrats, councilmen, and a few people in theater. They would be thrilled to meet someone as exceptional as you."

Thessa didn't know how to respond. Back in Sallis, securing her fortune for the rest of her life was a matter of marrying the right man—or it would have been, had she had the choice. Could Larence open up the world that she got shut out of when her parents disowned her?

"You don't have to decide anything right away," said Larence. "I'll make sure you know where to find me once you're back home."

Neither of them spoke again while they came up to the villa. Having rounded the hill's crest, they approached from the east and had to ride past the back wall to approach the stables. The sun was slowly setting, and a stiff breeze rolled down from the Lancum mountains in the distance. At the corner of the house, they passed the kitchen window and heard Donella singing to herself as she made the final preparations for dinner.

A few yards away from there, about a third of the way along the wall, a sharp popping sound from under the hoof of Larence's horse prompted both of them to stop.

"What was that?" asked Larence.

"It sounded like something broke," Thessa replied.

She slid off of Avalanche's back and crouched down. Larence pulled the brown mare aside a few steps, but remained in his saddle. When the horse's foot moved, Thessa had to pinch herself.

There, in the grass behind the back wall of the house, lay the crushed remains of what was unmistakably a medicine bottle. Moreover, the label was still on it. The writing was sloppy and somewhat smudged where it had been trod on, but stayed mostly discernible.

"Did you find something?" Larence's voice startled her.

Thessa's mind raced. Should she tell him? There was no reason to suspect he was involved in the poisoning. He might be able to help. After all, he knew the family much better than she and Corlis, through an outsider's point of view. Besides all that, after the talk they just had, lying to him would be almost a betrayal.

But letting him in on the secret without Corlis's knowledge would be an even worse betrayal.

"It's just some pieces of glass. From a wine bottle, I think." Thessa pulled out her handkerchief and hastily gathered up the bits, careful not to tear the paper. "I'll take this to the heap. It could hurt the horses if they step in it."

She accompanied Larence to the stables, where they left the horses in Iolinos's care. Before they parted ways at the side entrance of the house, Larence reminded her of his offer once again, but Thessa was barely listening. The bundle of glass shards were burning a hole in her purse. She thanked him for the ride and his kind words, then rushed back to her room.

* * *

To Thessa's immense relief, Corlis awaited her inside. He sat up on the bed and read her face at once. "Did you find something out?"

Thessa bolted the door behind her on instinct, then went over to the bed and unfolded the handkerchief. Corlis didn't waste any words acknowledging the sight. They both knew

215

it could only be one thing.

"I tried to read the label right there," Thessa whispered, "but there wasn't enough light." She carefully picked up the pieces held flimsily together by the glued paper. "I swear, apothecaries have the worst handwriting. I can barely make out what it says."

Corlis pulled her hand toward him. "Let me. I got plenty of practice reading Borgeo's notes while Aunt Mira was sick." He tilted his head and fixed one eye on the blurred ink strokes, spelling out the letters one by one. "T-C-T… that's short for tincture. N-S… and… F-L-T."

"Nightshade and fading lancetip," Thessa said. "Those are the two main ingredients in sleeping drops."

"Doesn't leave much to the imagination." Corlis sucked his tooth. "Where did you find this?"

"Behind the back wall. That's where most of the gallery windows are."

"Someone could have thrown it from there easily enough."

Thessa poked at the remains of the bottle. "Does it say who the recipe was for?"

"I'm trying to see." Corlis leaned closer. "This one is B-E-N, and the rest is just one long scribble, but it's safe enough to guess it says Benuarte. This other one must be the initial."

Thessa squinted at the label, trying to get a better view without getting in the way. The glass had snapped directly between the two parts of the name, and the paper was slightly torn, making it especially difficult to decipher. But from where she sat—

"Is that a G?" she asked. "Gretia…?"

Corlis's nose was nearly touching the pieces by now. He studied them like some sort of soothsayer trying to tell someone's fate from a pile of rocks. "No," he finally said. "It's an E. This belonged to Ernio."

Chapter 25

Corlis trotted up to the gallery in a surlier mood than usual.

The discovery of the bottle jammed yet another stick between the spokes of his and Thessa's investigation. While they now had enough to make a convincing case about the poisoning to Lord Hestor, presenting the evidence would invariably mean accusing his beloved firstborn. There was no way that could go over well—which meant that Corlis and Thessa would have to continue digging in secret.

Provided that their dig was a secret at all. Ceci could easily have shared what she knew with Alendro. Larence was also there when Thessa found the bottle, and if he was involved in the murder, then he knew what it was. The rest of the family were more difficult to guess if they suspected anything. Alendro caught on to Corlis and Thessa's plan that morning, so it was entirely possible that others did as well.

All things considered, they weren't much further ahead, and Corlis wondered what they hoped to achieve in the first place.

Someone poisoned Aunt Dalma, perhaps originally intending Livia. It was a strong suspicion, but for the time being, it was nothing more than that. If they wanted to make Lord

Hestor even consider involving a judge, they'd practically have to do the prosecutor's job and come forward with a suspect, evidence, and motive. Until then, they were merely outsiders stirring up trouble and besmirching the family's noble reputation.

So, if Corlis wanted to take up the name of Benuarte, he'd have to keep to himself, work unnoticed—and potentially endanger Livia's life by refusing to raise the alarm. Which, as he thought of it, was despicably selfish.

Yet at the same time, the other option wasn't much more sensible. Supposing that Corlis ran straight to Lord Hestor and told him everything, consequences be damned—what then? The family wouldn't know who to suspect, and the killer would get a chance to escape.

Both choices were equally bad. Corlis might as well take the one that had a chance of benefiting him.

The entrance to the gallery was wide open, and the others were already inside. Corlis's gaze drifted instinctively to the window under which Thessa had found the bottle. Much like the doors, all shutters were thrown open to allow the cool evening winds to weave across the room. Three tables had been moved to the middle, where the family huddled around them.

Ernio was the first to spot him as he entered. "Come, come, we're all set up. It's time to draw the first group."

Every year, as part of their summer gathering, the Benuartes liked to hold an evening of cards among themselves. The ante was only in chips instead of real money—though on closer examination, those chips were worth more than what most workmen wagered in real games. Corlis had never seen ivory before, but the gleaming white under the colorful painted markings could be nothing else. A far cry from the wooden tokens he used to exchange for beer at The Lame Mare. Leave it to the rich to make something worthless so expensive.

For the first round of matches, the eleven of them were divided into three groups by drawing a series of lots. Corlis ended up in the only group of three at the middle table, alongside Gretia and Lord Harmon. Each player was given a stack of chips for betting, and the game began.

Corlis never was a gambling man. In his life, risk had not been a source of enjoyment. Nonetheless, he had spent enough time around gamblers to be familiar with the most popular games, and to his relief, what was good enough for the common folk was good enough for the Benuartes. He wouldn't win anyone's pretended fortune, but he wouldn't make a fool of himself, either.

At first, the bets and calls were the only words spoken at the tables, but as the first few rounds rolled past—and the wine glasses emptied—sprouts of conversation cropped up. Most of them were contained within a group, but now and again people talked across tables as they overheard one another. That was what Corlis had counted on.

Around the middle of the second hour, he pretended to stifle a yawn. Then another one a few minutes later, and then one more, making an increasing show of it each time. At the fourth one, he gaped wide open. That one did the trick at last.

"In polite company," Lord Harmon said in a low voice, "we cover our mouths when we yawn."

"I'm sorry," Corlis said, trying to sound contrite. "It came on so quick. I barely realized I was doing it."

Lord Harmon sniffed, but turned back to his cards without further comment.

Luckily, Gretia took his stead. "Did you not get enough sleep?"

"No, I'm afraid not," Corlis replied. "I haven't been getting much sleep since I got here."

"Still?" Thessa asked from the next table over. She was in on the plan, but they agreed she'd mostly keep herself out, so as not to give themselves away before Alendro again. Over at his table, it was hard to tell how much attention he was paying to the discussion; he merely flicked his cards and juggled one of the fake coins along his fingers.

Lord Hestor chimed in, "I would have thought after sleeping above a tavern and next to a railroad for so long, some peace would agree with you."

"You have been awfully exhausted these past days," Livia's voice came from the other side. "Is something troubling you?"

Now the whole room was listening to him. Just as he wanted.

"I think it's only the change in the surroundings," he said. "But I did think I might go down to the village and get something from the apothecary to help."

"We have some peppermint and lavender from—" Gretia began eagerly, but bit her tongue mid-sentence with a look at her sister. "From two days ago."

That was not what Corlis had aimed for. "That sounds terrific," he said, fiddling with a token while he racked his brain for an excuse. His eye met Lord Harmon's, and he switched to a discreet tone. "But in polite company, I'd rather not say what peppermint makes me do all night."

The air hissed with the sound of suppressed laughter from all tables, with the obvious exception of Lord Harmon.

"I might give it a try," Corlis went on. "Last night it got so bad, I thought about getting sleeping drops, but that might be too drastic."

Ernio said, "Maybe it's the sound of a train you need."

"That works for me," Larence replied. "The train, I mean. As long as I'm on it, not next to it."

"I know how you feel, Corlis," said Rosilla, dealing out cards at her table. "After Berto was born, I all but begged our physician to give me nightshade, but he refused because it might affect my milk. Thank the stars, Millie is so much calmer."

Corlis sat tense as a bow, waiting for a reaction from the others.

"That she is." Ernio nodded. "Berto's more like me, right, Father?"

"Most definitely," Lord Hestor said. "Your mother used to say you were born eight pounds heavy, and seven of those were your lungs."

"I would have thought those seven were his head," Gretia teased.

A few minutes of back-and-forth ensued between the siblings, with the occasional anecdote from the lords or Rosilla. For all Corlis cared, it was only noise. What mattered to him at that point was all that *wasn't* being said. Mostly on Ernio's part.

He didn't say anything about the sleeping drops. That confirmed the bottle with his name on it was not meant to be seen by anyone, which made sense. By his own account, he trained every day in preparation to compete again, and a man would scarcely need help falling asleep after a day of exercise.

But there was something else that stood out to Corlis. Something much subtler—not about what was or wasn't said, but *how*. When Ernio mentioned the resemblance between himself and his son, he said Berto was "like" him, not that he "took after" him. Any person could be *like* another, but only offspring could *take after* a parent. Was that distinction intentional? And if so, was someone else meant to notice that, too?

Before he got too lost in thought, Lord Harmon's voice pulled him back to the outside world.

"Dealer has double eights and a crown." He flipped his three cards over.

Gretia laid out hers excitedly. "Nine and ten, three crowns. You?"

Corlis barely remembered what the game was, let alone what he had. Without looking, he revealed his hand. Gretia's optimism evaporated in a drawn-out whine.

"Nine and ten, six crowns," Lord Harmon read out. He pushed the pile of tokens in the middle toward Corlis with his nose twisted in begrudging respect. "Good luck in the second half, I suppose."

Eventually, Corlis caught up to what they were talking about. Somehow, while he wasn't paying attention, he won the game.

Maybe he should gamble more, after all.

Chapter 26

Once all three groups finished their respective games and declared a winner, those three moved to the middle to compete for the grand prize. Having won at her table, Ceci thus found herself opposite the two men she despised the most—Corlis and Larence. Even good luck found a way to turn sour.

She thought over her options on how to leave first. If she complained of a headache or some sudden bout of nausea, Alendro would surely want to accompany her downstairs. That would not work. If she simply lost all her chips, it was more likely he'd want to stay and see how the rest of the game played out. Fortunately, Ceci was good enough at the game to know how to lose quickly, but not conspicuously.

And in the meantime, she could try and find some pleasure in her situation.

"Larence," she said when it was her time to deal. "How long have you been working for the family?"

"Oh, for about"—Larence gazed pensively at the ceiling—"eight years now?"

Lord Hestor replied, "Almost nine. Since winter of forty-eight."

The rest of the family, who weren't playing, each gathered

behind one of the three people at the table. Ceci had Alendro on her right, almost cheek to cheek and with one arm around her shoulder; as well as Livia off to the left, who had joined her out of pity so that Ceci wouldn't be left out. A waste of sympathy, as she'd much rather have been alone with her thoughts. Not to mention having two pairs of eyes on her cards made it harder to lose on purpose without making it obvious.

"Winter of forty-eight," Ceci repeated. "Must have been an important time, if you remember so clearly."

Behind Larence, Lord Harmon cleared his throat.

Lord Hestor gave the diplomatic answer, "The state of affairs around the family estate had recently changed, and we needed someone to help sort things out."

Alendro added in a helpful tone, "He means my parents' divorce."

Lord Harmon glared daggers at his son from across the table. Outside of Ceci's view, she could tell Alendro grinned back at him with the innocence of a newborn lamb.

She took the opportunity to wrest back the reins of conversation. "And before that?" she asked, as if to disperse the tension. "Had you been working in Ardonne for long, or were you in Brasthe?"

"Some here, some there," Larence answered, glued to his cards. "I had a few clients, but hadn't quite settled down yet." He didn't show it, but he was squirming. Before Ceci could enjoy herself too much, he turned the question back against her. "How about you two? You said you met in New Montres?"

"Yes," Alendro answered in Ceci's stead. "You introduced us."

Larence furrowed his eyebrows in confusion. Ceci did the same, except she only did so as an act. She knew exactly what Alendro alluded to. And while he was correct in a way, she absolutely did not want anyone else to get that idea.

"Do you remember when Father and I met up with you two months ago?" Alendro went on, playing with one of Ceci's curls as he spoke. "You took us to that salon by Crescent Bay. The one with that Chalimnean songstress you were so fond of."

"Ah, yes," Larence said with a small smile of recognition. "The Honeysuckle, on Westward Bank Street."

"I remember," Lord Harmon butted in. "That gaudy place with all those mock gold decorations and the smell of patchouli everywhere. Practically a cathouse."

"The one and the same," Alendro said. "After the two of you left, I stayed around to enjoy the music for a while. And who else should be sitting by the table across from mine, all alone and forlorn in the harsh New Montres night?"

He grazed Ceci's cheek with the back of his hand. As much as it made her stomach churn, she was compelled to face Larence with overjoyed astonishment. "*You* were the reason he was there that night?"

Larence said nothing, only gave an awkward smile.

Ceci was not the least bit happy about the direction this topic had taken, but the dumb little sister came to her rescue.

Gretia clasped her hands and sighed theatrically. "See, Father? You never let *me* go to the salons in Pont Lanca, when the love of my life might be waiting for me there!" She pouted at Lord Hestor in accusation.

Before the lord could answer, Ernio said, "If those salons are frequented by men like Alendro, that might be the wisest choice Father could make."

Next to Ceci, Alendro took the ensuing chuckles with good grace.

"That's right, Gretia," Rosilla added from the other side. "Keep yourself to the stadiums instead, and you can hook a man like mine." She spoke with a tone that could just as easily have been sincere or vicious mockery.

"I'll take my chance with the salon," Gretia said, in a tone that left no such ambivalence.

Amidst the family squabble, took note of her stack of chips. She was close to losing altogether. It was time for the next step in her plan.

With one hand, she pretended to adjust one of the pins in her hair. It was one she had borrowed from Livia, since her own good jewelry was hidden somewhere in Corlis and Thessa's room. The tip of the pin was in the shape of a butterfly, with sharp, pointed wings. As she reached up, she stuck her finger with one of them enough to release a few drops of blood. She then hid her fingertip behind her cards and waited.

From the corner of her eye, Ceci saw Thessa raise a hand to her mouth like she was about to be sick.

"Is everything all right?" Lord Hestor asked.

Thessa almost gagged on her words. "Yes, I—think I need some air. It's a little stuffy in here. I'll be back soon. Good luck, Corlis."

She patted his shoulder, then got up and left. Now all Ceci had to do was drop out of the game before she got back. She made a plausibly careless bet to raise the ante and revealed an underwhelming hand. By this point, she was barely paying attention to the game. The whole time she counted out twelve chips to Larence, she was focused on the double doors, willing

Thessa to stay outside for only a few minutes longer.

Finally, after one more round, Ceci was free.

"Oh dear." Livia put a hand on her arm. "Sorry, Ceci. Luck wasn't on your side tonight."

Ceci played up her disappointment. "Victory made me careless." She handed over the rest of her chips, kissed Alendro on the cheek for his support, and made him promise to tell her who won when he joined her in the bedroom later. Without waiting for his answer, she congratulated the remaining players and left. In truth, the real victory was ahead of her.

* * *

The inner courtyard wasn't particularly big, about seven yards on each side. The walls of the villa rose two stories tall around it, and besides the moon and stars above, it was only illuminated by whatever meager light found its way down from the gallery windows. From the top of the stairs where Ceci stood, it was like a gaping pit. At the bottom, by the edge of the fountain, was Thessa.

She didn't notice her right away. Only when Ceci's sole rustled the gravel on the footpath did she stir. The way she jerked made it clear she was tense. Tense and afraid.

"Are you feeling better?" Ceci joined her at the fountain. Without the warm flecks of sunlight dancing around, it was as if the statue's overturned jar spewed ink instead of water.

Thessa's voice was stiff with apprehension. "Yes."

"I'm glad to hear it. I hoped we could have a minute to talk between ourselves."

"Why?"

"Why not?"

"I know you're trying to get your bag back." Thessa's eyes were as black as the night around them, but glistened with a fire that seemed to come from within.

Ceci sat down. "You don't think I should have it?"

"Not if you're up to something."

"And why would you think that? Because Corlis said so?" Ceci regarded Thessa's face from up close. "No, that's not it. You know a grifter when you see one, don't you. You've known since we met. You think I'm only around Alendro for his money. But I can tell you, you're wrong."

"Do you love him?"

Ceci scoffed. "He loves himself enough for the two of us." She glanced up at the gallery, where a blend of elated and disappointed cries sounded. "I needed him. To bring me here. I needed to get close to someone."

"Who?"

There was no way Ceci would answer that. If she revealed or merely hinted that Larence was her target, Thessa would try to stop her out of some great conviction that killing was wrong. Even if she told her everything—even if no one in their right mind would judge Ceci for her intentions, knowing what Larence had taken from her.

Truthfully, some part of Ceci did want to tell her. She wanted to confide in her. Not to explain or justify herself, but merely to lessen the load on her mind. It was the same part that had watched Thessa and Corlis throughout the past days, bitter with envy at the obvious and unconditional trust they had for one another. Ceci had not had anyone to trust for so long, she almost forgot what it meant.

Almost—but not entirely. And like the clean spot left on

a wall when a painting is removed, the absence of that trust only made the walls of her own heart all the more barren.

"I heard you were kicked out of your home," she said to Thessa. "What was that like? How did it feel to be left alone, with nothing and no one to take care of you? To spend each day thinking of the life you once had, the life that was ripped away from you?" She welled up. "If you could punish the one who did that to you—wouldn't you want to?"

Thessa mulled over Ceci's words. Above, Lord Hestor's indistinct voice talked over the others' chatter. Beyond the house walls, the noises of the country night were less than a whisper.

"My parents have caused me a lot of pain," Thessa said at last. "Not only when they disowned me. I wouldn't wish it on anyone. But if I hurt them now, the same way or worse, nothing would change. It wouldn't make the years of suffering go away, and I wouldn't be any happier—only as bad as them."

Ceci expected nothing less. Thessa may have liked to believe otherwise, but she was no better than Gretia. "So, I should just forget everything? Let him walk away like he did nothing wrong?"

"I don't know what you should do." Thessa got up and smoothed out her dress. "But I won't let you do anything that could hurt Corlis."

"I'm not trying to hurt him."

"You could hurt his future. That's enough for me." She started across the yard, considering the discussion over.

But Ceci was far from done.

She caught up to Thessa in the passage by Lord Hestor's study, right when they reached the outer courtyard from where the guest rooms opened. Once she was in arm's reach,

Ceci took out the borrowed pin from her hair and pressed it against Thessa's naked shoulder. Thessa froze up and hissed in pain.

"If you don't want to hurt Corlis's future," Ceci said, "you'll give me back my bag."

Thessa's eyes widened at the sight of the pin. The slim bit of metal glinted in the moonlight.

"This?" Ceci asked. "It's one of Livia's. Since you took my gold, I had to settle for silver." She stepped closer. "You fooled everyone at the lake this afternoon, passing off your little spell as being sick from blood. But I got to see you closer than the others, before you dunked yourself under the water. I saw the bristles of hair on your back and your claws pushing out."

Their faces were now only inches apart. The fire behind Thessa's eyes vanished and gave way to sheer terror.

"Are you that surprised?" Ceci went on. "Didn't you know, werewolves and bloodsuckers come from Brasthe. Our mothers have been scaring children into obedience with your kind for a century."

Thessa's voice trembled. "Nina is your real name, after all."

"My real name is none of your concern. What is your concern is that unless you give me back what's mine, I will tell everyone what you are. I will slice my arm open in the dining hall if need be. Then we'll see how much the family wants you and Corlis around."

If anyone had asked her, Ceci would have considered threatening a werewolf about the dumbest thing a person could conceive. Even then and there, knowing that Thessa would never actually try to attack her, it was reckless. But Ceci was beyond care or caution.

Across the passage, the clatter of a dozen lazy footsteps

came from the stairs where the family made their way down from the gallery. Ceci threw an irritated look over her shoulder at the small crowd approaching them, with Alendro at the forefront.

"You have until dawn," she threw at Thessa before she went back, ready to swoon over her lover for the remainder of the night.

Chapter 27

Corlis had lost, unsurprisingly. Not that he had much investment in the game to begin with. Out of his two opponents, he was more comfortable losing to Larence, only so he wouldn't have to endure Alendro's smug face over a victory that wasn't even his own.

After the decisive round of play, the family lingered about in the gallery for a little while, until everyone was ready to turn in for the night. The lords, their sons, the sisters, and Rosilla all filed out of the room. As Corlis was about to fall in with the rest of them, Larence grabbed his shoulder.

"Would you mind staying behind?"

Corlis obliged, curious. While the others left, Larence uncorked a decanter on a sideboard, smelled the contents, and poured out two glasses. Corlis sat down on one of the plush benches by the back wall, under a window overlooking the east slope of the hill. A waning moon rose on an immaculately clear sky, surrounded by more stars than Corlis had thought existed before he left the city.

"I hoped we could have a minute to talk between ourselves," Larence said, passing one of the glasses to him.

"What about?"

"Earlier today, at the guest-house." Larence took a seat

at the other end of the bench and rested one elbow on the windowsill. "You got very quiet when Lord Hestor said you'll need to get rid of the inn. Quieter than usual, I mean. He wants to go through our options tomorrow, but I thought it might be fairer to ask you first." He took a sip. "Do you have any plans?"

"That would imply thinking beyond tomorrow."

"Not so easy to get used to, is it?" Larence stared up at the stars. "You spend years and years concerned with nothing but being able to wake up the next day. You wish for comfort and peace of mind. Then you get it and realize—"

"—how much easier it was when you didn't have choices to make," Corlis said. "When did you have to face that?"

"When I was twenty-four. Growing up with no mother and a father who saw the bottom of his tankard more than my face, I wasn't exactly off to a good start in life. I spent most of my early years falling in and out of bad company on the streets of Oldavici. Did some things I'm not proud of."

Corlis had never been to Brasthe, and Aunt Mira hadn't spoken much of it either, so he didn't know exactly how bad the streets of its capital were. In general, Brasthe had the reputation of being a poorer imitation of Ardonne— according to the Ardonnese.

"After my father drank away the last of his mind," Larence continued, "I left the city and drifted across the countryside. I wasn't much use as a farmhand, but I had a decent head for figures. A grain trader hired me to run his books and later started letting me make my own deals. That was when I found my wings, so to speak."

He topped off his glass. Corlis suspected more was to follow, but decided to play along. "Then how come you're not known as the greatest grain trader in Brasthe today?"

"Because it wasn't the grain that got me where I am." He stuffed the cork back in the decanter. "It was the people I met while trading. Many of them weren't involved in the deals and most I never saw again. But my name got out there, and eventually into the ears of people who needed someone like me. *That* is why I'm here today."

It was such a blatantly well-rehearsed story, yet Corlis didn't mind. There was something to Larence's effortless confidence that made it hard to imagine this man had once been a street urchin in rags. It was in all the little things, from the way he held his glass, to how he casually swept the lint off of his trouser leg. Much like his clothes, sewn from exquisite materials with almost no decoration, everything about him was elegant without being pretentious.

For the first time since he arrived at the villa—or indeed, for the first time in a decade and a half—Corlis found himself in genuine admiration of someone. He wanted to be like Larence. He wondered if he could.

"What happened when you were twenty-four?" he asked.

Larence hastily swallowed his mouthful. "Oh, that's right. I bought my first house. More like a cottage. I don't have it any longer." He sounded almost embarrassed by the thought. "But after spending more or less half my life on the street, I felt like a king.

"The first night, I invited all my friends, who got drunk and smashed most of the furniture. But the next day—that, I spent alone. That was when I realized life was no longer solely about today. And the only thing I remember is knowing how happy I should have been, and yet being everything but."

He did understand, then. Corlis thought back to his last

months at The Lame Mare. That short time when he was close to paying off his debt, after which he could do as he pleased. At that point, the prospect of that freedom scared him. But when disaster struck and took that prospect away, he was devastated. As if nothing could make him happy.

He shook off the memory. "I had a night like that," he said, "When Uncle Patrell and Aunt Mira took me home from the orphanage, and for the first time, I got my own room."

Larence frowned. "They were your adoptive parents, weren't they? How come you don't call them mother and father?"

"I wanted to, as a matter of fact. But Ulmira would have none of it. She insisted I call them by their names. In the end, Patrell got us to meet halfway with aunt and uncle."

"Sounds like he was a good negotiator."

"He wasn't. He just always wanted to make everybody happy. Most of the time, he found some way to do it, even when you thought it'd be impossible. But not always. And then, one night, some drunks in the tavern"—Corlis bit his lip—"resisted all negotiation."

An image floated up from long buried recesses of his mind. Corlis, as a boy of eleven, crouched at the top of the stairs. Peeking between the balusters at the pool of blood on the floor. Aunt Mira screaming at him to get back to bed.

"When he died, me and Aunt Mira could barely stand each other. I was almost sure she would throw me out, but she didn't. Both of us stayed to keep the inn running. Beneath all the pettiness and the name-calling, there was an understanding that neither of us said out loud. We both knew it, and we knew the other one knew it. *This is all we have left.*"

He trailed off. Aunt Mira was long gone now, Uncle Patrell

for longer, and soon, The Lame Mare would follow.

"Never underestimate the power of sentimental value," Larence said.

Corlis swirled his wine. "It's not so much the thought of giving it up that bothers me. It's that, with the state it's in, whoever buys it will for sure tear it down. That's what I would do. But when I think of Patrell's legacy being pulled apart brick by brick, it's like I'm betraying him."

How stupid was that? Not only the thought of betraying someone dead, but doing so by making such an obvious and reasonable decision. He had thought about that many times. Wondered if his uncle, had he survived, might have tried to get rid of The Lame Mare himself, once he saw what a poor investment it was.

"And if that wasn't the case?" came Larence's voice again. He now leaned forward, elbows on his knees, looking Corlis in the eye. "If we found a buyer who agreed to preserve the inn as it is—maybe with a new coat of paint—would that ease your guilt?"

"It would take a lot of convincing," Corlis said tactfully. Whoever wanted to buy, renovate, and keep running an inn at the edge of the Wall District would have to be a rare breed. Rare and supremely naive.

Larence pulled back. "When you have the Benuarte name behind you, it's not out of the question." Once again with his offhand charm, he made Corlis believe the impossible was in reach. "Let's pick up tomorrow. Remember—if you're part of the family, that means I work for you now. And I'm very good at what I do."

Corlis finished his wine by the window alone before leaving the remnants of the family's game night behind. Unlike after the First of Summer feast, it didn't occur to him to clean up after himself.

* * *

When he got back to his and Thessa's room, he found it inside out. The covers from both beds lay on the floor, as did all the pillows. One of the mattresses was askew, three of its corners hanging off the bed frame. All the drawers and chests were open, clothes strewn about like a whirlwind had ravaged the place.

In the midst of the chaos, with her hair undone and her dress half off her shoulder, was Thessa. At the sound of the door, she froze, holding a bunched-up gown that she was stuffing into a trunk. Her eyes were red, and her lips were bitten bloody.

"What's going on?" Corlis hurried across the room, nearly tripping on a mound of undershirts.

Thessa followed his gaze along the mayhem around her. Then, she continued to shove the loose half of the gown into place. "I have to leave."

"Why?"

"Ceci knows about me." Thessa snatched up another garment at random. "I didn't have the time to tell you, but when we were at the lake, one of Gretia's friends cut her foot, and I almost transformed again. I could barely stop myself. But Ceci noticed."

Corlis moved closer. Thessa ignored him, and continued to fill the trunk in stiff motions with no rhyme or reason to them. She wasn't really packing. She was giving herself something to do before her wits gave out.

"And now, up in the gallery, I smelled blood," she continued, her voice shaky with repressed panic. "No one was bleeding, Corlis. It was only a game of cards. I'm losing my mind. I can't stay here."

"Let me get you a drink."

"I don't want a drink."

"Let me get you a drink," Corlis repeated, "and we'll talk about it. I don't want you to leave."

Thessa tore herself away from her packing. "If we don't give Ceci the bag by dawn, she'll tell everyone about me."

She darted frantically around, as if the family was about to burst in to mob her right there. That was when the upturned beds and emptied wardrobes finally made sense. She'd been trying to find where Corlis hid Ceci's things.

"If we do, she'll kill someone," he said slowly. "Unless we figure something out and beat her to it."

"It's too risky." Thessa shook her head. A half dozen loose locks around her face echoed the motion. "You know she's ready to take us both down with her."

"Fine, so let her have the damn bag. I need *you* here."

"Corlis, please—" Her voice cracked, and for the first time, shifted from a manic whisper to something softer and weaker. Something that put a stake through Corlis's heart. "Don't make this any harder."

Corlis only asked, "Where are you going?"

Thessa stopped to get a grasp on her surroundings and resume packing with purpose. She took out the gold-trimmed evening gown, gathering up some less glamorous but much more practical underwear.

"I'll take the train to New Montres, first thing in the morning."

"And from there?"

"I don't know."

Corlis pressed on. "What will you do about your condition?"

"I don't know."

"Are you just going to keep running for the rest of your life?"

"*I don't know!*" Thessa slammed her hands down. Her cheeks glistened in the unmoving light of the quartz from above. "I don't know what I'm going to do. I don't know what I *can* do. All I know is, I can't put you in danger. Why won't you understand that?"

She lunged at Corlis, who stumbled back on instinct. But instead of slapping him, shoving him, or yelling in his face, she merely threw her arms around him and buried her face in his neck among a torrent of sobs. "You mean too much to me."

Corlis led her back to the bed and sat both of them down. There, he held her in silence, while she cried for however long she needed. The little sister he never had. Corlis wished he could be a good brother to her; a wise pillar of strength, who knew all the right things to say or do in her hour of need. Instead, he only sat there, awkwardly rubbing her back, his fingers getting tangled in her hair, and hers tugging at his equestrian drape.

Minutes crept by, and the sobs ebbed away. Thessa straightened up, produced a handkerchief, and made an unsteady attempt to clean herself.

Corlis took her hand. "If you're going to leave, take the evening train. Say your goodbyes to the family. To Nykhe and Iolinos."

It was cheap of him to trot out their names, but it worked. Corlis got up to the window and opened the shutters. The steep slope before him, as well as the rolling hills further away, dissolved into the black of the sky. A chorus of insects filled the cooling air with a buzz so ubiquitous it might have come from the soil itself. As if nothing existed beyond the walls of the Benuarte villa but an endless sea of trees.

"Remember when we had lunch at the pier?" The void outside compelled Corlis to lower his voice. "When you said that sometimes, one boring day is all you need? I could kill for a day like that right now." He ambled back to the bed and sat down. "I'm going to miss you."

Thessa didn't say anything. Before them yawned the unending, peaceful emptiness of the Forterne night, and Corlis wondered how much more joining this family would cost him.

VI

Part Six

Chapter 28

Ceci let her head fall back toward the ceiling in the morning light. At long last, she was in control again. She got her belongings and had unbeatable leverage over Corlis and Thessa. Larence was back in his own room and didn't suspect a thing. The plan was once again within reach.

Her gaze drifted downward, from the pale blue mock skyscape painted above them, to the flaming brass arms of the clock over the richly carved headboard, eventually settling on her own naked body. Her breasts heaved gently with each indulgent rock of her hips, and between her thighs was Perfection.

In the mornings, Alendro preferred to be under her. Less likely a gesture of surrender on his part and more likely another way to, as usual, get what he wanted without putting in any work. All the same, Ceci enjoyed this arrangement because of what it allowed her to see, if only for a short while.

She brushed her hands over his sculpted torso. Eyes closed, Alendro's lips parted slightly while she felt each crevice up his stomach, the cords of muscle under his chest, and the massive arms that clung possessively to her legs. When she first saw it, she would have called Alendro's body a work of art, but she had since rescinded that judgment. It wasn't art. It was artifice.

Growing up in rural Brasthe, Ceci had seen plenty of strong men. Blacksmiths with hands like a bear and a grip like a vice. Woodcutters who were all skin and sinew, but could swing an ax for ten hours and make it look easy. Alendro was nothing like them. Since he left the legion years before, the only thing he needed his strength for was beating up drunk louts when he got bored. The real reason he honed his body to an ideal was to show he could afford the time to do so.

For what it was worth, he could call his body a work of his own. His face and his station, on the other hand, were pure dumb luck. In the great raffle of nature, he ended up with all the best features the Benuarte blood had to offer, along with whatever he nabbed from his mother's side to round out the flawless picture. Anyone besides Ceci only saw that face in a permanent expression of conceit.

But when they lay together in the mornings, she got to see something else. As Alendro approached the little death, that veneer of superiority cracked, as he strained in anticipation of a release that not even he could get quicker or easier than any other man. His brow creased up, his nose twisted, his teeth bared, while he could do nothing but wait for the laws of nature to run their course.

In those few moments, Alendro Benuarte looked almost like a human being.

His hands fell to the mattress, limp and slick with sweat. He slowly lifted them behind his head and leaned back on the pillow as if he was doing it a favor. Ceci stayed in place and allowed a few minutes to herself.

Alendro's dry lips parted in a smack as he drawled, "What

time is it?"

"It's almost ten," Ceci replied, glancing up while she played with a lock of her hair. Should she curl it in the afternoon? It was definitely losing its hold. Then again, she wasn't planning to stay another day. The prospect of not spending hours to look her best every day enticed her nearly as much as revenge.

"Are you sure?" Alendro asked.

"I know you don't love me for my wits," Ceci teased in an overplayed voice, "but I can read a clock face."

For the first time since she climbed on top of him, he opened his eyes and bore them straight into hers. His grin was there too, but it was different. Mixed with the usual self-satisfaction was something sharp. Something cruel.

"Are you sure it's ten?" he repeated. "Not *tine?*"

Ceci's finger froze mid-twist, but she retained her cool. She tilted her head at him in feigned confusion.

Alendro moved one hand to caress her arm. "You were very distracted last night. Especially during the second game. The others were too far to hear it, but I was right there when you counted out those tokens for Larence." He took her hand and counted her fingers with his. "Seven, *eet*, nine, *tine*. Whatever troubled you, it was enough to let your Brasthen accent slip through the cracks."

No one had ever noticed Ceci wasn't native Ardonnese before. Could she have been that careless last night? She wanted to kick herself. One damn mistake after the other. She couldn't squander her chances like this.

"Alendro, sweetheart—I think I know what language I speak." She flicked his earlobe with her free hand. "Maybe *you* were so distracted that you were hearing things?"

"Maybe," he echoed. "I had a lot to think about."

Ceci wasn't about to stumble into another obvious trap. "Then how about I leave you to it and get ready?" She got off of him, slipped on her dressing gown, and took a seat before the mirror. "You should do the same, you know," she said, picking up a hairbrush. "I'm sure they're missing you in the study."

"Hardly. Father, Uncle, and Ernio do a good job taking care of the estate. They don't need a good-for-nothing like me meddling in their grown-up business."

"Didn't your father say he'd like you to pay more attention?"

"No, he said I'd know more about the estate *if* I paid more attention. But I save it for other things. Small things." He threw his legs over the side of the bed. "Like when we found Aunt Dalma's body, the quartz light was open on her nightstand, despite how famously she hated those things. She brought a candle with her to Larence's room."

An image flashed into Ceci's mind—one she had tried to scour from memory. Aunt Dalma's lifeless, purple-gray face in the lamplight. The light that Ceci had left open.

Alendro sauntered over to the writing desk. "Then, of course, everyone stood respectfully around the bed, except for the shameless layabout that I am. I sat on the bench and noticed something hard under the cushion. When Uncle ordered me to go back and cover the dead hag, I checked under it." He picked up the letter opener and felt its point. "You know, this thing is sharp enough to stab a man, any day of the week."

Ceci watched him in the mirror without a word. Anyone else would have thought Alendro was raving, but he wasn't. And Alendro knew that she knew.

He set the knife back in its holder and sighed. "I have to

admit, I completely forgot about the bag. You know, the one the maid found? Somewhere out in the hall, behind an urn? Strange place for a bag to linger, after everyone had unpacked days before. Stranger yet, I went back after they took the body away, and it was nowhere to be found, though the room was supposed to be locked in between. The window was open, naturally—but what respectable person would be caught dead clambering through windows?"

At last, he looked at her. Not her reflection in the mirror, but her real self in front of it, compelling her to turn around. Despite being fully nude, he was more threatening than ever. Not for any physical danger he might pose, but for the cold confidence with which he spoke. It was as if they were back at the gambling table, and he was revealing double tens and thirteen crowns, one card at a time.

"I can't know what was in that bag," he said, "but I do know you've been wearing my cousins' jewelry for two days. Precisely since that mysterious bag appeared and vanished, after someone snuck a knife from our room into Aunt Dalma's—which, at that point, everyone thought to be where Larence slept. The man who hails from the same country as you—which you never once mentioned at the table last night, or since I've known you."

He made his way to the dressing table and loomed over Ceci.

"Let's add this all up, shall we? You showed up in my life out of nowhere, right after I met with Larence. You come from the same country as him, but you kept that from everyone. You packed up your best jewels in a bag and hid it out of sight—then, somehow, a weapon made its way from this room to Larence's."

One damn mistake after another.

As much as Ceci searched for a retort, it was an occasion where the honest response was the most suitable. "Darling, whatever are you trying to say?"

Alendro caressed her cheek, but there was no affection in it. Whatever fleeting shreds of humanity he had shown a minute earlier were nowhere to be found. He merely asked in a tone at once sinister and playful, "You wouldn't be plotting a murder, would you?"

Whether or not Alendro believed it, Ceci was committed to her act. She waited long enough to make it plausible, then burst into laughter.

"Brilliantly done, sweetheart." She clapped for his performance. "You belong on the stage, next to Valinne Miatti. For an instant there, I believed you were serious."

She opened the top drawer of the dressing table and made a show of taking out all the jewels Alendro had gifted her. She silently praised herself for, after all her other slip-ups, having the foresight to take them out of the bag after she wrested it back from Corlis.

"Now, if you don't mind, I need to finish up here." She picked up her gold headband and held it up against a dress she had laid out earlier. "What do you think? I do like Livia's taste as well, but these two go better together, wouldn't you agree?"

Alendro was unfazed by the display. Maybe he wavered in his theory; maybe not. What mattered was that Ceci could disprove his accusation, and he knew it.

He went to his own wardrobe and pulled out some underwear. "Whatever you put on, make sure it doesn't stain too easily. I don't know how well the laundresses here can deal with blood."

* * *

What respectable person would be caught dead clambering through windows?

Alendro's question echoed in Ceci's mind as she pushed herself over Larence's windowsill once again, this time from the outside. Respectable or not, this was her only way not to get caught, dead or alive. Larence was in Lord Hestor's study and should stay there for another hour or two. Ceci could only trust it would be enough for her to find what she needed.

Except, she had no idea what that was. Not exactly. But she'd know it when she saw it. It didn't need to be perfect, only close enough.

Ceci crept to the massive chest by the writing desk and gingerly lifted the lid. As far as she could tell, Larence carried his entire office around with him. No stricken deed, no expired contract, no random list of names was too insignificant for him not to have in his luggage while visiting the Benuartes. In some way, this made Ceci's quest more likely to succeed—in most ways, it only made it more taxing.

Alendro was on to her. What wasn't clear was what he planned to do about it. He might let her do what she wanted, or he might try to stop her. That was what made him so frustrating. At first, he came across like any other rich idiot, but in truth, the man's mind was a damn puzzle-box. Beneath the polished surface ticked a dozen hidden thoughts and schemes, and while all of them twisted in different ways, in the end, every last one pointed at his own interest.

Ceci couldn't take any chances. She had to find a way to

divert suspicion away from herself, whatever it was.

She was midway through a stack of documents when footsteps came from outside. Thinking quick, she grabbed a pen from the desk and crawled to the door, where she wedged the pen under it, then waited with bated breath. If anyone tried to come in, it should give her enough time to cover her tracks and jump out the window again.

The steps passed by and faded into the distance. Ceci resumed her search. So far, nothing, and she was over halfway through. *Curse that bastard and his bottomless pile of scraps.* She couldn't give up. She wouldn't. If it wasn't this paper, then the next. Or the one after that. Or—

Her hands stopped. Her heart might have as well.

At first, she didn't fully understand what the drawing spread across the page was, but her eyes picked it up on instinct. It was a map. A superficial but accurate map, clearly drawn by a professional. The right-hand margin featured various markings in bright red ink and several more in a different color. Most of the notes meant nothing to Ceci, save for one. That, and the printed header at the very top. When she read which office the document belonged to, her spirits lifted even further.

She found all she needed and more.

She folded up the paper and put everything else back the way she'd found it, as if she had never been there. The only exception was the pen, which she left there solely to annoy Larence. Come evening, a stuck door would be the least of his trouble.

Chapter 29

Within a short time, Corlis was reminded on no fewer than three occasions to be careful what he wished for. Two months before, he wished he didn't have to worry about what to do with the inn after he paid off his debts—then came the accident. As a child, he wished his parents would find him and take him to a grand country villa—then came the murder of Aunt Dalma. And as recently as the evening prior, he wished for one boring day—then came the annual reckoning in Lord Hestor's study.

Back at The Lame Mare, Corlis had been in charge of all decisions, but Addie was the one who ran the books. Corlis used to say it was because her handwriting was actually legible, but in truth, the mere thought of poring over ledgers for hours on end made him numb. Here, there was no such escape. The lords Hestor and Harmon disagreed over a great many things, but both of them insisted on being fully in the know about every detail of the family's finances. And there were a *lot* of details.

To make matters worse, since Corlis had some catching up to do, Lord Hestor suggested that he meet with Larence ahead of time for a quick rundown. After breakfast, Corlis sat there for well over an hour, while Larence went over the endless facets of the Benuarte estate: the title and lands in Forterne that the lords inherited as their birthright; the properties that Lord Harmon was awarded for his supposed heroism; the Lazewic inheritance that went to the Benuarte sisters after their mother passed; the apartment houses Ernio and Rosilla got after their wedding; as well as the multitude of minor investments, loans, bonds, and who knew what else.

By the time lunch rolled around, which Lord Hestor had ordered to be served to them in the study, Corlis felt like moss was growing over his brain. It wasn't until mid-afternoon that they shut the last of the books and proceeded to the master drawing room upstairs to reward themselves with a few drinks.

Corlis emptied his much-needed glass of cold wine punch and muttered to Ernio next to him, "I never imagined being rich was this exhausting."

Ernio chuckled. "Good thing we only do this once a year. The rest of the time, we have Larence and the people at the Golden Lion to count the beans."

"And Alendro has the rest of you to do everything." Corlis sucked his tooth and looked around, noting his cousin's conspicuous absence.

"That he does," Ernio said with a scowl. "Some people will walk all over others, only because they know they'll get away with it. You know he's never done a day of honest work in his life, right?"

Corlis bit his lip. He wouldn't exactly have described Ernio's accomplishments of being born into one fortune and marrying into another as honest work, but this was not the time to bring that up. Instead, he poured himself another drink. "Yes, he said so himself. But he was in the legion, wasn't he? If that counts for anything."

"If you wanted, you could give him that. Not that he saw anything outside the training barracks. And needless to say, he dropped out before he could be saddled with any real responsibility there, perish the thought."

Over at the other end of the room, the two lords and Larence stood in discussion over a map of the province. Corlis wondered aloud, "Has Harmon ever tried to push Alendro a little harder? He controls all the money on their side, after all." That much Corlis knew for sure after Larence's lesson. "He doesn't seem to appreciate his son's lifestyle."

"No, he doesn't *seem* to. In fact, he doesn't." Ernio hunched over to bring his towering height closer to Corlis. "But as long as Alendro depends on his dear father, he's on a short leash. He can't move out of their house in Tarnecia—he can't even take a week trip. Alendro can play the golden boy all he wants, but he's a lapdog, plain and simple."

"Why is that so important to Harmon?"

Ernio was at a whisper now. "Something's fishy about that divorce of his. His wife didn't tell anyone why she left him, but everyone knows it wasn't for another man. I think Uncle Harmon wasn't exactly the model husband he claims to have been." He straightened up, but kept his voice low. "Who knows? We might be meeting another long-lost cousin soon. Whatever it is, Alendro's in on it—I'll put my neck on that."

Despite how close Ernio was to the truth, Corlis didn't correct him. Things were messy enough as is, and Alendro's threat at the guest-house was fresh in his mind.

Ernio finished his wine. "All right, I'm off. I've been meaning to take Berto out to the stables for days but never got around to it. Rosie and I are thinking about buying him a horse, so I figured I'd show him the ones here first."

Corlis raised his eyebrow. "Does Berto like horses?"

"Sure, he will." Ernio rolled his shoulder. "I wonder if we should get a Comarnian Pacer or one of the Laerithian breeds."

He crossed the room in excited thought about the horse that his son would surely like. Right as he was about to open the door, there came a knock from the other side, and he opened it to reveal Donella's stout frame in the hall.

"Pardon, my lord." She bowed out of Ernio's way and waited for him to pass, then stepped inside. "Lord Hestor, if you please—the village physician is down in the study. She'd like to have a word with you about Lady Dalma."

"Dalma?" Lord Hestor asked. "What is it?"

"She didn't say, lord."

"Then *ask* her, woman," Lord Harmon butted in. "Better yet, tell her to come back tomorrow. We're having a family day."

"No, no." Lord Hestor hobbled reluctantly toward the housekeeper. "Best get this all over and done with. I don't want this whole thing around my neck like a dead albatross."

When he left, Larence and Lord Harmon turned back to the map, mercifully ignoring Corlis. He pretended to fiddle with a loose thread on his shirt, while in his mind he pictured the pace at which Lord Hestor made his way along the hall, down the stairs and to the study. Once the time was right, he left the drawing room and followed him at an innocuous speed, which would allow him to pass by the study just in time to accidentally catch the first morsels of conversation.

Or so he would have done, if Larence hadn't called after him before he reached the doorknob.

"Corlis! Before you go—can you stop by my room in an hour?"

"An hour? I think so." Corlis tried not to fidget. "Thessa might need help with her packing. She's leaving with the evening train."

"Oh?" Larence asked. "That's welcome news. It'll be nice to have some company. Though, I might be asleep for most of the trip."

Corlis had entirely forgotten that Larence was leaving with the same train. Was that any cause for concern? It didn't feel like it. Not as much as catching up to Lord Hestor before Corlis missed anything important.

"Anyway, it'll only take a few minutes of your time," Larence said. "It's to sort out the paperwork so I can represent you to buyers for the inn."

"Right." Corlis's hand twitched on the door handle. It was almost hot under his palm. "Sure, I can drop by."

Then at last, he stepped out into the hall. In a rare twist of good fortune, his calculation proved correct. Lord Hestor must have taken his sweet time on the stairs, as the physician— a sturdy and tall woman of some forty years, sporting short dark hair and the traditional green jacket of her profession— was in the middle of shaking hands with him when Corlis reached the courtyard. He slowed his steps and stuck to the wall, barely within earshot.

"I apologize for the sudden and late call, my lord." The woman's voice was as deep as her stature suggested, and while it was respectful, it retained a ring of authority. "I needed to discuss a few things regarding the late Lady Lazewic, and I felt it's best if I saw to it personally."

"I thought we settled everything with your aide," said Lord

Hestor.

"I thought so too, but there's been a development that you should be informed about. As it stands, my aide misjudged the cause of death."

Corlis's stomach crept into his throat.

The physician continued, "While it is true that the lady suffocated on her vomit, my aide was mistaken about the underlying cause of that vomiting. His first assumption—which, in all fairness to him, I too would have made—was that Lady Lazewic had drank too much."

The sneer was audible in Lord Hestor's voice. "That was everyone's assumption."

"When I prepared her body this morning, I examined it myself, and noticed some telltale signs. Chief among them a rash on the lower back, as well as strongly dilated pupils. These would indicate a fatal dose of sleeping drops, instead of ordinary drunkenness."

Neither of them noticed Corlis, who stood so motionless he may as well have been part of the wall. He couldn't predict what reaction Lord Hestor would have upon receiving the news, only that it wasn't the one he actually heard.

"Huh."

Whether or not the physician was as taken aback as Corlis by the lord's indifference, she didn't let on. She merely asked, "Do you know if she had a habit of taking them?"

At this point, Corlis figured he may as well let himself be seen. He strolled casually inside the study, as if listening out of passing curiosity. The other two noticed him but showed no particular reaction. It was all in the family.

"No idea," Lord Hestor replied. "I'd wager the wine had a role in it anyway. Likely, she tipped half a bottle of the stuff in her drink. You needn't have come all the way for this."

"It's part of the duty." The physician bowed. "I thought I might also double-check about the arrangements for laying her to rest. You said she'll be buried in the Benuarte family plot?"

The lord let out a dismissive sound. "It wouldn't have been my first choice, but she has no other living family that could take her off my hands, and I haven't the faintest if she made any preparations in Callex. Knowing her, I'd be astonished if she had that much foresight. And if she had, well"—he threw up his free hand that wasn't holding the cane—"whoever wants to can come get her."

"Very well," the physician concluded. "Thank you again for your time, Lord Hestor." And in a minute, she was gone.

Corlis stood rooted to the spot. Was that it? He could understand that Lord Hestor would so apathetically chalk up Aunt Dalma's death as her own fault. It was the physician that stunned him. Physicians were bound by law to report any suspicious deaths in the home to the local guard. Corlis knew that all too well from experience, when he used Lokenn's vial to put an end to Aunt Ulmira's suffering. The only reason he wasn't taken in and questioned was because both the local physician and guards had known his aunt and agreed it was for the best.

But, as ever, things worked differently in the province. When Hestor Benuarte shrugged off a relative's death, Vertussi Hill shrugged with him and minded their business.

The lord shook his head at the pointless visit. Corlis fell in with him as he ambled back across the courtyard. He wanted to take a stab at the topic—the only question was how much he should reveal about what he and Thessa had found out.

"Isn't it a little strange?" he opened.

"What is?"

"I wouldn't have thought Aunt Dalma took sleeping drops."

"You never know with her," Lord Hestor replied, keeping his eyes straight ahead. "I'm sure Livia could tell you a thing or two."

Corlis screwed up his face in feigned thought. "But didn't she say she was tired? Why would she take them?"

"Why did that woman do anything? Don't trouble yourself. It's not worth your time."

It is, if I'm about to join a family of murderers. "Did anyone find a bottle in her room when her things were packed up?"

"You'll have to ask Donella and Nicki." Lord Hestor furrowed his brow. "Why are you so set on this?"

This was as good a time as any. "Yesterday, Thessa found an empty medicine bottle outside, under the gallery windows. The label said it contained sleeping drops, and—it was made out to Ernio."

Once again, he awaited a reaction. Once again, he was let down.

"Ernio? That's odd. I wouldn't have thought he needed them. In any case, there's your answer. Dalma must have got them from him."

"Maybe," Corlis pressed. "I'm only thinking… What if she didn't know she took them?"

"What do you mean?"

"What if someone else gave them to her? Without her knowing?"

Lord Hestor stopped. He studied Corlis's face at length with a puzzled look, as he tried to make sense of his words. Then their meaning reached him, and his expression changed.

His mouth stiffened in the corners, and his nostrils flared ever so slightly, while he took a long, slow breath. He stepped closer and put a soft hand on Corlis's shoulder.

"I understand that you haven't had an easy life in the city." His voice was low and almost hoarse. "Growing up in an orphanage, and then some seedy tavern on the outskirts. I can see how that would make you always imagine the worst—just like Fabreve wrote in his letter after you met. But in the long run, that kind of thinking doesn't help anybody, especially not yourself. If you're going to be part of this family, you need to let go of it."

His fingers tightened slightly as he spoke, reminding Corlis of Alendro's grip at the guest-house. This one was less of a threat and more like concern—misguided, narrow-minded, and obtuse, but concern nonetheless. Whatever it was, it hit the last nail in the coffin of any chance to get help from him.

"You're right," Corlis said. "I'm sorry. I didn't mean to accuse anyone."

Lord Hestor answered warmly, "No harm done."

Chapter 30

Thessa closed and latched her trunk, then weighed it in her hand. It was hefty, but not uncomfortable. She had to bear in mind that no one would be around to carry it for her like on the way to Forterne. It only held the essentials—undergarments, a pair of shoes, and some of her simpler dresses. A load she was well versed with from her days on the road with Hanna. Days she might have to relive soon.

She gave the luggage one last tug, then lowered it on the floor next to the dresser. Over by the wardrobe, Nykhe folded up the last of her intricately embroidered gowns. One of the many that Thessa couldn't take with her.

"Did you get to wear this one?" Nykhe asked, carefully gathering up the fabric along the seam.

"No," Thessa said. "I'm not sure when I was supposed to. Back in Sallis, I only wore something like this to a wedding."

Nykhe ran her fingers over the fine threadwork. "What a pity. It would have looked splendid on you." She sounded more disappointed than Thessa, who personally didn't mind. Family occasions had not been a good time for her back home. Not that this one had turned out any better.

"It'll look splendid on anyone," she said. "I'm sure Gretia

won't mind taking it off my hands."

Nykhe finished with the gown and laid it on the bed beside the rest. They both gave the room a quick scan. The beds were immaculately made, the drawers and cabinets neatly shut, and not a single thing was out of place. Save for the clothes on the bed and the trunk by the dresser, it was as if the previous night had never happened.

But it had, as Thessa could not afford to forget.

"Will you be staying for dinner?" Nykhe asked.

"I'm afraid I can't. I'm taking the evening train, and I want to be early, for good measure." After Corlis had given Ceci her bag, all they could do was trust she wouldn't rat Thessa out for the last few hours she was at the villa. Having to risk one more night was out of the question. "I should go see Rosilla and the sisters, and I need to thank Lord Hestor and Ernio for their hospitality."

And they can give my regards to Lord Harmon and his horrible son, she thought.

"Thank you," Nykhe blurted out as Thessa was about to leave. "For your kindness. I hope we'll see you again soon."

You won't. Thessa touched the girl's arm. "I hope so, too."

* * *

The inner courtyard was empty in the mid-afternoon lull. Larence and the Benuarte men had given themselves a break from their ledgers and gone up to Lord Hestor's drawing room for a drink. The only person downstairs was Rosilla, sitting on a bench, balancing Millie in one hand and a book in the other. The spry paper slid out from under her finger, forcing her to retrace her steps with an irritated click of the tongue, all the while trying to keep the bundle in her lap asleep.

Thessa ventured a greeting. As Rosilla raised her head, a handful of her permanently frizzled reddish locks came undone and flew in her eye. On instinct, she brushed them behind her ear, and the book beside her flipped closed. It was a roadbook about the Midorean Valley.

"How are you, Thessa?" Rosilla greeted her wearily.

"Good, thank you. Is Ernio around?"

"He's out back in the stables with Berto."

Thessa sat down beside her. "Does Berto like horses?"

"Ernio does, so he has Ogde there to watch his son, while he takes up Julian's time and pretends to know what he's talking about."

It was a little disappointing to hear that Rosilla couldn't be bothered to use Iolinos's proper name, either. Maybe she never heard otherwise from her husband and father-in-law, and naturally, Iolinos wouldn't correct her.

"I should go see them later," Thessa said. "I'm saying my goodbyes to everyone."

"You're leaving already?" Rosilla asked while repeatedly attempting to prop her book up, to no avail.

"Yes, I need to go back to New Montres for my job."

Only half of that was a lie, but that half must have struck a nerve with Rosilla. A fleeting shadow flashed across her haggard complexion at the word "job." Something almost like envy.

"Right." She forced the book open and flipped it cover up. "Well, it was lovely to meet you, if only for these few days. Maybe we could exchange addresses before you go? I would love to hear how you get on by yourself."

Thessa had received this offer many times before, and without exception, it was pure formality. The album in her childhood room used to be chock-full of names and addresses, left to her by dozens of girls she had met at one of Papa's gatherings. Each of them promised a dozen letters and wrote none. But there was a naked earnestness in Rosilla's voice—one to suggest that she too owned such an album, and she had every intention to follow through.

"Definitely," Thessa said. "I'll make sure to write it down for you."

Rosilla tried to say something, but before she got a chance, Millie stirred awake with a troubled moan that quickly broke into crying. Rosilla craned her neck toward the side passage that led to the outside path. Ogde was nowhere to be seen, presumably occupied with Berto at the stables. Annoyed, Rosilla reached behind her neck to undo her dress.

"This clasp, I swear," she muttered, fumbling around behind her thick hair. Eventually, she gave up. "Sorry, would you mind?" she asked Thessa and turned her back to her.

Thessa obliged and undid the lock that held the front and back halves of the dress together. When Rosilla pulled out her breast, the loose back panel fell away, uncovering her skin. Like most Mountain people in summertime, her shoulders were rife with freckles. But as the fabric folded lower, it revealed something else. The entire lower half of Rosilla's back was covered in a faded but noticeable rash.

She faced away from Thessa, so she couldn't have seen her reaction. She only winced when Millie latched on and greedily started to suckle.

Throwing good manners out the window, Thessa asked directly, "Do you know about the hives on your back?"

Rosilla only let out a sigh. "More than enough. It's been coming and going for over a month, and none of my ointments were of any use. I took the mud baths down by the strand yesterday, hoping that would help." She shifted in her seat to get more comfortable. "In all honesty, I'd say it's all nerves, after what Ernio's been putting me through."

Thessa went on, "You said you don't take sleeping drops, right?"

"Millie sleeps through almost every night," Rosilla said. Gently tipping the baby, she added, "And even with Ogde around, I feed her myself now and then, so I couldn't if I wanted to."

That sealed it. There was nothing else to do.

"Wait here for a minute." Thessa got up and hurried to retrieve the broken medicine bottle for the thoroughly confused Rosilla. "I think you should see this. I found it in the grass out back."

Rosilla leaned as close as having Millie in her lap allowed. "What is it?"

"Nightshade and fading lancetip." Thessa pointed at the abbreviations on the label. "They're sleeping drops. It was made out to *E. Benuarte*."

"Ernio?" Rosilla frowned. She either couldn't or didn't want to understand the connection yet. "Why would Ernio take them? He sleeps like a log."

"I don't think he did," Thessa said carefully. "But… I know that a rash on the back can be one of the side effects."

At first, the only sound was the wet smacking of Millie's lips. Then, within an instant, a procession of emotion darted across Rosilla's face—realization, shock, revulsion, and finally, utter horror. She looked down at her daughter and pulled the nipple out of her mouth in a panic. A trail of milk and dribble stuck to the tiny mouth, which erupted in gurgling cries of indignant hunger.

Paying Millie no mind, Rosilla snatched the handkerchief from Thessa's hand and bolted toward the side passage. Thessa followed, wondering if this had been the right thing to do. The answer met her right outside the villa.

Ernio, Ogde, and Berto were on their way back from the stables, the latter enthroned on his father's shoulders, while the nurse kept watch from behind. The three of them sang a children's marching rhyme, and Ernio matched the beat with long, lunging steps.

He was about to greet Rosilla when she halted before him and shoved the handful of fragments in his face. "Is this yours?"

Though Thessa had spent several months as a grifter, thinking on her feet and talking her way out of trouble was not one of her strengths. That said, she knew that Ernio picked the worst possible thing to say in response.

"Where did you find that?"

"Thessa found it." Rosilla's eyes, wide with anger, were fixed intently on her husband. "Is this why I have hives on my back? Have you been giving me these without telling me?"

Ernio glanced at Thessa, then lowered his voice. "Let's go upstairs."

"No!" Rosilla shouted. "We're not going anywhere. Answer me right now. What—"

The impending tirade was cut off by Berto, who went red in the face and broke into desperate wails on top of his father. Ernio reached up to comfort him, but stopped mid-motion and made frantic noises of disgust while he hurriedly lowered

Berto to the ground. The boy's breeches now featured a rapidly growing, dark stain on the front.

In her usual taciturn manner, Ogde stepped forward to take both crying children—Millie in one arm, Berto in her other—and led them away from the commotion. Judging by the ease with which she did, this was not the first or second time she had to intervene.

Rosilla waited for the nurse to make her way through the passage. Thessa thought she should go too, but Rosilla held the most important evidence in her hand, and Thessa didn't want to let it out of sight. Besides that, something told her it would also be best not to leave these two alone.

Ernio took off his shirt and proceeded to wipe his back with the dry part. "This is exactly what I was trying to avoid," he said in a restrained voice.

"Avoid what?" Rosilla did not hold back at all. "Me finding out you've been drugging me for months?"

"Our son is almost five years old"—Ernio waved at the passage—"and he still wets himself because all he hears is us fighting."

Rosilla held up the bottle. "And *this* is your solution?"

"All I wanted was to help you get a good night's sleep, so we wouldn't go to bed angry. And look how well it's been working! You've been more rested than you ever were in your first two years with Berto. Everything was fine!"

"I don't believe this," Rosilla said. "You could have poisoned me! You could have poisoned Millie!"

"I was very careful," Ernio replied, outright offended. "I asked both the physician and the apothecary—"

"You asked them both, but not me?" Rosilla held her temples in incredulity. "You're impossible. You always have to know better than everyone else. You always say you want the best for them, but you don't really care. You don't care about anyone but yourself."

Ernio took the first half of the accusations in stride, but not the last one. The bearded yet youthful complexion, always so mild despite his intimidating size, suddenly grew cold. "When you got pregnant—"

Rosilla cut him off. "Don't start. Not this again."

"You and I met barely a month earlier," Ernio went on relentlessly, "and you were already showing. Everyone knew the child couldn't be mine. No one said it, but they knew. And I didn't care. I swore to raise that boy as if he was mine. I gave up *everything* for you two."

"I never asked you to!" Rosilla burst out. "You threw away your career when you didn't need to, and you've been holding that over my head ever since! What about me? You forced me to give up all of my plans, and now you're out chasing your glory days again, while I'm at home doing my own duty *and* yours!"

The way words flooded out of her, this had been a long time coming. The bottle was the spark that set the barrel of oil ablaze, but that barrel had slowly been filling up for years. Thessa had seen it happen back home and had a few such barrels of her own. The last one was her own engagement night, which was followed by her running away.

"*I'm* holding it over you?" Ernio echoed. "You never let me forget how close you were to going to the Academy. Every time a letter comes from your brother, I know I'll be hearing about Midorea for the rest of the day. *That's* what I'm trying to get away from." He regretted saying that right away, but there was no taking it back.

Rosilla threw her hands up. "I see, it's all my fault. I'm the one driving you away from home and your children. All right, then. I'll get out of your way. Do whatever you want, get whatever you want—like you always do." She threw the handkerchief with the bottle on the ground and stormed off.

Ernio reached after her. "Rosie—"

"*Don't touch me!*"

The response made him jerk back like he had grabbed a red-hot iron, and the famed athlete once again reverted to an overgrown child. He watched his wife go back into the house, while standing there forlorn and half naked, his wet shirt bunched up in his hands.

He unfolded it, found one of the remaining dry spots, and finished wiping himself. "You should have come to me first," he grunted at Thessa and went to follow Rosilla.

"Wait!" Thessa grabbed his arm. "I'm sorry for causing you trouble, but"—she picked up the handkerchief—"why was this out here?"

Ernio cast an irritated glare at the handful of glass, as if it had incriminated him by a will of its own. "You'll have to ask whoever took it from my drawer."

"Took it? You mean, it went missing?"

"On the night of the feast. Now if you don't mind, I need to wash down."

The two of them went back inside. While Ernio took to the bath, Thessa hurried up the stairs. Any concerns about her own departure from the villa were gone. This was her only chance to catch Ogde alone.

The double room where the couple stayed had belonged to Ernio in his youth, and his presence could not have been more glaring. The empty drawing room had become a shrine devoted to his many athletic achievements. Besides the range of laurels, medals, and other accolades, the walls and shelves were decorated with random pieces of utterly ordinary gear, from weights to javelins to a wrestler's loin cloth. Thessa couldn't help but compare it to Livia's room, which had seemingly remained untouched since she moved out.

Ogde was seated on the plush bench by the window with Millie over her shoulder. Berto was next to her, resting his head on her lap, making no sound apart from the occasional sniffle.

Thessa showed her the bottle. "Ogde, did you know Ernio had this?"

The Mountain girl cast a passing look at the pieces, patting Millie's back. "Yes," she replied, flatly as ever. "Berto found it. When we got here, we read a story about pirates, and he spent the rest of the day pulling out every drawer searching for treasure."

"What did you do when he found it?"

"Put it back where it was."

"And you never took it out? Either that day or later?"

"It's not mine," the nurse answered, as if nothing could be more self-evident.

Thessa pressed on. "Did you tell Ernio that you found it?" Anticipating the answer, she added, "Or anyone else?"

The slightest shadow of a wrinkle deepened Ogde's forehead as she thought back. "Right. I might have spoken of it to Lord Ernio's sister. We were down by the fountain where Berto was playing pirates, so we got talking about that."

"Which sister?" Thessa's mouth went dry. "Was it Gretia?"

Ogde squinted again. "Is she the one with the light hair?"

"Yes."

"Then the other one."

As if to punctuate the sentence, Millie let out a loud burp. Ogde rubbed her back and whispered in her ear about what a good girl she was.

Thessa left the room in a sleepwalk. Her legs moved on their own, leading her out into the hall, to the stairs outside, all the way across the yard, and to her room. The only sensation she had was that of the glass edges digging into her palm through the handkerchief.

Now that she had her answer, it was so obvious.

Aunt Dalma had mentioned that Livia could spend an entire evening sipping on a glass of wine. If someone had meant to poison her, she wouldn't have drank nearly enough for it to be effectual. Anyone in the family would have known that. It wouldn't make sense for them to try. And as it had just become apparent, they didn't.

Which begged another, more chilling question. Had Gretia not spilled her own drink on Livia's dress, forcing her to leave—who would Livia have given that wine to?

Chapter 31

Ceci patted herself down one last time to make sure she had everything she needed and all of it was well hidden. The paper, folded up and tucked away in her cleavage. The weapon, slid up her long, tight sleeve. She wouldn't bother with letter openers or anything of the sort this time around. A chopping knife from the kitchen was just fine.

This was her final chance. Tonight had to be perfect.

She crossed the yard and knocked on Larence's door.

"Ceci," he said as he opened. "What can I do for you?"

"Corlis asked me to call you over to his room. He wants to speak to you about something."

"Corlis? Is it about the inn?"

"I don't know, but it sounded important."

Larence threw a quick look at something on his desk and said, "All right, I'll be right out."

He rummaged around for a while, gathered up a bunch of papers, and joined Ceci outside. The two of them then walked back side by side.

"Are you escorting me?" Larence asked playfully.

"We're going the same way. Alendro's down in Pont Lanca, so Corlis and Thessa are keeping me company."

The first half was true. Alendro had, in a stroke of luck, gone to town for the evening—presumably in search of some friends he could pit against each other over a game. That left her free to do whatever she pleased, safely ignored by the rest of the family.

At the other room, Larence knocked and waited for Corlis to call him in. Ceci stood by the wall, out of sight.

"Good evening. Thessa, Corlis," Larence said as he entered.

"Larence?" Corlis's voice sounded from within. "I thought you wanted me to come over."

At that, Ceci stepped inside, locked the door after her, and pocketed the key.

"Didn't you—" Larence spun quizzically around and came face to face with the tip of Ceci's knife.

"Sit down," she told him. "Not a word."

Behind Larence, Corlis and Thessa regarded her, ready to interfere.

"What are you doing?" Larence asked in shock.

"I said, *sit down*." She stepped closer.

Larence lurched back and stumbled toward the bed where Corlis had been sitting.

Thessa moved forward. "Ceci—"

"Don't even think about it," Ceci said to her, but kept the knife directed at Larence. "If any of you try anything, someone's getting cut. Maybe him, maybe you—maybe me. But there will be blood." She leered at Thessa. "We wouldn't want that, would we?"

Thessa and Corlis shared a glance, and the latter nodded. He put a hand on Larence's shoulder and pushed him down on the bed. "Do what she says."

Larence frowned, but said nothing. Thessa sat down next

to him and put her hand on his other shoulder. Corlis stayed upright and kept one eye on Ceci.

She moved toward the bed, keeping enough distance between herself and the other three so they couldn't snatch the knife from her, but close enough that she could swipe at them in one step. Her gaze was locked firmly on her soon-to-be victim.

"What do you want, Nina?" Corlis asked.

Once again, Larence stuttered in confusion. "Nina?"

"That's right," Ceci said. "Nina Baior. Don't suppose that says anything to you," she added, seeing his blank expression. It only infuriated her more. "But maybe Temisciaru does."

There it was. The name of her village lured it out of him at long last. The first glimpse of recognition. The first, if ever so slight, hint of fear.

"Temisciaru?" Larence echoed. "You're from Brasthe?"

"What has he done to you?" Thessa asked.

Ceci held out with the answer. It was a sentence she had longed to say for years. If it wasn't so bitter, she would have savored it. As it was, she almost spat it instead. "He killed my parents."

Predictably enough, Larence played dumb. "This is ridiculous. You are out of your—"

He moved to get up, but was swiftly met with resistance from Corlis, who had the good sense to shove him back on the bed. He glared up at Ceci. "I never killed anyone. Not in Temisciaru, not anywhere else."

"Then tell them what you *did* do," Ceci replied. "Twelve years ago. Tell them what you did to my family and to a dozen others." She paused for a response she never expected to get. "No? Then I will."

And so, the long-held secrets came pouring out.

"It was a bad year for farmers all over, but especially the west of Brasthe. Long winter, cold spring. Droughts in the first half of summer, weeks of hail in the second. However thin anyone feared the harvest would be, it was thinner than that. What little grain we could reap, we needed to save for next year's sowing. It was going to be a tough year. But it was only going to be one.

"And then you came along. Came in with bags upon bags of cheap grain. From east, you said, where the weather hadn't gone mad, and the granaries were overflowing." Ceci gave a mocking sneer. "I was eight years old at the time. Didn't yet know the saying: 'A man who comes from far away can say whatever he pleases.'

"You convinced my father to sell our saved grains, and buy yours for cheap. I remember it so clearly. 'A smart choice is seeing an opportunity and seizing it,' you said. Father had the wits to doubt you, but you told him he'd risk letting his family starve. You used his love for us against him." Ceci welled up at the memory. "As if you knew what love was. You and your damn slick tongue sent us and half the village into ruin.

"Every last one of those bags was tainted. Black rust, they called it. Most of the crops didn't last until the end of spring. We had made it through winter on what little savings we had, but by the end of the summer, we were in debt. And that wasn't the worst of it. Black rust doesn't only kill the crops—it poisons the soil and everything that grows there. What should have been one bad year instead became three."

Ceci's voice trembled, but her hand was steady as a rock. No matter how many times she envisioned this moment, part of her couldn't believe it was truly happening. But the words gushed forth whether she wanted them or not.

"We had no choice but to sell our land for a fifth of its worth. We tried moving to Ardonne, but it was no use. All that hardship, all that debt, now we lost our home—and then so much more. My father couldn't face the thought of failing his family and hung himself. Mother was left to raise three of us on her own, and within a year, worked herself into an early grave. Three children were orphaned that day because of you. Three in my family alone, and who knows how many more in Temisciaru."

Thessa clutched her hands, while Corlis's face was stiff as a corpse, except that he tilted his snake-like head by a fraction of an inch, as if he was judging her words. Between them, Larence was intent on keeping up his pretenses.

"Ceci—Nina," he stammered. "I—I don't know what to say. I had no idea about any of this, I swear. But if I could have done anything to help your family, I would have, without another thought."

Ceci watched his pathetic act. With the crushing weight of her memories lifted from her chest, there was nothing left in her but contempt. "Lying through your teeth as always," she said. "You can't even be honest in the face of death." She spat at him and continued.

"My brother and sister were put in an orphanage, while I was sent away to work. In five years, I saved up enough to visit them, but they'd been given to another family in Brasthe. Took me months to find out where they lived, but as luck would have it, it was less than thirty miles from Temisciaru. While I was there, I could stop by and see what had become of my childhood home.

"The village was nothing like before. Half the old farms

and cottages were gone, rebuilt into villas. I wasn't allowed to go near the one on my family's land at first, but I got on good enough terms with the housekeeper to let me speak to the new mistress. She told me how fortunate they'd been to buy this excellent plot six years before, in such a quaint little corner of the countryside—and how grateful she was to the man who had led them to it.

"It didn't take much more asking to learn that everyone else in the village had bought their land through you. After that, my path was clear. I tracked you to New Montres and made a living there any way I could, all to get close to you. I haunted all the salons for over a year and almost gave up, until three months ago.

"That night, you were at the Honeysuckle with Alendro and his father. You left before I could get rid of the greasy bastard I had gone with, but I knew that was my only chance. I netted the golden boy and waited—waited for him to get me here. To finally look you in the eye one last time, before I put you in the dirt where you belong."

Larence had no more words after that. Thessa pulled away and stared at him like she'd never seen him before. In a way, she never had. She had no idea what kind of a man he was, but the truth was now laid bare, and whether she believed it or not, Thessa was horrified.

But Corlis, that scrawny pale lizard, stood exactly the same as before.

"Far be it from me to lecture you on how to commit murder," he began in that insufferable tone of his, "but in my experience, people usually try to have as few witnesses as possible, instead of several."

"That's because you're not witnesses," Ceci said. "You're

accomplices, now that you know the truth about me. And about this." She pulled out the document from her cleavage and offered it in her outstretched hand.

Corlis slowly reached over. On the bed, Thessa and Larence watched as he cautiously unfolded it. There was only the rustling of the paper, until its contents were fully revealed, and Ceci bathed in satisfaction as the last drop of color drained from Larence's face.

Chapter 32

Thessa waited for Corlis to say something, but he merely glared at the paper in his hand. After a minute, she asked, "What is it?"

The answer took a while. "It's a map. Made by the *New Montres City Council's Office for Expansion and Development*," he read out the official header. He then flipped the document around for them to see. "And this, I believe, is a planned new branch of the railroad, along with a new station."

He ran his forefinger along a couple of lines that had been drawn down the right side in red ink. There were a number of other markings as well. One of them was a crude rectangular shape in the same red, that must have indicated the place of the future station. The others were in blue and related to a number of the buildings nearby. Some of them were crossed out and had a few words scribbled next to them. One was circled.

During the weeks she spent preparing for her job as a messenger, Thessa had studied more than enough maps to recognize the area. It was the Wall District.

"It's right beside The Lame Mare!" she said.

Next to her, Larence tried to grab the sheet from Corlis, but was too slow. "That map is from years ago," he said with an annoyed scowl. "I forgot I even had it with me."

"Did you?" Corlis asked in an unimpressed tone. "Because these marked buildings right here—these are exactly the ones that have been under renewed construction for the past half a year."

By now, Thessa had put it together as well. "If they build a new station across the road from The Lame Mare, hundreds of people will come by every day."

"A pretty good investment," Corlis said. "Especially for someone who can snag it at a low price because of the state it's in." His voice sank to barely above a whisper. "How easy it must have been to bribe that worker to cause an accident."

Larence's gaze shifted back and forth between the three of them. "Don't you see what she's doing?" He pointed at Nina, as if she should have been the obvious suspect. "*She* marked the map! You heard her—she's been skulking after me for over a year! Who's to say she hasn't been after you too?"

Corlis looked at Nina, who steadied her grip on the knife's handle.

"Let's just say Nina and I have had some conversations of our own, and it's become clear that she never knew of me." Corlis flipped the paper toward him, then pointed at the scribbled notes next to the crossed-out buildings. "Not to mention I've seen more than enough of your handwriting today to recognize it."

"Corlis, listen to yourself," Larence said. "You're smarter than this. Are you honestly suggesting that I orchestrated this whole thing—the elevator, the lawyers, the invitation—all to strike a deal I could have made if I simply knocked on your door?"

"No," Corlis replied. "I'm saying you were a lucky bastard

who had the perfect coincidence fall in his lap. You heard about me from Lord Hestor, saw an opportunity, and seized it." He crossed his arms. "What I *didn't* say was that an elevator was involved in the accident. It was—but I didn't say it. Which makes it all the more interesting that you'd know."

Larence was at a loss for words, caught in a lie like that. Seeing he had no chance to sway Corlis, he pleaded with Thessa. "You have to see how absurd this all is. Help me talk some sense into him. Then you and I can go back to New Montres, and I can help you get out of that worthless job."

He reached for her hand on the bed, but she pulled it away. It was almost incredible how different he was. In Thessa's eyes, Larence had been nothing but the picture of worldliness before. Instead of that, he was now a panicked animal.

She got up from the bed. He followed and moved closer.

"You need me, Thessa." His tone was a mix of desperation and threat. "I'm the only one who can help you get back to the world where you belong."

Thessa backed further away from him, until she stopped next to Corlis. "I don't belong anywhere with you."

Thessa, Corlis, and Nina lined up together, with Larence on his own.

Nina's bright red lips dripped with venom. "All alone, with no way out. This is all I ever wanted."

"Good," Corlis said. "Because this is all you're getting. He's a loathsome, backstabbing son of a bitch, who deserves everything that's coming to him, but"—he moved in front of Thessa—"there won't be any bloodshed here. Not tonight."

Larence ventured extending a soothing hand toward Nina, but nothing beyond that. The motion did nothing to ease her fury, only stoked it, if anything.

She raised her chin in defiance. "He's not leaving this room alive."

Thessa joined in. "Nina, please. You don't know what you're doing." She struggled with whether she should say what she thought of. "I've killed a man before. It was almost a year ago, but it never stopped haunting me. You don't want that."

"Oh yes, I do," Nina snapped. "I waited for twelve years. You heard what he did to me and so many others! I'm not letting you take this away."

"Take what away?" Corlis threw his hands up. "Your chance to frame us for your crime? Don't pretend you're doing this for anyone but yourself. There are a thousand other Larences out there, just as rotten or worse, but they can run the whole world into ruin for all you care. The only reason you're so dead set is because you wasted twelve years seething for revenge. That's your fault and no one else's, and I'm not letting you drag me or Thessa into it."

Nina's eyes glistened. The tip of the knife dipped ever so slightly, as she was forced to adjust her sweaty grip around the handle. For an instant, it seemed she was about to relent.

Larence stepped around Corlis. "All right, let's all—*Ah!*"

He reached for Nina's wrist. Startled, she swung it to the side—perhaps in attack, perhaps merely to stay out of his grip. The blade flashed, and a row of bright red spots scattered on the wall. Larence cried out and grabbed his injured forearm, pressing rivulets of blood trough his fingers.

"Thessa!"

Corlis grabbed her by the shoulder, but she barely heard him. She barely heard her own thoughts. Within two beats of her thundering heart, her flesh was ablaze like molten iron, and her mind was devoured in a torrent of screams and howls.

Before she lost herself, the last thing she felt was a blunt hit under her ribs, a crash of splinters against her back, and a gust of evening chill as she plummeted backward.

Chapter 33

There was no time to think. As soon as Larence's blood spattered on the wall, all other concerns were gone, and a singular motive took over Corlis's brain. *Get Thessa out of here.*

With every ounce of strength he had, he tackled her and pushed her backward through the closed window. The evening chill hit him in the face, and the ground came rushing upward as they plummeted out onto the forested slope.

They were separated right after they landed. While the grass softened the blows a little, the bumps and ridges pummeled Corlis mercilessly on the shoulder, back, hips, and shoulder again as he rolled along. There was no telling where he went apart from down, so he buried his face in his forearms and gave himself up to fate.

In what he could consider a turn of good fortune, his path was broken fairly soon by a tree. The foot-wide trunk slammed against his stomach, knocking every drop of air out of his lungs. Momentum pulled his arms and legs forward, and he doubled over like a half-open pocketknife—but he stopped. As he was about to sigh with relief, he realized he couldn't breathe.

The trunk was wedged firmly under his ribs, and the

weight of his own limbs kept him from pushing himself away with the muscles around his stomach alone. He flailed his legs desperately, like a dog trying to swim. Meanwhile, he struggled to get a grip on the tree so he could lift himself off before he passed out.

After a sinew-ripping effort, his torso came free. Immediately, he flipped onto his back and breathed in with an ungraceful noise. His lungs flew into a panic, as if to make up for all the lost air. Though it was only evening beyond the canopy of leaves, his vision filled with stars. His head grew light, and his ears lost all sound, save for the rush of his own blood.

Clutching one hand over his mouth, he forced himself to slow down enough to recover his senses. That included his sense of pain, as he was quickly reminded when he propped himself up on his elbows, and a searing jolt shot into his chest. At least two of his ribs must have cracked. One by one, he tested the joints in his body, from the ankles up. Thankfully enough, nothing else was wrong.

Nothing else, apart from the whole wretched situation.

Slowly, he heaved himself into a sitting position and turned back to the house. It was oddly close—he had barely come twelve yards or so. The bruises all over his back and arms held a different opinion, but for now, he agreed to disagree. He calmed his breathing further, and listened intently to any noises from the room. Nothing came. That could either be good or very bad. Most likely, very bad.

Worse yet, he had no idea where Thessa was.

He clambered to his feet, and with unsteady steps, began to ease his way down the slope. In truth, the incline wasn't as sharp as he had judged from the window, but he wasn't in any rush to fall again in the deepening darkness. He shuffled from one tree to the next, feeling out their trunks with his outstretched hand. He went on like this for minutes before he heard something from up ahead. A frantic rustle in the undergrowth, accompanied by a series of angry, guttural growls that were neither human nor animal. Corlis stopped to pick up a broken branch from the ground, then proceeded with increasingly slow steps, until the source of the noises came into view.

Thessa was on the ground, scraping at it with both hands in single-minded frustration that did not suggest any rational thought. She kept trying to push herself up, but failed each time and slipped face-first back into the weeds. It wasn't hard to discern why. At the other end, her legs lay limp and motionless at an angle that was uncannily misaligned with her upper body.

Corlis had seen bodies like this, back while he and Aunt Mira ran their disposal business for the underworld of New Montres. This was the body of someone whose back was broken.

The sheer bestial fury that clouded Thessa's brain could only have been compounded by the pain she was in. There was no chance of talking or getting close to her without risking an attack. And even if she couldn't use her legs, she had ten sharp claws and many more sharp teeth Corlis had to be concerned about.

He took out the pin that held his equestrian drape in place and rolled up the fabric into a rope. Then he grabbed the stick with two hands and held it crossways before himself, as he slowly approached his friend and prayed that she would forgive him for what he was about to do.

Twigs crackled under his sole, and Thessa whipped her head toward him. On sight, she tried to lunge forward and snapped at him with her maw. Corlis rammed the stick forward and stuck it between her jaws. While she was caught off balance, he swung his leg around to straddle her, put one knee between her shoulder blades, and brought his weight down. Thessa splayed helplessly on the ground, but the real struggle had only begun. Corlis grabbed each end of his makeshift rope, hooked Thessa's neck in it to pull it backward, then crossed the ends behind her neck and held them tight.

Under him, Thessa growled and snarled, but her frenzied breaths soon ebbed into faint, voiceless wheezing. Corlis resisted every urge to release her, until she ceased moving altogether and went limp.

Corlis threw away the drape like it was red-hot. He leapt off of her and carefully rolled her on her back, making sure to straighten out her legs in their proper position. Using some more sticks and his drape, he made the closest thing he could to a splint to give her back some degree of support. By the time he leaned over her half-open mouth to check her breathing, she was already reverting back to human.

Having nothing else he could do, Corlis sat down and waited for Thessa's strange werewolf physiology to do its job. Minutes stretched into hours, and the sky deepened from evening to night. The unseen world of the undergrowth awoke around them, and the air filled with the chirps of crickets, cicadas, and sawflies. A million small lives, each so minuscule compared to Corlis or Thessa, and yet, so indifferent to their existence. Whatever happened to the two of them that night, whatever suffering either of them faced, the creatures of the forest would live on, unaffected and uncaring.

Thessa stirred at last and let out a small moan. It was weak and short—but it was her own voice.

"Don't get up." Corlis put a hand on her shoulder. "Can you hear me?"

"Yes," came the slow answer. Her eyes fluttered and wandered around. "Are we outside?"

"Yes. I pushed you out the window, and we rolled down the hill. You broke your back." Corlis decided that much detail sufficed. "Does it hurt?"

"Everywhere."

"Try moving your feet around. Only your feet."

A faint scraping sound, first from the right, then the left. So far, so good. Much like he had done after unwrapping himself from around the tree, he guided Thessa to check both her legs, until at last he was confident enough to untie her splint and let her sit up. Whatever the necromancers of Brasthe had done to create werewolves, Corlis had to salute them for their work—even if by all accounts it involved a lot of gruesome and unwilling experiments.

Thessa pulled up her knees and distracted herself by picking out the thorns and leaves from her hair. "Do you know what happened after?"

"No idea. I tried to listen from some ways down, but I couldn't hear anything."

Thessa looked up the slope. At this distance, the villa was nowhere to be seen from the hundreds of trees. "How far down did you stop?"

"I got caught on a tree by the stomach."

"You could have broken *your* back. You could have broken your *neck*."

That thought had caught up to Corlis as well, if only in hindsight. "I couldn't let you hurt anyone. I had to get you out of that room, no matter what." He swallowed. "You mean too much to me."

Thessa didn't reply, only wiped her nose. Corlis gave her some more time, then pushed himself off the ground, forgetting that his legs had fallen asleep. He buckled, not unlike Thessa had earlier, then waited on all fours for the tingling in his flesh to stop before getting upright.

Thessa followed suit, and after agreeing they had little choice, the two of them headed back uphill to the house. They were about halfway there when a light flashed in the distance. A small spot of cold white that could only have come from a quartz torch, bobbed and swayed along the uneven ground. Someone from the house. The only question was whether this meant relief or more trouble.

Before Corlis could guess, Thessa sniffed the air, then called out. "Iolinos!"

The spot of light stopped and pointed at them, then approached with hurried steps.

"Thessa?" the stablehand asked back in a hushed voice and emerged from the darkness, torch in hand. As he got close, Corlis too could smell the hay and muck on him. "Are you two all right?"

"We're fine," Corlis said. "Were you searching for us?"

Iolinos leaned closer and ran his torch left and right. "Not just me. The village guard, too!"

That was a bad sign if Corlis had ever heard one. "Why?"

"Larence Maiesco is dead. And"—the boy lowered his voice further—"Ceci Virago says *you* killed him. She says she found you over his dead body with a knife, and then you jumped out the window." He sounded more scared than the two of them combined. "You didn't, right?"

"No, of course not," Thessa said. "And she isn't only lying about that. Ceci isn't her real name. It's Nina, and she's from Brasthe."

"Not that we can prove that, after I gave her the bag back. Whereas, she likely has the map to show for motive, as she so carefully planned." Corlis sucked his tooth. He'd admire her, if he wasn't about to be tried for someone else's crime. Again.

Nina's betrayal wasn't a shock, but there was an upside—once again in what *wasn't* said. Namely, the stablehand didn't mention anything about Thessa. Nina may well have been holding that card for later, but for the time being, it was one less immediate concern.

"Is there any way I can help?" Iolinos asked.

Corlis wished for two easier questions instead. He wasn't sure what anyone could do to help, besides Nina confessing to the murder. He might as well hope to be appointed emperor.

"Has Alendro come back yet?" Thessa asked.

The stablehand shook his head. "He's down in Pont Lanca. Lord Harmon sent one of the guardsmen after him."

"Then there is something you can do. Help me saddle up Avalanche." Seeing Corlis's reaction, Thessa added, "We have to try. Alendro knows Nina better than either of us, and he has no interest in her revenge."

"He knows *Ceci* better than either of us," Corlis said.

"If anyone knows how to get a hold on her, it's him." She said to Iolinos, "I'll take the southern slope through the forest. If you lend me your torch, that should let me beat the guards to Pont Lanca and bring him back with me."

Corlis sighed reluctantly. Not that he could fault Thessa's

plan, or that he had a better idea—he just didn't like it when someone else was right. "All right. I'll do my best to drag things out until you get back."

"You're going up to the house?" Thessa asked.

"If I have to be taken back by the guardsmen, it'll only make me look more guilty. This way, I might be able to explain where I've been." Corlis surveyed his attire, full of scuffs and stains from the roll down the hill. "It'll be a challenge, but I might."

That was that. Iolinos and Thessa whispered their goodbyes and started up the hill, going diagonally to cut some of the distance to the stables.

Corlis waited a few minutes until they were gone, then started off the other way. If memory served him well, he should emerge from the forest near the road that led up to the villa. Once he was back, all he needed to do was present himself willingly to be questioned and stall the process until Thessa's return, all without incriminating himself or exposing her as a werewolf.

Should be easy enough.

VII

Part Seven

Chapter 34

Lord Hestor's study was a wholly different place at night. During the day, the furnished passage bathed in the sunlight pouring from the two courtyards on either side, but provided some welcome shade in the summer heat. Now, the only light came from the various quartz lamps strewn throughout—and while some of it fell onto the grass and gravel of the yards to give indication of an outside world, for the most part, it was swallowed by black emptiness.

It wasn't a comforting light, either. The crystals were encased under yellow-tinted glass to lend some warmth to their harsh glow, but that did nothing to change their unnerving stillness. Where real flames danced and flickered, quartz light was as steady as the rock it emanated from. Aunt Dalma had described it as "dead", and as he sat there waiting to be questioned, Corlis had to agree.

With the exception of Alendro, the whole family had shown up for the spectacle. Corlis was in the middle, with the sisters and Rosilla on a bench behind. In front of him, on one side, Lord Harmon leaned back in a chair with his arms crossed and his chin up, as though he was personally responsible for Corlis having been caught. On the other side stood two guardsmen from the village—some balding, pot-bellied sergeant and his bucktoothed underling. Towering over both of them, Ernio could have been more of a guard than the two put together. Nina sat a bit further away, where she put her "troubled eyes" to good use, playing up the part of the terrified witness.

"I want you to know that no one is accusing you of anything." Lord Hestor leaned forward on his ornate desk.

"The gentlemen are only here on a courtesy call, then?" Corlis indicated the guardsmen.

Lord Harmon huffed and muttered under his breath, "Not a respectable bone in his body."

Lord Hestor sighed. "Please, Corlis. Just tell us where you've been."

"In the last two hours, to be precise," the bucktooth added. He sounded exactly as dense as Corlis had imagined.

Corlis picked a stray blade of grass off of his shirt. "I was out for a walk in the forest."

The sergeant glowered at him, lips puckered under his overgrown mustache. "You were out for a walk in the forest."

"I've lived in New Montres my whole life," Corlis went on. "Never saw anything bigger than a public garden. I had a few hours to kill before dinner, so I thought I'd go explore."

"For two hours?"

Corlis shrugged. "I admit, I didn't plan it to be that long. But, as you can see"—he spread his hands, putting all his stains and creases on show—"I'm not very experienced. I got lost. It got dark. I tripped and tumbled down the hill. It's half a miracle I didn't break my neck. But it did take me a good while to find my way home."

"Do you have any witnesses?"

"I didn't think I'd need any."

"Is that a no?"

"Yes."

"Yes or no?" The irritation in the sergeant's voice grew with each sentence. It was a treacherous line to toe. Getting him riled could help muddle the questioning, but it could just as easily land Corlis on the short end of the stick.

"Yes, it's a no," Corlis said. "I don't have any witnesses. Thessa wasn't in the room with me when I left. I believe she went down to Pont Lanca."

"The second carriage is out back," Lord Harmon threw in. "Alendro took the first one, and he's still away." Despite his casual tone, his eagerness to catch Corlis in a lie could not have been more glaring.

"She took your horse," Corlis said to Lord Hestor, then to the guardsmen, "You can go see for yourselves."

The bucktooth looked to the sergeant for orders, who sent him off in the general direction of the stables. The underling then shuffled back and forth through the study for a minute in an effort to figure out which way to go, until Ernio pointed him at the side passage that led to the path.

Once he was gone, the sergeant continued. "How was your relationship with Larence Maiesco?"

"Superficial at best. I never met him until—what, four days ago?"

"And during those four days?"

Corlis picked his words. "He gave the impression of a very pleasant man. Cultured. Good with business." None of those were untrue. That was indeed the impression that Larence had made on him. What Corlis learned about him afterward was a different issue.

"I understand you're the proprietor of an inn in New Montres." The sergeant checked his notes. "The Lame Mare.

Did that ever come up in discussion between the two of you?"

That did not bode well. If all the sergeant had known was that Larence was found dead, he would have no reason to know about the inn, let alone connect it to the death. Nina must have planted something to suggest Corlis had a motive. Probably the map, but he couldn't make assumptions.

"Briefly," he answered. "Lord Hestor mentioned that, if I were to join the family, I would need to give up ownership. He said I should discuss the options with Larence."

"Did you?" the sergeant asked.

"We never got around to it." *As far as anyone knew.*

The sergeant continued to ogle him with mistrust. Before he could ask his next question, the underling came jogging back.

"I asked the stablehand," he said, slightly winded from what must have been the most effort he'd made all year. "Kalou did take Lord Hestor's horse. He showed me the empty stall. He didn't remember exactly when, only that it was before dinner."

Silently, Corlis thanked Iolinos for making up a lie that was in line with his. The sergeant, meanwhile, was anything but content to accept this corroboration. His opinion leaned evidently closer to Lord Harmon's.

In the lull of the questioning, Corlis scanned the room again. Nina sat straight and tense, leaning slightly forward so as not to miss a single word. Ernio rolled his shoulder, more awkward than anything to be there. The bench was mostly out of Corlis's view, but he saw Gretia fidgeting with the hem of her dress, much more nervously than she had any apparent reason to.

"With all due respect, Andassi," the sergeant grunted, "you

don't appear very shaken by Maiesco's death."

"I barely knew him."

"Even so—a man was killed in the same house you're staying in." The sergeant motioned at him. "In your room, no less."

After Iolinos, Corlis now wanted to thank the portly servant of the law before him. This was the exact sort of question he wanted to hear. "I grew up in a bad part of the city. Death doesn't exactly rattle me." He added, "Besides, three nights ago, a woman died in the same house we're all staying in. Apart from one person, who fainted quite spectacularly, no one else appeared very shaken."

He punctuated the sentence by once again running his gaze over the company surrounding him, at the same time surveying the results of his provocation. Ernio gaped like a boy caught out of bed.

Lord Harmon, reliable as ever, fell for the trap. "What is that supposed to—"

Before he got further, Lord Hestor put up his hand. "Dalma's death was an accident, Corlis. We've been over this."

"Was it?" Corlis asked plainly.

"Please, gentlemen," the sergeant interjected. "Let's stick to the subject." On the one hand, he was supposed to be in control of the scene, but on the other hand, he obviously couldn't reprimand a lord in his own house. He merely stood on the side and watched as Lord Harmon railed against his brother.

"Don't you see what he's doing?" Harmon sputtered. "He knows he's in trouble, so he's trying to distract you by befouling our family name! And you're sitting there, letting it happen!"

"Uncle, stop!" Livia chimed in from behind. "This isn't Father's fault."

Lord Hestor listened to the accusations with diminishing patience. Corlis recalled the morning they found Aunt Dalma's body—how he brought the room to order and shut up Alendro. If Lord Hestor were to raise his voice, and Lord Harmon put up a decent fight, they could keep the circus going for a good while longer. He snuck a peek at the main entrance, but it was impossible to tell in the darkness if anyone was approaching.

"Oh yes, it is," Lord Harmon seethed on, raising his finger. "I warned you, Hestor. I warned you long ahead of time not to bring this common scum into our home, but you didn't listen. And now, what has all your foolishness led to? A man was slain under your roof!"

"Harmon." Lord Hestor's voice rang with a distinct threat.

"This would never have happened in *my* house!"

That did it. Lord Hestor rose to his feet with impressive speed, given his size and his ankle, and leaned on his cane to bellow at his twin. "That's what this is about, isn't it? You don't give an ounce of piss about Larence. All you care about is your petty, lifelong grudge for not being first out of the womb. You've been sulking about it for sixty years, as if that was the reason for all your failures." He threw up his arm. "Look at your son! Look at your marriage! Do you think either of those would have turned out better, had you been head of the family?"

"Father!" Ernio stood rooted to the spot in a similar conundrum as the sergeant, wanting, but not daring, to restrain Lord Hestor.

Lord Harmon shoved himself out of his chair and stood

face to face with his brother. "You lecture *me* about being a husband? I'm not the one who sired a common bastard, and then let him loose to destroy our family!" He pointed at Corlis. "Everything was fine until this miscreant showed up!"

Seeing the perfect occasion for another splash of oil on the fire, Corlis said, "Everything except your nephew drugging his wife."

Ernio went pale. "How *dare* you?"

"*You* are offended at this?" Rosilla sprang to her feet, and the room fell into chaos.

"Is that true?"

"That's none of your business!"

"Stop it, all of you!"

"Is that your so-called model son?"

"How could you do that?"

"I didn't!"

"He's lying!"

The clamor of the Benuartes yelling over one another was brought to a sharp end by the sergeant's whistle, as he judged that the degree of disorder justified his intervention. He commanded everyone back to their seats and reminded them the questioning was officially conducted by the guard. From then onward, no one was to speak without his permission. Having restored order this way, he directed his ire at Corlis.

"All right, Andassi," he snapped. "You've had your fun. Now, answer me. Do you recognize this?"

Corlis indeed recognized the paper he held up, though not entirely in its current form. Besides the red markings denoting the new railway branch and Larence's own notes, a good quarter of the page was taken up by the words "I'LL MAKE YOU PAY." The letters were in such a generic hand that they could have been written by anyone.

"No," he said.

"This was found next to Maiesco's body," the sergeant pressed.

"And?"

"What did Maiesco have to pay for?"

"You tell me."

The sergeant slammed the map on Lord Hestor's desk and stepped forward, not two feet away from Corlis. There, he leaned over him and rested his thumbs in his distended belt.

"I'll tell you what I know, Andassi," he growled. "I know a man was found dead in *your* room, next to a map of *your* city, with *your* inn marked on it. And I know this man had been a good friend of Lord Benuarte and the rest of the family for nearly a decade."

"Do you *know* I killed him?"

Keeping his watery eyes on Corlis, the sergeant cocked his head toward Nina. "I have a witness who says she found you over his dead body, knife in hand, and that when she screamed, you jumped out the window. Unless you have someone to back up your side of the story, you'll be coming with us."

No, Corlis did not have someone to back up his side. But as he sat there, staring up into that blotchy red face, he merely kept quiet—and listened. From the depth of the Forterne night, that silence so vast you could hear the birds fart in their sleep, there came hoofbeats. The rest of them noticed it and turned to the outer courtyard. The battering grew ever louder, until the ghostly figure of Avalanche showed up in the entryway.

Corlis bit his lip. Having to be rescued by Alendro of all people was bad enough—having him gallop into the yard on an actual white horse was a handful of salt in the wound. Thessa wasn't any more pleased, as she was relegated to sitting behind him with her arms around his waist. Alendro led Avalanche into the middle of the yard, then pulled sharply on the reins, making the steed rear up and whinny. Because *of course* he was an outstanding rider, too.

Avalanche barely got all four feet on the ground by the time Alendro slid effortlessly out of the saddle, paying no mind to Thessa. He smoothed out his impeccable clothes during the few steps it took him to reach the study and stopped before the guardsmen, who had instinctively backed away from Corlis.

"Father, Uncle—gentlemen." Alendro bowed his head to the lords, then at the two uniformed men. He ignored everyone else, including Nina, whose eyes now went from troubled to panicked. He put his hands behind his back and added, "I hope I'm not too late."

"That depends, young lord," the sergeant said with an uneasy cough. "Too late for what?"

"To confess to the murder of Larence Maiesco."

If the night had been quiet before, at this point, a marching ant would have made an outright racket. Alendro's words left everyone in the room dumbfounded. This also included Thessa, which worried Corlis above all else. It meant that, whatever Alendro had planned—because he had planned something—he hadn't divulged it on the way home. Why would he keep his intentions hidden, unless they were bad news for Corlis?

Of the company gathered in the study, Ernio was the first to react, by letting out a dismissive scoff.

Lord Harmon arrived at a similar conclusion. "Son, this is no time for another one of your jokes."

"Then good thing I'm being serious," Alendro replied.

The sergeant cleared his throat at length. "Young lord," he began with another bow, "I must remind you of the gravity of the situation. Killing a man is a crime punishable by death."

"And that is exactly the fate that I don't want my cousin to unjustly suffer." Alendro paced solemnly over to Corlis and stood on his side, resting one hand on his shoulder—ever so slightly closer to the neck, as he had done at the guest-house. "If you intend to keep your oaths as guardsmen to uphold the law of the empire, then you will allow me to make my confession."

The guardsmen exchanged a series of bewildered blinks. The sergeant's air of authority evaporated, and he deferred to Lord Hestor.

The lord gawked at his nephew and asked, "Why would you kill Larence?"

"He was blackmailing me. Or rather, blackmailing Father through me. He claimed that, before she died, Aunt Dalma had told him some terrible secret." Alendro smirked. "How convenient for him that I couldn't verify that with her. He said that, unless I paid him, he would expose this secret to the highest circles of society and ruin father's reputation forever."

Lord Harmon's mouth twitched. "What secret was this supposed to be?"

"He didn't say. Only suggested it had something to do with your service as captain."

Corlis couldn't see Alendro's expression as he stood next to him, but his father's said all there needed to be said anyway. The usual veneer of pompous superiority was paper-thin. The bloodless, fleshy lips pressed stiffly together, sowing deep creases into his sagging cheeks, while his nostrils flared with each repressed breath.

"You killed him over some obvious fabrication?" Lord Harmon asked.

"I couldn't take any risks," came the dutiful answer. "You know I put my family before anyone and anything else."

The rest of said family listened in puzzlement, while father and son were locked in an unspoken duel of their own. Both of them knew full well Larence hadn't done any of what Alendro said. The real blackmail was happening then and there.

The sergeant coughed again. "Young lord, I apologize, but—your story doesn't quite add up. Neither with what's been said so far, nor the evidence."

Speaking for the first time since they all sat down, Nina piped up. "You couldn't have killed him! I saw Corlis over his body, and you were down in Pont Lanca all afternoon!" She must not have had any idea about what Alendro was up to either, and it clearly didn't sit well with her.

Alendro picked up the yarn. "I thought it would be the perfect cover. I took the carriage all the way to town and trekked back on foot. I already had the knife with me—all I had to do was catch Larence somewhere I could sneak into the house unnoticed.

"After skulking around for a good while, I spotted him in Corlis's room. They were going over some paperwork together. I waited for Corlis to leave, climbed in through the window, and stabbed Larence before he could call for help. I left the knife and jumped back out. But"—he spread his arms in surrender—"I guess I wasn't quick enough. Corlis arrived right as I climbed out. I heard him jump after me."

Once again, to his dismay, the attention in the room landed on Corlis. The sergeant's glare in particular was more accusatory than before. "Why haven't you told us any of this, Andassi?"

Why, indeed. There weren't many answers he could give to that. There was the truthful one, which was precisely what he'd struggled to avoid. And then there was the other one. The simple, straightforward lie that meshed almost seamlessly into Alendro's neat little story. The only problem was that the mere thought of it made Corlis want to gag with bile—worse yet, Alendro almost definitely knew that and set him up for it on purpose.

Corlis took a long, slow breath. "Because," he reluctantly said, "I didn't want to believe Alendro did it. And even if he did, I wanted to give him a chance to get away. I know it's wrong, but—I couldn't bear to think of my cousin being hanged as a killer."

He kept his head down as he spoke, partly to play into the rueful act, and partly because if he saw Alendro's smug grin, the urge to spit at him might prove too powerful.

"I almost did get away," Alendro concluded. "But when Thessa found me and told me you were being accused of my terrible deed, I simply had to come back. I would sooner die than let an innocent man be punished."

As he closed his monologue, the family's expressions changed little from their previous confusion. The sergeant ruffled frantically through his underling's notes. Everyone else merely stood and waited for someone else to do something.

Lord Harmon was the first to regain his voice. "No, no, no. I don't believe it. This must be *his* doing." He pointed at Corlis again. "You put him up to this. I know it."

Alendro stepped closer. "I can assure you, he had no part in it. Besides, Father—are you trying to say Corlis is some sort of mastermind, who's been pulling the strings this whole time?" He played his father like a fiddle, knowing Lord Harmon would choke before he commended Corlis in any way.

The sergeant picked up the map again, this time with noticeably less conviction. "So, this paper in the room—"

"Yes, that was my warning to Larence. I gave it to him yesterday, but he didn't listen. I must admit, it was something of a dramatic touch of me to leave it by his dead body."

It was impressive how quickly Alendro improvised the lie. Granted, he must have had a lot of practice. More so than his insufferable nature, what irritated Corlis most about him was how alike the two of them were.

The guardsmen studied the document at length, then slowly put it away with the rest of the notes, and paced nervously. Both of them knew what the next step was supposed to be, but neither was in any great rush to do it.

Before either one spoke, Nina got up from her chair. "Alendro!"

"Ceci, my love." Alendro moved past the desk and gently cupped her cheeks in his hands. "It breaks my heart that it has come to this. I wish I could be beside you until my dying day, but… I understand if you can't bear the sight of me after what I've done."

Nina was a great many things. She was a grifter, a killer, a backstabber—but not an idiot. She saw the way out she was being offered and gladly took it. She let out a gasp, buried her face in her hands, then ran from the study without another word. Alendro watched her go with a look of sorrowful regret that might have convinced someone who had been born yesterday.

"Very well," the sergeant said at last, pulling up his belt. "Officer, take the young lord down to the guardhouse. The lords may follow if they wish. Other than that, I thank the rest of you for your time. I believe we're done."

Lord Harmon promptly made it known that he very much wished to follow, and he did so as the lackey led Alendro away. The two of them would undoubtedly have a good, long talk in private at the guardhouse's questioning room.

And, like the sergeant said, that was the end of it. Lord Hestor suggested that everyone retire to their rooms for the rest of the evening. He assured Corlis and Thessa that the guardsmen had already taken Larence's body away, and Donella was close to done cleaning up the floor.

Rosilla darted off upstairs, with Ernio at a notable distance behind. He was followed by his father and the two sisters.

All of them left without so much as a word to Corlis, except Livia. While the others filed out, she touched Corlis on the arm and whispered, "I'm sorry you had to go through this."

Corlis thanked her for the gesture, and she went off with the rest of her family. Corlis and Thessa were left to themselves in the study, which was now a lonesome island of light lapped by darkness on both sides.

Thessa sidled up to him. "What do we do?"

In response, Corlis pulled out the pin from his shoulder and left it on Lord Hestor's desk, along with his rumpled and grass-stained equestrian drape.

"We go home."

Chapter 35

Thessa stood alone in a world that was nothing but light and beauty. She had gotten up before everyone else to go outside atop Vertussi Hill and take in the view one last time. The sun was already a good way up, and a mild breeze caressed the wildflowers that grew knee-high on the two sides of the path. All the way on the northern horizon, a small patch of clouds gathered at the foot of the Lancum Mountains, like the vanguard of an encroaching army.

For now, however, Thessa relished the cavalcade of vibrant blues and greens, the whisper of the leaves, and the caress of grass against her open palm.

One last boring day.

The announcement at breakfast that she and Corlis were both leaving was met with little protest from the family. Lord Hestor and his children expressed varying degrees of regret, but made no effort to change Corlis's mind. Lord Harmon saw it as all but an open admission of his guilt.

Alendro was there too. Nominally, he was under arrest, but needless to say, him spending a minute in a holding cell was never a question. His father vouched to ensure he'd remain at the villa until a formal judgment was passed—not that he showed any desire to abscond. He toasted Corlis with his cup of iced milk and said, "This family will be a great deal more dull for your absence, Cousin." Behind his usual tone, there was something that made him almost sound sincere.

He was in largely the same mood when Thessa found him later. His room was much emptier than a mere day before. Nina had made short work of leaving the house after Alendro's performance. Not so much as a stray hairpin betrayed that she had ever set foot in there.

"Did you see her at all when you got back from the guardhouse?" Thessa asked.

Alendro slouched in a chair by the window, resting his legs comfortably on a padded stool and picking out nuts from a bowl on the sideboard. "No, she was long gone. Didn't even leave me a farewell note." He sighed. "Did you come to comfort me?"

"I wanted to know why you did it."

"Did what?"

"Why you confessed to killing Larence."

"You make it sound like I did something wrong," Alendro said. Despite his features being so much sharper than Ernio's, he was just as much of an overgrown boy. In many ways, more so. "Is it a crime to save my cousin from the gallows?"

"I know that's not the real reason."

"Good to hear. It would be terribly disappointing if you were that gullible."

Thessa leaned against the frame on the other side of the window. "You're not worried then?"

"What is there to worry about?" Alendro gathered up a handful of salted almonds and threw one in his mouth. "Lord Harmon Benuarte won't let himself be known as the father of a killer. He will pull every string, call in every favor, make every threat it takes to keep my name clean—and, more importantly, his own.

"Then, once this whole inconvenience is over, he'll kick me out of the house. Not publicly, of course. That would make people ask questions. I'll simply pack up my things, and he'll give me a monthly allowance so I don't disgrace him by being poor." He smirked through a mouthful of nuts. "It'll be tough, but it should tide me over until I find some lonely widow with more money than days to live."

From the way he acted so eminently pleased with himself, anyone would have thought Alendro had single-handedly solved all the world's problems.

"You blackened yourself to get away from your father without having to make an honest living by your own," Thessa said. She shouldn't have imagined anything less petty.

"Again, you make it sound so selfish." Alendro tutted. "I helped Ceci get her revenge, didn't I?"

That caught Thessa off guard. "You knew she wanted revenge?"

"I wasn't sure. But I did suspect she was after Larence, and they were both from Brasthe, which she hid from me." He raised a finger to underline the personal slight. "It was only natural that they had some history. I went down to Pont Lanca good and early in the afternoon, leaving her ample time to make good on her plan before Larence left for the train."

"You… *let* her do it?" Thessa gaped. "You knew she wanted to kill Larence and didn't think to warn him?"

"I'm sure she had good reasons." Alendro picked at crumbs between his teeth as indifferently as if they were discussing the impending rain. His tone was flat out peevish. "Don't tell me you're getting teary-eyed over his death. The man was a bastard. I don't know what he did to Ceci, but I can tell you this much: no one gets as rich as him with only 'hard work and smart choices.' Families like mine have always seen to that. I can guarantee he destroyed more lives than you could count."

For a little while, Thessa was irritated—both at his callous and self-seeking attitude, as well as the fact that he was right. It made her more frustrated than she had been in a long time. But as quickly as the feeling came, it dispersed even quicker, when she thought back to the last time she experienced the same frustration.

"Corlis used to be so much like you when we first met. He had an excuse for everything too."

Alendro cocked one eyebrow. "And what happened to make him the paragon of integrity that he is today?"

Thessa pushed herself away from the wall. "He was stabbed in the back and left for dead, all alone."

She didn't think the answer would shake him to any visible extent. Surely enough, the usual grin crept back to his handsome face. "I suppose I should keep company to watch out for me."

Turning her back on him, Thessa only replied, "Good luck."

* * *

Seeing as how she'd already said her farewells once, Thessa figured there wasn't any point in going through those motions again. Instead, she decided to spend her remaining hours with one last ride on Avalanche. She'd miss that magnificent horse more than any actual members of the family. Then again, they

312

were never meant to be her family to begin with. She was as good as an intruder, who showed up alongside their long lost relative, ruined Ernio and Rosilla's marriage, and almost killed someone.

Strolling along the outer path, she reached the back corner of the house. The kitchen windows were wide open, and from the inside came Donella's deep voice as she sang idly to herself. She was already getting ready for dinner, though it was barely past lunch. It reminded Thessa of how hard she and Nykhe had to work this past week for all the guests' sake. Now, two rooms were already vacant, and a third one was about to follow. Ernio and his family would leave soon, along with Lord Harmon and his son. Little by little, the Benuarte villa emptied again.

As Thessa was about to pass the kitchen, a minor commotion sounded over the slightly off-key singing. A short but loud bit of clucking and some frantic flapping of wings, both of which were abruptly cut short. Then came the scent.

It was blood. Lots of it. Thessa froze in her tracks and spun around in a panic, searching for the quickest way out if her instincts overpowered her again. But the rush never came. The smell made it to her nose, and it was more pleasing than she cared to admit—but aside from that, it was like any other smell.

She snuck up to the nearest window and peeked inside. Donella sat on a three-legged stool, her calves and feet pressed against a metal bucket, which slowly filled up from the chicken she was bleeding out. Glancing up, she waved to Thessa at first, but her face changed at once.

"Don't look here, young lady!" She lowered the chicken and scuttled awkwardly on the stool in an attempt to block the bucket from Thessa's view. "This is no sight for you. It'll make you faint!"

"Oh, I'm sorry," Thessa said. "I'll leave you to it. Good afternoon!"

Retreating from the window, she all but sprinted back around to her and Corlis's room. She flung open the door to find him in the process of changing, with a shirt on and no trousers.

"Buckets of blood, Thessa—can't you knock?" He scrambled to cover himself, but once he saw her, his mood changed again. "What is it? Did something happen?"

"Yes! Or no. Except—" Thessa's mind reeled from the events. "I went past the kitchen window, and there was blood everywhere! From a chicken," she hurriedly added, before Corlis got the wrong idea. "Donella had just cut a chicken. That's where the blood came from. I smelled it, but nothing happened."

While she spoke, Corlis yanked a sheet from the bed to wrap around his waist. "You didn't get the urge to transform?"

"No, not at all."

"Do you think it's because you transformed last night?"

"I don't know. It might be." Thessa fiddled with her hair. "Now that I think back, I have been… relieved. Since last night, I mean. It's almost like when—"

"When you need to let something out?" Corlis asked tactfully.

"Sort of."

Keeping one hand on the sheet to stop it from slipping, Corlis rubbed his chin. "We can make that work. If all it takes is to let you transform now and then, you could do it at the inn. I can lock you in the cellar and stand guard to make sure you don't hurt anyone."

"You think that would be safe?"

"It's worth a try. We'll do it regularly to make sure we don't forget. Once a month, maybe. That should be easy enough to remember."

Thessa picked nervously at her nails. She wanted to believe it was that simple—but then, she had also wanted to believe it was only horse's blood that set her off; or that Nina would change her mind about revenge; or that Larence could help her back to the world she had ran away from. Things had a habit of not being the way Thessa wanted to believe.

"And if it doesn't work?" she asked timidly.

"Then we'll think of something else." Corlis moved closer. "I know how important you think it is to stand on your own. Not in the least because I had a hand in convincing you of that. But without my aunt and uncle, I'd have been less than nothing. Without Addie, I'd have run the inn into the ground. And without you, I would have been hanged. Twice." He stood in that utterly ridiculous position, with one hand on the sheet that guarded his modesty, and said, "Let me help. You don't have to do this alone."

Lacking any words to express her gratitude, in Ardonnese or any language, Thessa threw her arms around him.

The two of them stayed for a minute or so, leaning on one another, until Corlis said, "Can I finish getting dressed now?"

Thessa choked back her laughter and pulled away, wiping her eyes. "All right. Iolinos is waiting for me, anyway."

She left him and made her way to the stables once again. Avalanche was already saddled up and raring for more exercise. Thessa climbed on his back, and for one last time, she enjoyed the luxury of not having to think about tomorrow.

Chapter 36

Corlis made his way slowly up the stairs to the gallery. It was already late in the afternoon, nearing dinner—one that he and Thessa would miss, in order to catch their evening train to New Montres. It was for the best. He had no need to spend one more meal with his family that never was. Back in the room where he and Thessa had stayed, his trunks were all packed and ready to go.

There was only one thing left to take care of.

The music reached him before he got to the threshold. Its sound was nothing like the lutists or flute players who holed up in a corner at The Lame Mare and played bawdy shanties for a copper. It was low and delicate, almost faint, yet crystal clear and purposeful in each note. It was a sound that didn't need to be loud to command attention.

The harp stood by the back wall of the gallery. Livia sat on a bench next to it, dressed in her usual demure blues, her jet black hair done up in intricate braids, running her nimble fingers over the strings. Beside her, Gretia's hair hung in messy strands from her loose bun. She rested her chin in her hand, regarding her sister with the utmost admiration.

When Corlis got closer, Livia stopped playing to welcome him, but her face darkened as he pulled up a chair and sat down. She rested her hands in her lap and waited for him to speak. Gretia also straightened up, not so much out of poise, but rather as if she was ready to flee.

Corlis looked into Livia's somber, dark green eyes. "She was holding you hostage."

A shadow of fright shot across Gretia's face, but Livia merely said, "Not me. My career."

Corlis leaned back. "When Thessa told me you were the only other person who knew about the bottle, I was so disappointed. Larence explained how inheritance works in a family like yours. When a lady dies, her fortune traditionally goes to her closest living female descendants. In Aunt Dalma's case, you two." He bit his lip. "It was so hard to believe you'd kill for something as trivial as money.

"Then I thought back to something else I saw yesterday. We went over every last line in your father's books. It was the single most tedious morning of my life, but I can't say it didn't stick. Because I remembered the money that Lord Hestor sent your aunt to cover your expenses. Hundreds of silvers, and only growing each month." He turned to Livia again. "She was bankrupt, wasn't she."

Livia sank her gaze in agreement. "In more ways than one. She had three different creditors laying claim to her house alone. The banknotes from Father were the only thing keeping her out of debtor's prison."

Outside, the sun was high up, but its rays were weakening. The clouds from north had reached the lake and would be over Vertussi Hill in a few hours. Corlis and Thessa would barely make it to the train station before the downpour hit.

"I didn't understand why she'd call you talentless," he said slowly. "I don't know the first thing about music, but—

well, I think the whole point is that anyone can recognize if someone's gifted. But it makes a lot more sense if she had to undermine you to keep you there."

Livia pressed her lips together. "I'm ashamed to think of how long it took me to catch on. Every few months, she'd make up some excuse to find me a different tutor. Only after the third time did I realize, she didn't want me to get close enough to them that they'd recommend me for positions.

"After eight months, I heard about an upcoming audition for the Paleastre Hall Orchestra. I decided to take my chance and apply by myself. I snuck out under the pretense of meeting a friend." She allowed herself a small smile. "It went wonderfully. There was to be a second round, but the conductor said I might as well start preparing for it.

"Unfortunately, they were rule-bound to send me a formal answer by letter, and Aunt Dalma found it. She was furious. She called me a horrible, ungrateful wretch, and said that if I ever tried something like that, or told anyone about it, she would see to it that I never got to play anywhere bigger than a roadside tavern. She may have been bankrupt, but I knew she was capable of ruining me."

Capable, Corlis thought—*both as in "able" and as in "willing."* Goes to show, you could never know how much of a bastard someone was.

"I was trapped," Livia finished. "With or without her, my dreams in music were crushed."

"But was that reason enough to kill her?"

That was one of the two questions on Corlis's mind. The rest of it he had suspected based on what he knew, if not in all detail. This was the one thing he needed reassurance on. Whether Livia was *capable* of killing her aunt.

"No, it wasn't," came the plain answer. She gathered her strength before continuing. "I learned about Ernio's sleeping drops from Ogde and stole them from his drawer before we left for the village. Then, up here, I poured it into a glass of wine I planned to offer to Aunt Dalma and threw the bottle out the window. But then—"

"I saw you do it," Gretia blurted out. She had not dared to interrupt her sister's confession, but was unable to hold herself back any longer. "I saw the bottle in your hand. I remembered when we were little, how you'd only play *The Sun Rises from the Sea* when you were sad. When you dedicated it to Aunt Dalma, you secretly told me you were miserable with her. I thought"—she sniffled—"I thought you were going to drink it yourself. I pretended to spill my drink on you by accident, then I took your glass away before you could do it."

Livia patted her tenderly on the shoulder. "You should have let me, after what I almost did."

"Don't say that!" Gretia wept. "You're a wonderful musician who deserves to be famous, and now you're free! Free from that dreadful woman!"

She sobbed in a mix of sorrow and relief, while Livia sat there as much of a living statue as ever.

Corlis gave the two of them a minute before he went on. Because as much as he appreciated what they went through, there was one more thing he needed to address. It wasn't any easier than the first, but if he didn't bring it up, it would stick in his mind like a splinter.

"After you spilled your drink on Livia," he said to Gretia, "she left the gallery, and you had her glass of wine in your hand. Wine that you believed to be poisoned."

"Yes?" the girl asked back.

"Why didn't you just pour it out the window?" He left the second half of the question unsaid. Why, instead of getting rid of the poisoned drink, she had chosen to walk right past her drunk aunt whose own glass had freshly run out—or why she made no effort to stop her when she downed the whole thing.

Gretia licked her lips, fidgeted with the hem of her dress, and looked everywhere in the room, except back at Corlis.

"Right," Corlis said. The rest was practically small talk. "I take it your father knows all about it?"

"I couldn't live with myself if I kept something like this from him," Livia replied.

"We told him the next day," Gretia chimed in, "after they took away Aunt Dalma's body."

Which explained Lord Hestor's apparent disinterest when the physician discovered the correct cause of death, as well as his repeated efforts to dissuade Corlis from prying. In a way, his devotion to his daughters was admirable. In another life, in which Corlis was his legitimate offspring, Lord Hestor might have done something similar for him too.

"You must think we're horrible," Livia said as Corlis got up from his seat. "I wouldn't blame you for it. But please, don't judge Gretia too harshly. Whatever she did, it was because of me. She didn't plan to murder Aunt Dalma."

No, she didn't. She merely saw an opportunity and seized it.

Gretia tightened her grip on her sister's arm, and Livia rested her own hand on hers. In that singular gesture, Corlis saw more affection than he knew in his entire childhood.

In place of a response, he only said, "Good luck with your career."

* * *

Back outside, Lord Hestor called to Corlis from his usual place in the study. Corlis trotted into the furnished passage, which showed no sign of the previous night's events. All the chairs and benches were back in their original places, and the traces of chaos had been dutifully cleaned up by Nykhe, including the ragged drape Corlis had left behind. Taking a seat, he did notice his gilded drape pin standing in one of the holders on the desk.

The lord took the ever-present decanter from a side table and poured out a glass for the road. Corlis swirled the drink under his nose the way he'd learned during the tasting at the guest-house. He wouldn't drink something like this for a long time.

Lord Hestor waited for him to take a few sips. "All set?"

"All set."

Across the yard, next to the room where Corlis and Thessa had stayed, their luggage stood in an orderly stack—a considerably smaller one than at their arrival. Thessa had chosen to leave most of her expensive dresses behind for Gretia, and Corlis too only kept the garments that he might wear in the city without getting robbed or ridiculed. Besides, none of those clothes were truly theirs to begin with. Taking those few with them was more akin to theft than anything.

"Good." Lord Hestor nodded. "The carriage is ready for you out front. Take your time."

A hundred different feelings battered Corlis's brain from the inside, demanding to be let out. He wanted to apologize. He wanted Lord Hestor to apologize. He wanted to thank him. He wanted to condemn him. He was anxious, relieved, honored, and insulted, all at the same time.

Before any of that found its way to his tongue, Lord Hestor reached into his tunic and pulled out a familiar piece of paper.

"I had the guardsmen hand this over once Harmon and Alendro were back," he said and smoothed out the map. "Can't say anything for certain, but I'd reckon Larence had his sights on your inn for a while." His eye drifted toward the message Nina had added. *I'LL MAKE YOU PAY.*

"I didn't kill him," Corlis said.

The lord didn't reply. He was like a different man altogether. His jovial nature was nowhere to be found now, only a pensive melancholy playing around his bloodless lips while he weighed Corlis's words. There was no question he didn't believe Alendro's confession for a second. But without knowing everything about Nina—which would inevitably sound like something Corlis made up on the spot—there was only one alternative.

Lord Hestor slowly tore the paper in two, then four, then eight pieces, and tossed them to the side. "I couldn't prove it if I wanted to."

That should have been a relief. Somehow, it was only worse instead.

"But seeing how he might have had a hand in the accident that befell you, I do share some of the responsibility. I don't want you to leave on that note." The lord tapped his desk, which had the inkwell and sealing wax out. "I wrote to Fabreve at the Golden Lion and instructed them to arrange the repairs on your behalf, at the expense of the Benuarte estate. Everything will be taken care of, and we'll all forget anything happened."

Including this whole week, and the fact that I was ever here.

Corlis didn't answer. Words didn't feel right. Nothing felt right.

Lord Hestor rose sluggishly and placed a hand on his shoulder. "You owe me nothing, you understand? Whatever your name is, be proud of yourself. Build your own family and your own legacy."

They had a few more last drinks before Thessa arrived, and the three of them made their way through the outer courtyard. The driver strapped the diminished luggage on the back of the carriage, while Corlis and Thessa climbed in and bid their final goodbyes. The gravel crackled under the wheels, and they rolled out onto the path. The villa slowly but surely shrunk into the distance behind them, its many window panes reflecting the gray of the clouded sky overhead.

Chapter 37

Rain drizzled over the coach in a shower that never seemed to end. Thessa shifted closer to the middle of the bench, so that she could hold the umbrella over both herself and Porla. Their heads and backs stayed somewhat dry, but there was no shielding their faces from the wind that blasted them with cold spray in all directions.

"I can't believe it's only been fall for two weeks." Thessa pulled her cape tighter with her free hand. "It wasn't this bad last year."

"It hasn't been this bad in a long while," Porla said, chewing on her usual piece of entwood bark. "Folks are saying it's already the coldest and wettest fall in some twenty years."

"I believe them."

Mercifully, their goal was near, and their way was unimpeded. In stark contrast to the spring, when almost every street in the Wall District was a constant deluge of carts, workers, and deliverymen, the only thing flooding the roads now was the rainwater. If nothing else, it helped wash away the dust left behind from all those construction sites—every one of which had ceased back in the summer. The dozen or so half-finished buildings provided a glaring backdrop to the only one that had undergone a complete overhaul over the past months.

Porla pulled in the reins, and the coach lurched to a halt in front of the all new Lame Mare inn.

"There you two are!" Addie's surly face appeared in the peephole to greet them with the closest thing to warmth she was capable of. "Get in already before you're washed away in this damn slop. And mind your boots! I just mopped."

Like the outside, the tavern was a newer and better version of its old self. The floorboards were freshly laid and polished, and the walls were spotless with new paint. To Thessa's personal relief, the workers had kept the old mural on the ceiling, with all the charming figures depicting an idyllic country life.

Most of the tables were covered in the unused and upturned chairs, with a lone exception. It was the one closest to the massive stone fireplace, which had several thick logs on a roaring flame. At this table sat the trio of Corlis, Addie, and Ladec, each halfway through their own drinks already.

"Don't fret, we spared some for you," the guardsman said and slid two full cups of white wine before the pair as they took their seats.

Thessa lifted her drink. "Is this from Forterne?"

"I might have put away a bottle by accident while packing," Corlis said. "There was wine everywhere in that house."

Thessa frowned. "In bottles?"

"Fine, it was everywhere in the cellar."

"He's got more than one, believe me," Addie said, her blonde pigtails waggling as she shook her head. "And he won't let anyone near it! Says he's saving it for special occasions." She sneered at Corlis. "What occasion will that be? When the Emperor comes for a visit?"

"If you keep giving me that lip, it will be. And given we've just been made a republic, you'll be waiting for a long while."

"Ha!" Addie retorted. "That wine still won't be half as sour as you by then."

"All right, you two," Porla stepped in. "Don't jump at each other's throats before you've even opened the place. If you're like this now, imagine how it'll be when it's teeming."

"Speaking of"—Ladec stroked his beloved horseshoe mustache—"I've been meaning to ask, what's with that new station you said they were planning? Shouldn't they have gotten started by now?"

Corlis poured himself more wine and passed the pitcher around. "No, you're right. They should have." He took a comfortable swig of the liquid gold, while everyone around the table hung on his word, except for Thessa who had heard it the week prior.

"That map Larence had?" Corlis began. "The one from the Office of Expansion and Development? When me and Thessa confronted him, he said it was from years ago. Turns out, that was about the only bit of truth he told all that time. I went to the Wall District City Hall and asked them about it. The clerk told me right off the top of his head. There was a plan to extend the railroad some two years back, but they decided it wasn't worth the investment.

"Larence must have gotten his hands on an old document from that time and decided to put it to use the way he usually does—by scamming people. He went around telling everyone the Wall District was about to become a gold mine. With the seal and everything, it was convincing enough for some of his investor friends to buy up the abandoned buildings in the area. Once they were rebuilt, he was going to resell them to his other investor friends and take a cut of the profits."

"But surely, those other friends would catch on," Ladec said, "when they saw there was no railroad, no station, no nothing."

"I'm sure he had a plan for that too. Maybe he was going to blame the City Council for backing off. Maybe he thought to pack his things and disappear somewhere overseas before anyone came knocking. As much of a snake he was, you can't deny he was smart."

Everyone mulled over the news. Ladec twirled his whiskers, Addie drummed on the table, and Corlis stared into the fire.

Next to Thessa, Porla's freckled face broadened into a smile, and she raised her cup. "At least things aren't any worse."

"Is that something to drink to?" Addie asked.

"Well, just because you didn't make it further up the hill doesn't mean you slid back."

"That's reason enough for me," Ladec chimed in.

"I guess it is as good as we lot can hope for," Corlis said.

Thessa had to agree. Things may not have worked out the way she or Corlis had hoped, but they could also have gone much worse on so many occasions. In a way, she should consider herself fortunate. There was something to be said for staying in place.

She joined in the toast. "To health."

The five of them clinked over the table and continued to do so for the rest of the night, while the rain poured relentlessly outside.

* * *

Meanwhile, at the New Montres Central railway station, Officer Nella Dormanni stood by the platform in nervous excitement, awaiting the train from Midorea that would bring her a very special visitor.

About the Author

Jerry F. Westinger is a software developer by day, aspiring author by night, pastry chef on the weekends, and mortician by trade.

Also by Jerry F. Westinger

Coming soon!
Bad luck and worse choices continue in 2024

9 789152 724675